...to draw on for the stories
...iting ever since she can remember.

...ine isn't writing you'll find her listening to audiobook... while she sews or designs handbags, usually with a
rescu... ...er or two curled up on her feet!

@Romanceminx
LorraineWilsonWriter
lorraine-wilson.com

Also by Lorraine Wilson

Confessions of a Chalet Girl
Secrets of a Chalet Girl
Revenge of a Chalet Girl
Secret Crush of a Chalet Girl
Chalet Girl Plays Cupid
Rebellion of a Chalet Girl

Chalet Girls

LORRAINE WILSON

A division of HarperCollins*Publishers*
www.harpercollins.co.uk

Harper*Impulse* an imprint of
HarperCollins*Publishers*
1 London Bridge Street
London SE1 9GF

www.harpercollins.co.uk

A Paperback Original 2017

First published in Great Britain in ebook format by Harper*Impulse* 2017

A catalogue record for this book
is available from the British Library

ISBN: 9780008235789

Set in Birka by Palimpsest Book Production Limited, Falkirk, Stirlingshire

Printed and bound in Great Britain

For Pip, a very special rescue dog

Chapter 1

From: benross21@yahoo.com
To: lucy.ross@hotmail.com
Subject: World domination

Hi Lucy,
How's it going in the land of the millionaires? Mum saw something in the *Daily Mail* about chalet girls taking their tops off for cocktails and shagging in gondolas. She's now convinced you're up to no good.

Are you? I do hope so ;-)

Sadly, I suspect you're being a good girl, which seems like such a waste tbh. If Dad could spare me from the croft I'd be out there like a shot.

Anyway, you owe me one because I've been doing my best to convince Mum you're much more likely to be entering competitions and following in the footsteps of Jenny Jones, that chalet girl-turned-Winter Games medalist you keep going on about. If you could set yourself on the path to Winter Games stardom that would probably take the heat off.

I also showed her photos on the net of all the Royals and celebrities who holiday in Verbier to convince her you're not living in a den of iniquity.

So, I've stopped her getting on a plane to drag you home. All you have to do now is win a Winter Games' medal and bag a Royal. Easy peasy ;-)

Seriously, though, I do miss you, little sis. I hope you make it back home for a visit once the winter season's over.

I'll leave you with a joke:

Q- How many chalet girls does it take to screw in a light bulb?

A- None. Chalet girls screw in hot tubs. Ha ha.

Love from your exceptionally witty brother,

Ben

LUCY

As I read the email, two things occur to me. One – my brother Ben is a dillop-brain. Two – unfortunately he knows me far too well.

I slip my phone back into my jeans pocket. I've got more important things on my mind and thinking about Mum always puts a downer on my mood. I don't want to feel sad this evening.

Tash would appreciate the joke, I'm sure. Out of the four of us chalet girls sharing a dorm room at Chalet Repos this season, she's the only one who has almost certainly had sex with a guest in a hot tub. Rebecca would worry about being caught, Beth is new and has only been here for five minutes and I . . . well, it's the ski, not the après ski that drew me to Verbier.

I would love nothing more than to follow in Jenny Jones' footsteps. Chalet girl to Winter Games medalist is quite a leap, though.

'We need to get going.' I'm practically bouncing with impatience, keen to get everyone out of the dorm room so we can get on our way. 'The screening starts at eight o'clock.'

'We've got plenty of time.' Tash stares dreamily into her little compact mirror, perfecting her cat-like eye make-up.

Tash has been transformed in the time I've known her; her spiky edginess morphing into a more chilled and dreamy version of herself. Like a cactus transforming into a rose – fewer spikes, but still the odd thorn if you press in the wrong place.

She's lovestruck. I even heard her whistling while she unloaded the dishwasher this morning. It's weirding me out but I've no doubt her innate snarkiness will be making a come-back all too soon. Particularly now Holly's put Amelia and Matt in charge of Chalet Repos – a decision I think must've been made under the influence of baby-brain. The sleep deprivation of new motherhood has to be blinding Holly to the potential explosive danger of making Amelia Tash's boss.

At least for the moment there are no audible ticking bombs. Tash came back from her last visit with Nate blissed out and beaming, as though all her cocktails had come at once. Then she went on to describe in lurid detail how it wasn't just the cocktails, if you know what I mean. I never know what to say when the others talk about sex. I usually stay quiet and hope no one will notice. It wouldn't usually be much of a problem but they do talk about sex a lot.

I've not experienced the spell Tash is under first-hand. I'm curious – okay, maybe the teensiest bit wistful. It might be nice to be that blissed out by a man.

Not that I'd let myself mope around like that over anyone. I'm more of a doer.

I've always been practical. I suppose you have to be when you grow up on a Highland croft. To say my parents weren't exactly big on indulging emotions or talking about feelings would be a huge understatement. Duty to God, self-discipline and hard work were the Holy Trinity in our house. Let's just say Verbier has been a bit of an eye-opener.

Where I do take after Mum is that I've got no patience

with faffing. I've been ready for ages and am itching to get out of the tiny bunk room and into the fresh Swiss air. The scents of too many different perfumes mingle to fill the air in the bunk room, so it's cloying and sickly sweet.

'Hiya.' Amelia enters the bunk room without knocking. She had the luxury of getting ready in the double room she shares with Matt.

'What's this film we're going to see, again?' Amelia asks. She looks immaculate, as always, in designer knee-high boots and a silk, jersey-blend dress. Her high blonde ponytail swishes as she moves, reminding me of the cows back home, swishing their tails at milking time.

Beth squirts yet more perfume into the air and walks into the cloud.

I take a small step back, my legs bumping against the edge of the bunk bed behind me, and sigh. I close my eyes briefly and think of all the glorious, powdery white snow just a chairlift ride away that makes all this worth it.

'It's a film of the line Sebastien Laroche took at the Verbier Xtreme last year. You know, he jumped that cliff that had never been jumped before? I bet *Crazy White Lines* will win the Valais Freeride Film Festival. No one can beat Sebastien.' I look around, expecting to see dawning recognition in the others' eyes but find only blank incomprehension. How can they not have heard of Sebastien Laroche? The man's a legend.

'Ooh, our Lucy has a crush. I think Sebastien Laroche has a fan girl slash stalker in the making here.' Tash smirks, dropping the mascara back into her make-up case.

I glare at her.

'Okay, don't get your knickers in a twist, I'm coming. Impatient much?' She adds, her lips still twitching.

'I am not a stalker.' I narrow my eyes. 'But I do admire him, because he's an amazing athlete. He takes big mountain boarding to a whole new level. Did you know companies are fighting over his sponsorship and begging to film his runs?'

Tash rolls her eyes. She likes skiing and snowboarding but isn't serious about the sport like I am. I bite my tongue. She's agreed to come and keep me company tonight. I just have to accept that not everyone is as into the sport as I am.

'It'll be fun to watch. I can't imagine hovering over a mountain ridge in a helicopter and then having to jump out onto it.' Rebecca zips up her make-up bag and puts it into her locker.

'I bet he's totally bonkers,' Amelia adds. 'Has to be.'

I glower at Amelia. She's yet another casual skier with no sporting ambition beyond skiing to the nearest cantine for a champagne cocktail. Not that there's anything wrong with cocktails, but surely life has to be about more than getting hammered every night?

'What?' Amelia shrugs. 'Who but a nutter would choose to snowboard on ice and scree, knowing every line they take could be their last? It's mad.'

I bite my lip, resisting the urge to argue with great difficulty.

'I'm glad we're guest-free for a few nights,' Rebecca, ever the peacemaker, changes the subject and drops her lip gloss into her clutch bag, clicking it shut. She's wearing a silky grey cashmere top and designer jeans. She's also perfectly made up, with pearly-pink lips and smoky eye shadow. Everyone is looking super-glam compared to me, but I guess I have different priorities. I'm going to watch the film, not to be watched myself.

Still, maybe I should've made an effort with make-up, but I rarely bother these days. My skin is beautifully clear from all my time out in the fresh Swiss air and bathing in pure mountain water. I've never felt better. Plus I've got a healthy tan from spending every spare minute on the slopes.

I've never been a girly girl; it just isn't me. Growing up on a croft in the Scottish Highlands in a tiny village near Drumnadrochit didn't inspire much interest in clothes or fashion. Mum never wore make-up and would've come down hard on me if I'd spent precious money on anything so frivolous and selfish. As far as she was concerned vanity was a sin and, boy, didn't I know about it! She reminded me often enough.

Instead I filled any free time I had with hiking and skiing when we had enough snow. I always dreamt of skiing in the Alps one day, maybe even competing. Skiing in Scotland wasn't enough for me, the snow coverage far too unreliable. Moving to Verbier was a huge deal, given no one in my family has ever moved further away than a ten-mile radius of Drumnadrochit. You'd have thought I was denouncing my Scottish heritage, God and my family from the way Mum and Dad had reacted when I'd told them where I was going. Well, I say Mum and Dad, but it was Mum who did the talking, as always. Dad just gave me the silent treatment, refusing even to say goodbye to me.

They still think this is a passing fancy for me but landing this chalet-girl job was the start of living my dream.

One day I'd love to be a big-mountain skier. Not that I ever admit this to anyone. They'd probably laugh and I've had a lifetime of being disparaged, I can't face anyone else trying to crush my dreams. But why shouldn't I compete one day? I'm good, and I've been told I'm getting better every month. If I could find someone willing to coach me, well, who knows . . .

'Earth to Lucy.' Tash waves a hand in front of my face. 'What are you thinking about? Or should that be 'who'?'

'Nothing,' I mumble and look away, embarrassed to be caught daydreaming. 'Can we get going now?'

Tash smirks but finally we're out of the bunk room and I slip into my ski jacket. It's not stylish, but it's the warmest coat I own. The walk back to the chalet will be a cold one, resort temperatures plummet rapidly once darkness falls. You forget your gloves at your peril. I'd rather be warm than look pretty on the offchance of meeting someone interesting.

'No Matt? I thought he was coming too?' Beth asks as she steps into her Ugg boots.

'He's got some work to do.' Amelia slips a stylish, no doubt expensive faux-fur-lined wrap over her shoulders. 'We need all the freelance web-design work he can pick up, given we've got a wedding to pay for.'

Tash rolls her eyes; something she's taken to doing whenever Amelia mentions her wedding. To be fair, it happens a lot. Tash said we should start a swear jar going but instead of putting money in when she swears Amelia should be made to add a Swiss franc every time she mentions her wedding. For some reason, Amelia wasn't amused by the idea. Let's just say that the relationship between the two of them is as frosty as the icicles hanging down from Chalet Repos' roof.

As we troop out of the warmth of the chalet into crisp, fresh snow there are thick snowflakes swirling silently overhead. They land on our hoods and hair, brushing our eyelashes and cooling our warm cheeks. After the stifling atmosphere of the dorm room it's a relief to be out in the snow.

We head en masse to the car park in town, where a number of large white marquees have been erected for the film festival. I fish the tickets out of my jacket pocket as we merge with the crowd hurrying out of the cold and into the warmth of the main heated tent. We're cutting it fine. I crane my neck to see if there's a group of empty seats together. No such luck.

There is one empty seat at the front. I gaze at it longingly.

'Go on, go sit at the front. You can take that chair in the front row' Tash gives me a none-too-gentle push. 'We'll meet you afterwards. You're the one who's really into this, after all.'

I don't need any more urging. I rush forward before any of the other late-comers can get to it. I'll get a fantastic view of the screen from the front row. Once seated I'm twitchy, eyes directly ahead on the screen, waiting for the film to start and hoping to God none of my neighbours try to make small talk.

You'd think, given how much I love the mountains and winter sports, I'd have loads in common with my fellow seasonnaires, right?

Wrong.

As far as I can tell, most seasonnaires are here for the après ski, with a bit of skiing thrown in. Any illusions I had of meeting a serious boyfriend here in Switzerland took a flying leap off a mountain and crashed on the rocks below long ago. It should've been obvious, if I'd thought it through properly. Seasonnaire. The very name of the type of job we do suggests a temporary arrangement – only for a season. Most of the relationships that spring up in resorts, if they last beyond a one-night stand, span only a few weeks, not even the whole season. I keep telling myself it isn't a big deal. After all, it's not the main reason I came to Verbier. But still. I had hoped. . .

My skin prickles to attention, my sixth sense telling me I'm being watched. I cross my arms and stare rigidly ahead. Thankfully the screen finally flickers into life, showing a holding page, a photograph of an alpine ridge. The general hubbub dies down to the odd cough. One of Sebastien Laroche's sponsors from a popular outdoor clothing company comes to the front and lists some of Sebastien's previous triumphs by way of introduction – three times European Boardercross champion and a place on the French Winter Games team last year, only narrowly missing out on a medal.

Of course I admire him. He's achieved things I can only dream about. Okay, he happens to be easy on the eye too. Maybe I have just a teensy wee crush.

When the introduction is over the holding screen disappears and the screen is filled with the image of a helicopter in flight. The camera pans to the open side door. Inside is Sebastien Laroche, a huge grin lighting up his charismatic face. He has wild black curls and his face is as craggy as the mountaintops he loves. His skin is tanned, with that weather-beaten look truly outdoorsy people get, and there's a jagged scar on his chin. Maybe he's not conventionally handsome, but when he smiles, like he's smiling now, his face glows with a fierce, dancing light.

He's utterly mesmerising.

Okay, so it might be more than a wee crush.

'Snowboarding is my life, my reason to live.' On screen, Sebastien's eyes shine with anticipation of the jump, lit with pure joy.

I shift forward in my chair, my gaze trained on Sebastien as he jumps down from the helicopter onto a metre-wide snowy ridge. The camera pans out and down to show a two-thousand-metre drop to the valley below, broken only by sheer, razor-sharp rocks.

The crowd gasp, united in their incredulity at the precariousness of Sebastien's position.

'*Il est fou*,' a woman behind me mutters. With difficulty I resist the temptation to turn around and give her my death glare. How can she dismiss his bravery as madness?

Although, when I see the line he takes down the mountain, sliding on virtually vertical stretches of scree and accelerating when he hits patches of ice, the breath catches in my chest. A small part of me reluctantly agrees. But where do we draw the line between madness and bravery? And who gets to decide where it lies?

Perhaps he's both mad and brave, essential characteristics for a pioneer, someone capable of transcending the ordinary with the extraordinary.

The camera follows his path down the mountainside. Whenever he leaps to a decent patch of snow he part-glides, part-dances on the snow's crust. He moves so gracefully it's like he's in tune with the mountain. As though he's dancing in time to a mountain heartbeat no one else can hear but him.

I expected his skill but didn't anticipate anything so beautiful or so moving. It stirs me deep down, opening up a visceral yearning.

Could I ever move that gracefully? My grandmother was the one who taught me to dream big. Before she died she told me to go out into the world and take all the opportunities she never had. She never left the Scottish Highlands to travel and she always regretted it. I know she loved Granddad but he was traditional and controlling. She made me promise never to tie myself to a man who tried to crush my dreams. I'll always be grateful to her for giving me the courage to defy Mum and Dad and come to Verbier.

When the film ends the crowd erupts in enthusiastic applause. I ease back into my chair, disappointed it's over. Only now do I finally breathe out properly. I'd no idea I was even holding my breath.

My skin prickles again and I sense an intent stare from the person sitting beside me, demanding my attention. I bite my lip. It could be someone I know. I wasn't really looking when I sat down, I was too busy nabbing the seat. It would be rude not to acknowledge them. Reluctantly I turn and my eyebrows shoot up.

'Oh my God.' I'm staring directly back at the subject of the film, at Sebastien Laroche himself. His eyes flicker with amusement.

'I've been called a lot of things in my life but never God.'

He grins, a hint of wickedness in the curve of his mouth. 'I'm not sure I'm cut out to be a deity. Too badly behaved.'

His English is heavily accented with his native French accent but he speaks with a confidence that tells me he doesn't give a damn.

Heat floods my cheeks and I don't know where to look. Why did I have to sound so naïve and starstruck? Along with the prickling embarrassment, I'm aware of something more – a stirring deep inside me. A quickening and an awakening. The look in his eyes when he says ‚badly behaved' makes my stomach flip over. I have to say something, right now. I swallow hard.

'Um, that was amazing.' I gesture towards the screen, admiration finally breaking through my embarrassment.

'I was watching you while the film played. You get *it*.' He places a heavy emphasis on the word 'it' and, before I realise what he's doing, he takes my hand and places it over his heart. 'You get it right here.'

I feel the steady thrum of his heartbeat through his cotton cashmere crewneck, it pulses against my palm. I can feel hard muscle beneath the soft, silky fabric. My cheeks burn even hotter.

'Er, yes, I think so.' I blink and kick myself for umming and erring. This has got to be the most bizarre conversation I've ever had. Yet, as embarrassed as I am, I don't want it to end.

Ever.

'I saw it in your eyes; you were up there, with me.' His intense gaze is fixed on me, as though I'm the only person in the room. I always thought that was a cliché, but it's how it really feels. Surely he must be aware there are lots of people waiting to speak to him? I'm sure everyone must be staring at us, but I can't break eye contact with Sebastien. He's even more mesmerising and twice as charismatic in real life as he was on screen.

'Do you have a name?' His lips quirk. I try not to fixate on them but it's difficult not to imagine what it would be like to be kissed by him.

'Yes. . .' I'm flustered. He still has my hand against his chest and is acting as though the way he's behaving is perfectly normal. 'I'm Lucy.'

'Lucy,' he tries out my name, his accent making it sound musical. He smiles. 'You can call me Seb. Now I'm afraid you'll have to excuse me. I have to go and make nice with the very generous people who give me money to do what I love. Will I see you at the after-party?'

He lets go of my hand and I instantly wish he hadn't broken the connection between us.

'I don't think I'm invited.' I bite my lip, torn between desire and the urge to scurry back into my shell.

'Pffft.' He shrugs, a quintessentially French gesture of dismissal. 'Consider yourself invited. Say you are my guest. Then we can talk some more.'

'I'm not sure. . .' I'm wasting my breath, as he's dropped my hand and turned and is already in deep conversation with two men in expensive suits.

Okay then. I remember to breathe and slip out of my seat, heart thumping, as I make my way out of the tent, gaze lowered to the ground.

That was. . . surreal. I'm going to assume I had some kind of meltdown or fell asleep and daydreamed that encounter. There's no way I'm going to some after-party. Parties are hellish enough when you know people, but making small talk with lots of strangers? It's not going to happen. The only place I'm going is back to my bunk at Chalet Repos.

Chapter 2

From: sandratrent@gmail.com
To: sophietrent@hotmail.com
Re: The Lodge Hotel

Sophie darling, didn't you get my other messages? I really need you to get back to me ASAP so we can start planning the wedding.

I know you said there's no hurry but I don't think you realise how far in advance wedding venues get booked up. Rita from the WI has a daughter who works at the Lodge Hotel – they've had a cancellation for the second Saturday in May next year but we have to act quickly if we want that date.

I'm so looking forward to planning you a wonderful wedding, darling. I can't wait.

Anyway, I must go. There's a pile of ironing to be done and your dad's calling for his coffee. We both know how grumpy he gets when he's caffeine-deprived so I'd better get on.

Give our best to Luc.
Love,
Mum

SOPHIE

I thrust my phone to the bottom of my bag, wishing it were as easy to squash down my anxiety. Emails can be ignored, for a little while, at least. Emotional procrastination is more difficult and worse for your health. I can feel a stress headache pulsing at my temples but force a smile to my lips and make an effort to tune back into the conversation.

'Wow. This chalet is freakin' amazing. Can we go and see the basement spa now? Pretty please?' Tash practically bounces on the spot, her childlike glee at odds with her immaculate and elaborate make-up.

'Absolutely, but no stripping off.' Holly catches my eye and grins. We both know there's no containing Tash when she's in one of her exuberant moods.

'Spoil sport,' Tash pouts.

'Well, not until after midnight anyway.' Holly concedes. 'The other guests should be mostly drunk by then. But, given it's Sophie's engagement party, maybe you should check with her before you do anything, erm, too outrageous.

My engagement party.

The words cause another worm of anxiety to squirm in my stomach.

'Please, like I've ever been able to stop Tash stripping off.' I shrug. 'But we're celebrating Amelia's engagement tonight too and I'm not sure she'd be happy about it.'

Amelia got engaged a while before me, but when planning the party Holly realised she hadn't done anything for Amelia and was worried she'd take offence. Holly was probably right, but I actually don't mind in the slightest. I've got no problem with sharing the party with Amelia and, if anyone else wants to take some of the limelight off me, they're very welcome to it.

'Who's stripping off?' Nate comes into the room with Scott and Luc.

'Your girlfriend,' Holly says.

Nate rolls his eyes but they twinkle with good humour and the gesture is accompanied by an amused quirk of the lips. 'That's my girl.'

'You're all looking very glamorous.' Scott makes a show of looking us up and down. 'Especially my lovely wife, of course. It's nice to see you all in dresses for a change.'

'I love you very much, my sexist dinosaur husband, but I would like to point out that party dresses aren't exactly practical clothing in a ski resort.' Holly pretends to huff. 'Anyway, glamorous clothes also tend to be dry-clean only. In other words, they're very baby-unfriendly.'

'You know, I think you look gorgeous in anything.' Scott smiles fondly at Holly, tucking a stray strand of auburn hair back into her up-do. 'Now, who'd like a private tour before the party guests arrive? I think we're all set up now.'

Luc slips behind me and plants a kiss on the top of my head. When he wraps his arms around me some of my tension ebbs away and I almost believe everything might be okay.

Almost.

'Thanks so much for this. We really appreciate it.' I follow Scott and Holly down the corridor.

'No problem, Sophie, it's our engagement present to you,' Scott smiles. 'Holly and I wanted to do something special for you and Amelia. Plus we really want to show off how Chalet Amélie is coming along.'

'It's gorgeous, Scott. I thought Chalet Repos was special, but this is something else.'

I mean it too. It hits just the right note between traditional Swiss chalet and modern home. I adore the mini library and snug on the mezzanine gallery looking down onto the double-height living room. The whole wall facing the valley is glass with an arching timber frame and we're looking straight out onto snow-capped mountain peaks. I love the double-sided fireplace facing out onto the dining area on one side and the huge u-shaped leather seating unit festooned with silky faux-fur throws on the other. The kitchen is all modern – sleek black units, granite worktops and shiny chrome fittings. Not to mention two large island units. I've never had a kitchen big enough to house even one island unit.

'I think I have kitchen-envy,' I whisper to Holly. 'Actually, scrub that, I have chalet envy.'

I love the cosy little flat I share with Luc above Bar des Amis, but I dream of living in a chalet like this. Maybe one day we'll be able to build our own little chalet further away from Verbier where land prices are cheaper. I enjoyed my time living and working at Chalet Repos, but definitely don't miss sharing the cramped dorm room with three other girls.

'I know,' Holly whispers back, looking over my shoulder to check Scott isn't listening. She needn't worry, the men are all engrossed checking out the fancy espresso machine and talking about controlling the under-floor heating with an iPhone app. 'It seems such a shame to waste all this on paying guests, but Scott and Nate keep reminding me it's a business. We've had to up our game a bit. People are starting to expect more from a luxury chalet rental.'

Scott catches the end of the conversation. 'And they're getting more. Come on, I'll show you some of the chalet's special features. The guest suites aren't quite finished yet but the cinema room and games room are done.'

'There's a cinema room?' Luc raises his eyebrows.

'Yes. It's expected now, for this class of chalet. We also have an indoor heated pool, indoor and outdoor Jacuzzis, a steam room and sauna, a spa treatment room, a gym with plasma TV, DVD and music system, a games room with pool table, a party area with disco ball and bar, oh and a wine cellar.' Scott ticks the features off on his fingers.

'I think I want to move in,' Luc sighs. 'Will you adopt us?'

His words, so carelessly spoken, make the worm of anxiety writhe and squirm inside me.

'If you like,' Holly grins. 'I want to move in here, but Scott won't let me. He says paying guests won't appreciate a crying baby in situ and I suppose having our own space is best. Never mind, it's perfect for a party, and there are no guests booked in until Christmas.'

Holly breaks off to check her phone, forehead creased.

'I'm sure Maddie is fine, Holly. The babysitter will ring if there's a problem,' I say for the umpteenth time this evening.

'I know, I was checking the signal, in case there's no reception.' She pulls a face. 'It is the first time I've left her for an entire evening and she's still so tiny. It's hard. Like I'm missing a limb or something. Although, I'll admit it's nice to be wearing something other than pyjamas at seven p.m.'

We make our way down to the spa. Dark slate tiles and mood lighting create the ambience of a cave. An extremely luxurious cave with sleek S-curved loungers and coloured lights dancing on the turquoise pool's surface.

'It has an aromatherapy shower and a cold plunge pool.' Scott leads us along the side of the pool to the spa area and treatment room with massage table.

Voices upstairs interrupt our tour.

'That's probably Amelia and Matt.' Holly touches Scott's elbow and tugs him away from a discussion with Nate and Luc about how the aromatherapy shower works. 'And the guests will start arriving soon. We should go up.'

We head back upstairs and when Amelia sees me I'm greeted to a no-contact double air-kiss that's more like assault by perfume fumes than a friendly greeting. The whole air-kissing thing is so phoney. When we were both working at Chalet Repos and sharing a dorm room we never greeted each other with air-kisses. Getting engaged and then promoted has changed her – and not for the better.

I catch Tash rolling her eyes behind Amelia's back. Funny how Amelia doesn't try to air-kiss Tash. Now, that would be entertaining.

'So, how are the wedding plans coming along, Sophie?' Amelia asks once she's finished doing the double-kiss thing with Luc. Although I notice he didn't get the no-contact version – there was definite lip-brushing cheek action going on. Funny that. Hmm.

'Um, well it's still early days,' I avoid looking at Luc and try to suppress my rising panic.

'Oh, you shouldn't leave it too late. I've been planning since the day after Matt proposed.'

'If not before,' Tash mutters.

I suppress a giggle. 'Really? Have you had a tour of Chalet Amélie yet? The spa looks amazing.'

'Not yet.' Amelia's fixed smile doesn't waver.

'I bet you wish Holly had put you and Matt in charge of Chalet Amélie instead of Chalet Repos.' Tash is also smiling, but the hint of snark is unmistakable.

'Which chalet did Holly put you in charge of? Oh wait, she didn't. Sorry, I forgot.' Amelia steers the conversation into treacherous waters.

Time to head for the lifeboats.

'We're going to get a drink.' I steer Tash away before she can open her mouth.

'Ignore her,' I whisper in Tash's ear. 'You've got a whole season to get through. Pace yourself.'

'I might need more than one drink,' Tash sighs.

While helping ourselves to champagne cocktails we bump into Emily.

'Hi Sophie, how are the wedding plans coming along?' She smiles brightly.

Arghh. Why does everyone assume I must have a one-track mind because I'm engaged?

'It's a bit. . . complicated,' I hedge. It's going to be a long evening. 'Have you and Jake moved in here yet?'

'We're moving in at the weekend so we can be on site to oversee the rest of the work,' Emily beams. 'Oh hi, Tash, how are you?'

'Great thanks,' Tash mumbles. 'I'm going to find Nate.'

'Sorry, Sophie, I've got to head off too. I need to find Holly. I'll catch you later.' Emily grimaces apologetically and follows Tash.

I make my way up to the snug on the gallery before anyone else can ask how the wedding plans are going. I'm keen to see what books they've put in the library area. Books have been my escape my whole life, from reading *Sweet Valley High* novels in the school library to hide from bullies to romance novels – a pleasure I refuse to feel guilty for. What's so wrong with feel-good escapism? I don't need depressing realism when I'm trying to relax.

After a happy ten minutes scanning the books I settle into an armchair with my drink, preparing to be thoroughly anti-social until Holly or Tash appear to drag me back into the fray.

It's then that I spot him on a sofa below.

Him.

Thomas.

The ghost of ski seasons past. The cause of so much misery and pain.

Something twists painfully deep inside me and my stomach cramps. It's far worse than the anxiety worm this time; it's bigger and more dangerous. It has fangs.

Fangs that have dripped poison into my relationship with Luc.

I press back into my chair, even though he's not looking up and I'm well hidden.

Crap. Crap. Crap. What do I do?

I stay where I am, frozen, heart thudding until Holly, Tash and Lucy come up to find me. Part of me is glad of the friend armour now surrounding me but I'm in too much of a state to hide anything from them. They know me too well.

'It's your party, Sophie, you can't hide up here.' Holly peers down at me, narrowing her eyes and frowning. 'Hey, what's up?'

'He's here. What's he doing here?' I whisper. Something wet splashes on my lap. I look down to see my hands are trembling, spilling my drink onto my dress. Lucy takes the glass off me and Tash kneels down beside my chair, squeezing my hand.

'Who are you talking about, Soph?' Holly asks, forehead creased. 'Who's here?'

'Thomas,' I whisper, trying to sink further down in my seat. I take my hand back from Tash and wrap my arms around my still-cramping stomach.

'Oh.' Holly's eyes widen.

'What? *That* Thomas?' Tash's voice is much louder than I'd like.

'Ssh, yes, *that* Thomas.' I squeeze my eyes tightly shut and take a deep breath before opening them again. I think I might be sick.

'Which Thomas?' Lucy looks furtively around us and down to the packed room below the mezzanine.

'He of the 'fat girls try harder' and 'I don't use condoms' fame,' Tash replies, eyes flinty.

Recognition dawns on Lucy's face.

I wince and take a shaky breath.

'I'm so sorry, I don't know why he's here Soph. He certainly wasn't invited.' Holly's eyes are wide, she looks stricken. 'He must've come as someone's guest. I'll get Scott to ask him to leave.'

'No.' I reach for her wrist before she can leave. 'Luc might guess. He'll see I'm upset and could put two and two together. I never gave Luc the name of the guy responsible, you see. Things are a bit. . . difficult at the moment. I'm worried he might decide to teach Thomas a lesson, you know, to defend my honour.'

Holly chews her bottom lip, hesitating. 'I suppose, but it's your party, Soph. I want you to have a nice time. I hate that you're going through this because of that jerk.'

Anger flares in her eyes. By 'This' I know she means more than his presence tonight. She, more than anyone, knows the grief Thomas has caused and continues to cause.

'Was he the one who used to place bets with his friends about who could pull and shag the ugliest girl?' Lucy asks, face contorted with disgust.

'Yes,' I reply shortly, face burning.

'Oh, Soph, I'm sorry, you can't possibly think I meant you. . .' Lucy adds, colouring when she sees my face.

But no matter how many times my friends tell me that can't have been what Thomas was doing the night I went home with him, I've never totally shaken the suspicion.

Tash and Lucy have described Thomas' charming personality perfectly. As well as his aversion to using protection he also has no scruples regarding forcing a girl to do what he wants in such a way that he only just falls short of date rape.

Barely.

The whole 'fat girls try harder' – a comment I overheard Thomas make when he talked about our night together with his friends, haunted me for a long time. The bloody annoying part of it was that when it happened I was a healthy weight for my height for the first time in years of struggling with diets. Compared to the Verbier skinny-blonde clones I'm on the plump side, but Luc says he loves my curves. I think he really means it too. He always seems very, ahem, appreciative. Anyway I'm not technically overweight, not according to the charts I've found on the internet.

Crap, Thomas is doing it to me again. Screwing with my head. It's bad enough his actions had consequences Luc and I have to live with for the rest of our lives but now I'm supposed to sit here watching him drink and chat up some other poor girl?

I can't do it.

'Could we go down to the cinema room?' I plead. 'I don't want a fuss. Trust me, Luc might lose it.'

'I'm not sure I've ever seen Luc angry.' Tash stands up.

'He rarely gets angry but anything that threatens me or Max stirs up his inner caveman.' I get up from my chair. 'Please, let's go somewhere else. I don't want to waste another minute tonight thinking or talking about Thomas.'

I refuse to hand Thomas that power. It's bad enough that

I have to be constantly reminded of what he's done, of the choices he's taken away from me.

His poison has seeped into our relationship and we can't find the antidote, no matter how hard we try. Heat flushes up my neck and burns my cheeks. My hands ball into fists at my side. Never mind worrying about Luc hurting Thomas, I need to get far away before I take one of the marshmallow toasting forks and go for Thomas myself.

Chapter 3

From: eva.johnson@gmail.com
To: beth.chapman@yahoo.com
Subject: Okay?

Hello Beth,

How are you getting on? I'd love to hear all your news. Have you learnt to ski yet?

I know we disagreed about the wisdom of you taking this job in Verbier, but please know I'm here for you, whatever choices you make. Our spare room is yours whenever you need it. I was worried it might be too soon, but I hope you'll prove me wrong. I only worry because I care, Beth. I don't want you to get hurt. You're like a second daughter to me.

If things do get difficult, remember you're stronger than you think you are. You're a remarkable young woman and I'm proud of how far you've come.

Lots of love,

Eva

BETH

I'm having a bad day. The kind of day when the past feels as tangible as the present and no matter how much make-up I put on, or how bright I fake my smile, I can't get away from the heavy sadness tugging at my bones. It's true, these kinds of days are happening less and less recently and I've learnt techniques to manage them but. . . Well, let's just say today's effort is a crappy one, like I've been driven over by a tank.

I wish I could escape it all forever, but no matter where I go, I can't seem to leave it behind. I thought in Verbier, a world away from my native Streatham, I would feel safe and be able to drop my hyper-vigilance, but I still can't sit with my back to a door and I sleep lightly, with one ear open, like a dog. That's if you can call patches of unsatisfactory rest broken up with nightmares sleep.

I should feel safe. It's clean and beautiful here and there's hardly any crime in the mountains. I know, I checked the statistics. But, as I stand outside Chalet Amélie wearing my best black dress and knee-high boots, I'm gripped by the sudden sense that I'm adrift.

Like I could just float away.

'Are you coming in, Beth?' Holly's voice cuts through my particular brand of crazy. Her tone is kind.

As bosses go I've had far worse than Holly. I've not really spent much time with her because she's just had a baby, but what I've seen of her I like. I meet her eyes, touched by the kindness I find there. I wish I could open up to her. But that's really not a good idea. That way madness lies – the proper losing-the-plot kind. The only hope I ever have of leaving the past behind is to never talk about it. Never think about it.

'Sure, I was just getting a breath of fresh air,' I lie, not convincing either of us.

Get. It. Together.

I need to use tonight as an opportunity to meet someone, to find a way to distract myself. I'd like to feel safe and grounded, even if it's just for one night. To not be alone in my head. I think I'm going to drive myself nuts otherwise. I want to be touched. I need the affirmation of sex, to know I can still do it, that I'm strong enough.

'How are you settling in at Chalet Repos?' Holly's kind voice jolts me.

I try to drag myself back down to earth, to grab hold of the rope Holly is throwing me. Who knew I'd be so grateful for small talk?

'Well, thanks. It's so beautiful here and I can't wait to learn to ski.' I reply stiffly, like a second-rate actress reciting her lines.

Again. Not kidding anyone.

Holly slips her arm through mine. 'It must be hard not knowing many people here. I'm sure Rebecca and Lucy aren't that far away. They went down to the spa, I think. Let's go and find them.'

'Okay.' My smile is genuine this time. I'm grateful to Holly for pulling me out of my mental quick-sand. 'Amazing chalet, by the way.'

Chalet Amélie is truly out of this world. I've never been

anywhere so fancy. It's nicer even than Chalet Repos and much bigger. As Holly shows me round my jaw drops.

Fancy having so many rooms you have spares left over for a games room, dance floor and cinema room. I think the games room alone is bigger than the dingy flat I used to share with Mum. When we get to the spa suite I think I've walked into heaven. You couldn't get further away from the public swimming baths back home. No smell of chlorine – instead a sweet scent of orange blossom is piped out of discreetly placed diffusers. And instead of the usual public baths accompaniment of shrieking kids there's mellow lounge music filling the air. Chill-out music.

It's working. The ambient peace washes over me, easing the kinks out of my tightly wound nerves and taut muscles. I gaze around and then stiffen. I'm sure that couple in the Jacuzzi aren't wearing swimsuits. Um, perhaps there's such a thing as being too chilled. Or maybe I'm being too buttoned-up. Too English. Part of me kind of admires anyone with the body confidence to be that brazen. I turn away, cheeks burning, desperate to pretend I'm cool with it and to hide the evidence I don't belong in this world. I'm ashamed of the buzz of arousal humming through my body. It makes my need to be touched flare into life, the visceral ache in the pit of my belly gripping me, demanding attention.

Holly has turned to talk to Rebecca, so I walk around, taking everything in and trying to relax. When that doesn't work I store up details to share with Eva and Debbie in my next email instead.

'Fancy a skinny-dip?'

I turn to see who's spoken and find I'm face to face with a scruffy surfer type with light-brown hair, laughing eyes and a large grin.

'No thank you.' I reply, sounding horribly prim and proper. I'm irritated with him for making me into ,that' girl. For laughing at me.

'Only I saw you watching.' He nods over at the Jacuzzi.

'Excuse me?' I arch both my eyebrows and fix him with my best piss-off glare. How dare he? 'I wasn't, you know, watching them. I was just looking at the Jacuzzi.'

A hot flush creeps up my neck. His being right does nothing to placate me, it's just winding me up. In a way, I'm telling the truth, though. I've never actually been in a Jacuzzi and I do fancy going in one, but not naked. At least not naked in public. With the right man, well maybe.

'You were so.' His grin stretches ever wider. 'And why not? They wouldn't do it in public if they didn't want an audience. Are you sure I can't persuade you? There's nothing nicer than feeling the warm water against your naked body, bubbles tickling your skin and getting you in the mood.'

I wish his words weren't getting me hot and bothered so easily. I feel desire uncoiling deep inside me, unfurling tendrils of sharp arousal. It doesn't help that he's really attractive. I mean the drop-dead gorgeous, totally shaggable kind of attractive you hardly ever come across in real life. I bet he knows it too.

'I'm Dan.' He smiles. He totally knows it.

When he reaches out a hand, I shake it on auto-pilot,

confused by conflicting emotions and the ability of this stranger to get under my skin so quickly.

'I'm not skinny-dipping,' I reply firmly, ignoring the stirrings of desire.

'Interesting name.' He grins. 'Can I go and fetch you a drink Miss Not Skinny-Dipping? Is that hyphenated, by the way?'

'Very funny, and no thanks. I always fetch my own drinks at parties. I had a friend who was roofied at a party once. No offence.' As soon as I say it I regret my reply. It came out far brusquer than I intended. Why am I scaring a drop-dead gorgeous, twinkly-eyed sex god away?

I sigh inwardly. Luckily I'd been out with Debbie when her drink was spiked and I was able to get her home. Eva made us both promise to be ultra-careful after that. She's always been much more of a mum to me than my own ever was. I'd be jealous of Debbie if she hadn't chosen to unselfishly share her mum with me. Eva's been amazing. It's not an exaggeration to say she saved me when the myth I could cope alone exploded so spectacularly. So I take her advice seriously.

'Ouch, I think I've just been shot down and accused of being a date rapist in one sentence.' Dan places a hand over his heart.

'Well, you did try to get me naked before I even knew your name.' I point out and try to soften my response with a smile, but I don't think it works. Dan's body language no longer mirrors mine. I've blown it.

'Can't blame a guy for trying,' he laughs. 'See you around, Miss Not Skinny- Dipping.'

Then he turns around and walks off. I'm pierced by a pang

of disappointment he's giving up so easily. Should I go after him, apologise, explain? Hardly. One question usually leads to another and then another. It's easier to let him go.

I need a drink.

There are no cocktail-laden waiters or waitresses in sight down here so I head to the bar. I really do need a drink. Everyone else seems to have had the same idea, though, and I can't get through the crowd.

'What are you after?' The man standing next to me turns and smiles. He has short dark hair and a five o'clock shadow. He possesses an undeniable charm, even if his smile doesn't quite reach his cool-blue eyes. 'I'll push through and get it for you.'

'Anything fruity and alcoholic please.'

I suppress any unhelpful comparison with Dan. He walked away, didn't he? Whereas Mr Five-o'clock-shadow is here and giving me all the right signals. I smile at the stranger, determined not to muck it up this time. If I walk around to the side of the bar I should be able to keep my eye on him the whole time so he can't drop something in my drink.

I bite my lip. I hate being like this. Why can't I be normal? If I'm not careful I'll end up totally paranoid like Mum. Bipolar disorder often runs in families. I've done the research. At three am I lie awake worrying there's a rogue gene in my DNA, just waiting, like a ticking bomb, to ruin my life.

My doctor said if I think I'm mad, then I'm probably not. I can't believe a modern GP still uses the word 'mad', but he did. He said mad people usually think they're sane and ordered me to stop worrying. As if it were that easy. I'm not sure I'm capable of doing that, but I do have to start taking chances again. If I see danger around every corner I'll never be free to live the life I want. For so long all I cared about was surviving. That's not good enough any more. If I live a curtailed life, then I'm the one being constantly punished and that's wrong on so many levels.

I'm going to have sex tonight. It's a start and it's just sex. Only sex. A meeting of bodies, nothing more. I can keep my mind locked tight, metal shutters down and padlock on. I'll keep the two separate. I have to. I need to be touched really badly. I want to feel hands on my skin and be caressed and made love to. I need the connection, a tether to stop that floating-away feeling.

The dark-haired guy comes back bearing two bottles. He's tall and good looking. A sporty type. There's a confidence in the way he holds himself that I like. Something in me wants to cling to that confidence. As though I can acquire it by osmosis.

'Thanks so much. I'm Beth.' I say, trying to dispel images of a scruffy surfer sex god with laughing eyes.

'I'm Thomas.' He chinks his bottle against mine. 'Cheers.'

I sip the fruity alcohol a little too quickly and warmth spreads through my chest.

'Do you live in Verbier?' I ask, searching in vain for interesting conversation to hold his attention.

'I'm based here but I have to travel a lot because I compete. Boardercross.' He says, as though that's supposed to mean something to me.

'Oh? I don't know much about the sport, I'm afraid. I've only just arrived here. I'm a chalet girl.'

'A chalet girl? Ah.' A wolfish smile crosses his face.

It should make me run, but it's actually kind of sexy. My body is letting me know, in no uncertain terms, it would be happy if Thomas gobbled me up. It's good to feel desire again. For a long time I felt nothing, nothing at all.

He places a hand on my back to guide me away from the bar. It seems conversation isn't going to be required. Well, that's . . . okay, I suppose. This is what I came here for, wasn't it? I've got something to prove to myself. That I'm no one's victim. I'm taking control.

Adrenalin surges through me, but I'm split. I've got the mind-body disconnect thing going on, making me separate from the sensations of attraction. As if this is happening to someone else.

It's a feeling that triggers alarm bells.

Maybe Eva is right and I'm not ready to be out doing this. But I can't hide from the world forever and why should I have to? Plus, it's not like staying in on my own is such a great option. Being alone is when I feel most afraid.

On my own is vulnerable, unprotected and unsafe.

I get enough attention to reassure me I'm reasonably attractive to men who are into willowy redheads, or want to be. I'm willing to trade anything I've got for someone who might make me feel safe. When Thomas's hand snakes down to my hip I lean in closer, craving the contact. Part of me wishes he was interested in small talk. This is giving me far too much time to think.

I don't give a flying fuck if I'm being anti-feminist. Alone is unsafe. I learnt that the hard way, growing up essentially alone. Mum was there physically, but she was never great at being the grown-up. Some days she was great. When she was spiraling up she'd cook me a meal like a normal mum and maybe want to watch a DVD with me or go shopping. But even then there was a manic quality to her happiness that created a distance between us. I could never quite believe it. I never knew how long it would last. On other days she wouldn't get out of bed or eat, or even drink unless I made her. When she took her medication things improved but I still felt shut out. She'd feel better and then she'd stop taking her tablets because she didn't feel as if she needed them any more. Then she'd get worse again.

It was a seemingly endless repeating pattern.

I thought everyone grew up feeling alone, that it was normal to be afraid all the time. Until I was paired up with Debbie for a geography project at school and she took me home to meet her family. Then I realised what Mum and I had wasn't anything approaching normal.

We did a good enough job of pretending, though. I remember a social worker coming to see me once and I lied through my teeth. I had to protect Mum and our version of family. We were very lucky. The scarce visits had coincided with Mum's good days. Although being ‚lucky' meant I had to deal with everything alone. There was no dad on the scene to protect me, to help me, to be there for me. Well, he was around for a bit when I was a baby, but I don't remember him.

Thomas guides me upstairs and we step out onto the terrace, the cold night air assaulting us. I shiver. My fantasy of a man who'll take care of me and defend me against the monsters under my bed seems really foolish. Am I doing the right thing?

'Shall we go back to my place?' He pulls me closer.

'Sure, why not?' I smile, my heart hammering. So Thomas probably isn't going to be the guy who sticks around to help me slay monsters, but at least tonight I won't be alone in bed and that might keep the nightmares away for a while.

On the short walk back to Thomas's flat he doesn't bother to get to know me, but that's fine by me. I will my body to respond to him when he gropes me in his apartment block's lift, but I only feel numb as he runs his hands over my breasts, kneading them like they're dough, tweaking my nipples so they hurt. And not in a good way.

A shiver of fear runs down my spine. I ignore it. I've got to get back to normal. I need this. I give him the benefit of the doubt and try to kiss him back with enthusiasm. I've committed to this and I'll see it through. Like an experiment. As we enter his flat my fragile desire ebbs away and I'm starting to think I've chosen the wrong man to experiment with. The surroundings are cramped and bare. There are dirty dishes in the sink and the place needs a good vacuum. This is nothing like I imagined; it doesn't match Thomas's charming veneer. A veneer that's showing a good few cracks now he's confident of getting into my pants.

A detachment creeps over me, a disconnected sensation that leaves me stone cold. Is it too late to change my mind?

Before I can speak he pulls my dress up to my waist and is tugging my knickers down with one hand and undoing his flies with the other. Before I know it he's nudging between my legs without even bothering to warm me up.

'Condom,' I gasp and try to pull away, but his fingers are digging into my upper arms, gripping in a way I know will leave bruises.

The forceful grip triggers a first flicker of real panic.

'Oh, for fuck's sake.' His handsome face clouds with irritation.

It's the irritation that does it.

'We need to use a condom,' I repeat, resisting the urge to flinch, fuelled by anger that he's trying to make me feel unreasonable in asking for basic protection. I stare round at the grubby flat and realise he's making me feel grubby too. 'Tell you what, let's not bother, if it's that much of a problem to you.'

His cold, blue eyes glint maliciously and the grip on my arm tightens.

Rage surges up in me so ferocious it practically chokes me. Never again.

Never again.

Even if I have to fight with tooth and nail and every trick in my arsenal, I'm not going to let another man hurt me without fighting back. The rage gives me strength to wrench out of his grasp and pull my knickers back up.

He follows me down the hallway as I make my escape. I can feel him behind me, his breath on my neck.

I spin around and confront him.

'Don't you dare.' I hiss the words, one hand on my hip, the other pointing towards his chest. Rage still surges through me, spewing molten lava.

Giving me strength.

'You're a frigid bitch and you know what else you are?' His upper lip curls.

'I really don't give a flying fuck what you think of me.' I barely recognise my own voice. My legs are trembling and I can feel the sweat trickling down my back. 'But take one step further and I'll call the police. I'm sure you've left bruises on me they'd be very interested in seeing.'

The red marks on my arms sting. For once I'm glad I bruise easily.

That halts him in his tracks but doesn't stop the stream of filth coming out of his mouth. I slam his front door on the words, trying to block my ears as I make my way down the stairs as fast as my shaky legs allow.

Soon I'm walking through the snow, wondering if tears can freeze on your face. It certainly feels cold enough. I stick to the darker side of the street, wanting to skulk in the shadows. Hoping to disappear into a giant black hole.

'Stupid, stupid, stupid girl,' I whisper. This wasn't part of the plan at all. Am I so desperate for physical affection I'm prepared to put myself through this?

God, I don't think I even want to know the answer to that.

I force myself to take a deep breath and focus. So, tonight was crap. But I have to put it behind me. I've coped with far worse than this. Men much crueler than Thomas have tried to crush me and didn't succeed. I won't let them.

I always promised myself if something like this ever happened again I'd fight back, no matter what. My trembling fingers itch to ring Eva but she'll tell me to come back home.

I can't do that, it's too awkward to be at Eva's and, anyway, I can't bear to be in London right now.

I pause and squeeze my eyes shut so tightly I see stars. I have to get my emotions under control before I get back to Chalet Repos. You'd think sharing a bunk room with three other girls would mean I felt less alone but it seems to highlight my isolation. I feel more trapped in my head than ever, without someone who gets me and knows how to draw me out.

They all know each other; I'm the only newbie. It doesn't help that I'm so used to holding things back I struggle to connect with other people in a way that means anything. I'm worried they think I'm aloof and snobbish. I hope they don't. Maybe they could become friends in time if I really make an effort.

I brush tears away from my cold cheeks. I'm fine. I'm absolutely, totally fine and my plan is going to work. I'll bloody well make it work.

From: debbie.johnson@gmail.com
To: beth.chapman@yahoo.com
Subject: Having fun?

Hi Beth,

Long time no hear! Let me have all your news, please. Apart from the photos you posted online when you first arrived you've given me nothing.

I really miss you. Mum misses you too and so does Mark. Did I tell you he's got a new girlfriend? Emma is very bubbly. There's just this one really annoying thing about her – she has this weird laugh, a bit like an asthmatic seal. But I suppose she's okay really.

Have you met any sexy ski instructors yet? Or future husband material?

I know Mum says what you're trying to do is anti-feminist, but I get it. If anyone deserves a rich man who wants nothing more than to take care of his wife, it's you. You so deserve some good luck.

Give me some decent gossip and I might tell you about the rubbish internet date I went on last Saturday.

Love, Debbie xxxx

Chapter 4

LUCY

'Think you'll see your crush tonight?' Tash elbows me as we make our way over to Chalet Amélie for Sophie and Amelia's engagement party. Unfortunately there are some parties it's impossible to avoid. Not without offending people anyway.

'My crush?' My cheeks flush, burning with embarrassment. Crap, I am so bad at hiding my feelings. Hopefully the dark will hide my blushes.

'The very tasty Sebastien Laroche, of course, who else?' Tash teases. 'Unless you've got something else to confess? Have you got multiple crushes you're hiding from me?'

'Huh, as if.' I snort.

I've got nothing to confess. More's the pity. I'm starting to wish I had. Not that I dare confide as much in Tash or she'd do her best to set me up with someone utterly unsuitable. I'm just not wired for casual relationships. They seem such a waste of time. I want to hold out for the right man.

'Sebastien definitely likes you.' Tash persists, watching me, presumably to gauge the effect of her words. 'I saw the way he looked at you.'

'I don't think so.' I stare at the ground, at the fresh, powdery snow we're crunching underfoot. The flare of hope I feel at her words troubles me.

'Oh, I think you know he likes you. You're afraid of it, that's all,' Tash proclaims triumphantly.

That's all?

'Hmm. When did you get so perceptive Tash?' I grimace.

'Ha, I'm right, aren't I?' Tash grins.

I wish she wasn't.

'I expect he likes a lot of girls. He looks the type.' I bite my lip. 'I doubt he's ever serious.'

It's confusing. On the one hand he's almost definitely unsuitable, but he's also my snowboarding idol and a free-riding God. Not to mention he's bloody gorgeous and I've not been able to think about anything else but him since the night of the film festival screening. The skin on my hand still tingles when I think about him holding it. I've replayed the way he put my hand over his heart and how it made me feel a thousand times. How mad is that? I find it disturbing that a man can have the power to do that to me.

The gesture was casual and yet at the same time intensely intimate. What does that mean? Probably that Sebastien treats physical intimacy with a casual disregard. So, he's not right for me.

Desire and fear race through me, competing for dominance, neck and neck. I don't know which is going to win.

'Just because he likes women in general it doesn't mean he

can't like you in particular.' Tash slips her arm through mine. She's wearing a short asymmetrical jersey dress with chunky boots and she hasn't bothered with her coat for the short walk between the chalets. Her trademark cat-like eye shadow makes her stand out from the crowd. She's cool. Or whatever the cool word is for cool. I don't even know that.

I'm dowdy by comparison in my best dark indigo jeans and silky black top. I just don't do glamorous. I feel most comfortable in my sports gear. When I'm skiing I'm in my element, it's the only time I feel like I truly fit in.

'Why would he like me, Tash?' I blurt out. 'I mean, I'm nothing special.'

Tash stops dead on the path and turns to me. 'Are you kidding? What do you mean you're nothing special? You're pretty, you're a fantastic skier and a loyal friend. Also you don't bullshit people. That's pretty rare, you know. He'd be lucky to have you. Plus you're really into the things he loves.'

I smile and squeeze her arm. 'Thanks, Tash.'

I wish I believed it. Growing up with a hyper-critical mother who saw it as her mission in life to make sure I didn't get 'above myself' hasn't done much for my self-esteem. She once told Dad off for praising me for good test results at school, saying I'd get a big head.

So, no matter how well I did, how many A grades I got or what team I made at school I never got more than a nod and a criticism that I could've done better. I should've got an A star or made team captain.

'How long is it since you had sex?'

Tash's question catches me off-guard.

My cheeks flame even hotter. Thank God it's dark.

'I don't know exactly,' I mumble.

'Roughly then?' Tash is like a terrier with a tuggy-toy. She's not going to let go of this anytime soon.

I sigh. 'I don't know.'

'Well, you've not hooked up with anyone out here that I know of.' Tash has stopped on the path again and as we're arm in arm she jerks me to a stop too. 'Fuck a duck, you're never a virgin?'

The incredulity in her tone stings. I bite my lip and look away.

'Really? I don't think I know any other virgins.' Tash seems genuinely astounded. 'How do you get to your mid-twenties and keep your virginity? Because you've had boyfriends, right?'

'Yes but. . . where I come from it's very church-orientated.' I jerk my chin up. I've nothing to be ashamed of. 'I used to belong to the church youth group. It was one of the few places my parents would let me go and that's where I met my boyfriend. There was a lot of fuss made about staying pure for marriage.'

'Really?' Tash raises her eyebrows. 'I can't imagine it, but then I've never known anyone religious. At least I don't think so.'

She makes it sound like I'm suffering from a rare disease.

'I'm not. . . well, I used to be, but when I got older I questioned things more. My beliefs are a bit more fluid now. I suppose that's the best way to describe it,' I sigh. 'My boyfriend was more. . . rigid.'

'I bet he was, all that time without sex.' Tash laughs.

I smile and roll my eyes. 'Well, we did other stuff, you know. Just didn't go all the way.'

'So, what's stopping you now?'

'I think if I've waited this long I should probably save having sex until it's perfect. I have to wait for the right man. I kind of fell into my first relationship. I said yes to the first boy who asked me out. Looking back, there was no way he was right for me.'

'But it's never perfect, Lucy. Life isn't like that.' Tash resumes the walk to Chalet Amélie. 'If you want my advice, you need to get losing your virginity over and done with, preferably with someone you don't care about, because the first time is usually crap. If you don't sleep with multiple partners, how will you ever really know if you're a good match in bed with the guy you ultimately deem perfect to settle down with?'

'Um, I'm not sure I like that idea. I'd rather wait for it to feel. . . right.' I squirm beside her, half-relieved my secret is out and half-terrified this will be the catalyst for a change I'm not sure I'm ready for. But maybe I'm hiding behind the excuse of waiting for it to be perfect before I commit to having sex. It means I've never had to put myself out there or risk getting hurt. Also I've never had to expose my sexual ignorance to anyone.

She pulls a face. 'You might find yourself waiting a long time if you're not prepared to compromise at all. Actually, thinking about it, Nate is pretty near perfect but he can still annoy the hell out of me at times. Sometimes you have to adjust what you think you want for what is actually right for you. Or for what's right in front of you.'

Anxiety grips me as we approach Chalet Amélie. Any relief I felt at confessing my secret is overshadowed by fear of ridicule or even ending up the subject of a bet.

'Tash, please don't tell anyone.' My jaw clenches.

'Of course I won't.' Tash squeezes my arm. 'I do think we should try and get you laid, though.'

We?

She lets go of my arm and walks ahead of me into the chalet.

'Tash, no.' I hurry after her, unease churning in my stomach. I really, really don't want to fall prey to one of her schemes, however well-intentioned she might be.

When I leave the fresh, cold night air and enter the chalet after Tash a wall of warmth hits me. I hope she's going to drop the subject now we're surrounded by people.

We find Sophie hiding out on the gallery and have to talk her into rejoining the party. It seems a shame some idiot from her past gets to ruin her engagement party. All the more reason to be very careful who you sleep with and wait for the right person. I head off to find a drink and bump into Rebecca in the crowd.

'So, what were you arguing about with Tash earlier?' Rebecca raises an eyebrow, clearly a seasonnaire on the scent of a secret. She's sipping a Kir Royale. I definitely need one.

'Oh nothing much, it doesn't matter. You know what Tash is like.' I avoid her gaze and look around to find a circulating waiter so I can grab a much-needed champagne cocktail.

I can't believe I kept the secret of my virginity all this time and now it's been out five minutes I'm already struggling to contain it. I might've known it'd be Tash who'd winkle it out of me. She's too canny by half.

Will she keep it quiet? I trust her, she's a good friend but not great at either keeping her voice down or being subtle. If she makes getting me laid one of her projects, well. . .

I reach out for a glass of Kir Royale from the tray of a passing waiter and sip the blackcurrant bubbles with champagne kick, the warmth spreading down into my chest. Mum might think cocktails are the invention of the devil but my family drink whiskey like it's a religion, so I don't see why cocktails get such a bad rap. It's just one of the many things I'm not allowed to question.

Whenever I questioned anything as a child Mum would say ‚because' and her mouth would tighten in a way I learnt to dread. Religion was the main subject off limits, though. I once questioned why God wouldn't want me to use the swings in the village playground on a Sunday and Mum and Dad refused to speak to me for days. The worst part was the way they looked at me, as though I was the worst disappointment ever and I'd been deliberately wicked when really I was just baffled. I'd just wanted to understand.

I sigh and swig back more of the cocktail. The girls out here would think I was nuts if I tried to explain the strict Presbyterian culture I grew up in. Tash clearly thinks I'm some kind of alien or perhaps a cult survivor.

'Salut.' A voice cuts through my thoughts and I'm being embraced before I can look up.

When I do glance up Sebastien's large, sensual lips are

already on my cheek. He kisses me enthusiastically on both cheeks and then directly on the mouth. I barely have time to register the casual intrusion of his lips and hint of tongue before it's withdrawn again.

'Uh, hi.' I blink. Did that . . . Is that . . . Okay, my brain has frozen, speech and thought resolutely refusing to obey me.

'Where did you get to the other night? Come, come.' He neither waits for, nor seems to expect, an answer but takes me by the hand and leads me away from an open-mouthed Rebecca. His hand is rough and large compared to mine. The contact is startling but by no means unwelcome.

It doesn't occur to me to refuse. Why doesn't it occur to me to refuse?

He draws me into a quiet alcove and pulls me down next to him on a small brown-leather sofa. The sofa is covered with the softest faux-mink throw I've ever touched, it's so silky beneath my fingers. There's not much room, so I'm pressed up against him, my thigh making contact with his. I'm achingly aware of his close proximity and the corresponding flare into life of desire, deep inside me. It's like he's dropped a match onto a pile of dry kindling.

I've never felt a desire this compelling before. Going without sex honestly hasn't bothered me that much, but then I've never met anyone like Seb before.

Sebastien rests his hand on my thigh and leans in. I think he's going to kiss me but his lips don't make contact with my skin. I realise, with a jolt, that I really want them to. Boy, do I want them to. I am so confused. God help me.

'Have you been thinking about me?' He whispers. 'Because I've been thinking about you. Do you know what I've been thinking?'

He trails his hand up and down my thigh, rhythmically stroking my leg. It's surprisingly arousing.

'Uh, no.' My breath catches in my chest as desire floods me, an overwhelming breach of my defences. I'm unfurling, coming undone beneath his fingers. Every reason I ever had for waiting is disintegrating and being washed away along with my resolve.

'I've been thinking about all the things I'd like to do to you.' His lips brush my ear and hot breath tickles my skin as he whispers. 'Very wicked things that will bring us both a great deal of pleasure.'

I inhale sharply, startled by the jolt of sexual electricity coursing through me. I never knew. . . I didn't think. . . Oh my. . .

His hand trails higher up my thigh and then gently squeezes my hip bone. A gentle moan escapes my lips and heat sears my cheeks. At the back of my mind I wonder if anyone is watching us but I'm too far gone to check.

Seb's breath catches and the amused desire twinkling in his dark eyes morphs into something deeper, more intense, as though he too is losing control.

Finally his lips brush my neck, my collarbone and the skin exposed at the neckline of my top. My nipples harden, sensitive against my cotton bra. This is fast, far too fast. Yet my body is crying out that this isn't fast enough. I want him! Oh, God do I want him.

His lips are now on mine and I forget everything as his tongue explores my mouth, tasting and teasing, thrusting against my tongue in a promise of what else he could do to me. There's a buzz between my legs, sharp, intense need flaring into life, spreading through my body like wild fire.

My body's capitulation is so quick it scares me. It's too fast. I need to find the brake or pull the emergency cord to stop this. I pull back reluctantly.

'What's wrong?' Sebastien eyes me quizzically, continuing to languidly stroke my hip and making all the little hairs on my arms stand erect.

'Erm, well, we don't know each other. This isn't what I do. It's. . .' I run out of words. I don't know what it is. The throbbing need inside me makes it impossible to concentrate on what I'm saying.

'You don't like it? Shall I stop?' he asks immediately.

'No, I mean yes. I mean I like it. I don't want you to stop exactly, just. . .' I break off, flustered and afraid I'll push him away.

'Sorry if I'm going too fast. You're utterly irresistible. My fault.' He pulls a funny face. 'Shall we do things the English way? We can be stiff and awkward and pretend to ignore our attraction for each other.'

I narrow my eyes. 'I'm actually Scottish, not English.'

'Ah I see. There's a difference?'

I almost launch into the kind of well-practised diatribe I have to use on idiots, but see Seb's lips twitching.

'You're mocking me.'

'Not at all.' He grins, a hint of laughter lines around his

eyes. It's a face used to smiles and laughter. 'I just want to make you comfortable.'

'Thanks. You're right. It's all a bit fast for me.' I tense, hoping he'll understand and not lose interest.

Seb takes my hand and cups it in his. 'No worries. I'm far too used to getting my own way. It will be good for me to wait. But there's nothing to be afraid of. Attraction is an amazing thing, it would be wrong to fight it.'

'Would it?' I can't help but smile. He looks so sincere at the utter wrongness of ignoring sexual attraction, but I sense an undercurrent of mockery, not of me but of himself. A man who can laugh at himself. Hmm, I'm totally done for.

'Are you sure you wouldn't like me to leave?' Seb examines me closely.

'I definitely don't want you to leave. I just need to go, you know, slower.' I will him to understand.

Seb shrugs. 'Really, it's not a problem. We go slow. Slow can be good too. Can I kiss you?'

I nod and part my lips as his mouth meets mine. I could do this all night. My lips are tingling where they meet his. I once read that the skin on our lips is the most sensitive of anywhere on our body. Now I can quite believe it.

I'm falling deeper and deeper, taken up by desire and Seb's muscular body pressed hard against mine. His scent intoxicates me, so clean and manly, so enticing I want to press myself even harder into him. I've moved little by little and so has he. We're as close as we can be without me actually climbing onto his lap.

A very enticing proposition. Doubt presses in at the corner of my mind. Why on earth did I say I wanted to go slow? Right now my body would be happy to move at the speed of light, all my senses tingling. Feeling vibrantly alive.

My mind is flooded with images of what Seb could do to me, if I let him. Am I nuts to be holding back? I doubt many women say 'no' to him. I have a lifetime of experience of not crossing the line, but this is by far the hardest test I've ever faced.

When Seb stops kissing me and pulls away it's hard to ignore the unfulfilled ache between my legs.

'Shall we go for a walk?' Seb's eyes are dark and his breathing hard.

Maybe pulling back is hard for him too. That's flattering. As we stand up I remind myself of all the reasons why I have to control myself. I can't lose my virginity to a one-night stand, however enticing the proposition. And it is enticing. I might not have held out so long if Seb had been around when I was younger. I assumed I didn't have much of a libido, but it turns out it was merely slumbering, waiting to be roused and coaxed into life by the right man.

'Maybe we can go and look round the chalet?' I suggest. 'You know, I'd love to know more about the film-skiing you do and your trip to the Antarctic. It sounds amazing.'

I watch Seb closely for any signs of irritation or impatience. Normally this is the point in proceedings when I cease to be interesting and men suddenly remember they were supposed to be somewhere else. What's the point of wasting time on a girl who's not going to put out?

'Sure.' If Seb is disappointed he hides it admirably and puts as much enthusiasm into his tales of snowboarding as he did into kissing, a grin splitting his charismatic face.

We stay close as we make our way around the chalet and I listen to his stories. I'm happy to take his arm and snuggle into his side. I can't give up the physical contact. It's as if he's magnetised me, somehow, and I couldn't pull away even if I wanted to.

Which I don't.

'Have you seen the view from the terrace? It's too crowded in here. Would you like to get some air, perhaps?' Seb asks, once we've seen round the chalet.

'Yes, that would be nice.' I smile, my face practically splitting in two at the idea of being alone with him. Maybe the champagne cocktails have gone to my head a little. Perhaps they are wicked after all.

Seb's grin widens too and he takes my hand, leading me to the way out as he tells me how amazing it feels to be on top of the world and at one with the mountains. We both fall quiet outside on the decked terrace and stand looking down over the twinkling lights of houses in the dark valley far below. As my eyes adjust, I realise that it's not totally dark out here. The snowy mountains reflect the pale, white moonlight. The sky is clear and the stars glitter like diamonds. It's magical. I could never get bored of this. Never. I'm falling in love with Switzerland and maybe a certain mountain boardercross champion too.

'I could never leave the mountains. I hate the city.' Seb leans over the rail. 'I have to be able to see the horizon. In the cities there's so much concrete everywhere, it's stifling the earth. The earth can't breathe in the city and neither can I.'

'That's very poetic. I feel like that too. I come from the Scottish Highlands.'

'Ah, the Highlands. I have been to Inverness and Loch Ness, where you have your famous monster. Have you ever seen it?'

I snort. 'No, there's no monster. Just miles and miles of space to breathe.'

Seb's hand rests over mine on the rail. I wish I could believe that this is the start of something, but I know sex isn't a big deal for Seb. When I finally have sex it has to be with someone who cares about me, someone I'm in a relationship with. Sex itself is a leap for me. Casual sex is a leap too far.

'So why did you leave Scotland?' Seb turns and fixes me with an intense gaze that pierces through my defences.

It's as if he can see me, really see me. All the extraneous things of life – small talk, social niceties, external filters – have been stripped away. He's taken the time to look at me properly. Is this what love feels like? I don't want to lie to him. I feel I owe him the truth for not running as far away from me as possible. For being different from the other men who've tried their luck with me since I moved to Verbier.

'I tell everyone I came to Switzerland for the skiing, the snow is unreliable in the Highlands, after all,' I pause. 'And that is partly true.'

'And what is the other reason, Lucy Lu?' Seb strokes the side of my face.

He's given me a nickname. Warmth spreads through my chest and my lips curve into a smile.

'I had to get far away from home. Nothing really bad. My family are good people, but I needed space from them, to escape the life they expected me to live. I know I said there's miles of space to breathe in the Highlands, but at home I felt suffocated.'

'So you spread your wings. I get it. Families . . . pffft.' Seb shrugs. 'They are difficult. My family are in France and I live in Switzerland and visit once a month or so. It's a perfect arrangement.'

I love how animated his face gets. Every craggy feature lit up with joy, amusement or desire, ever changing with his mood. Full of life. I feel a little more alive just for standing next to him, conjured into being more, feeling more by the touch of his hand on my skin.

'Do you come from a big family?'

'Yes, I have three brothers. We are very competitive.' Seb raises his eyes to the stars. 'My brother Michel got a bronze medal in the last Winter Games and I was placed fourth. I have never heard the end of it. He's never beaten me in the Verbier Extreme, though. Do you have brothers?'

Seb's eyes shine with humour, as bright as the starry canopy above us.

'Yes, funnily enough I've got three brothers too. I guess it's a little different being a sister. My parents are pretty old fashioned, only the males of the family matter.' I grip the rail tightly. 'Their only ambition for me is that I marry a local farmer.'

'They don't approve of you coming to Verbier?' Seb moves closer. I can feel the warmth of his body, the enticing pull of his chemistry.

'You could say that.' I bite my lip and edge closer to him.

'Well I'm very glad you did.' Seb cups my face with his hands, eyes sparkling and my heart skips a beat.

Before I know it I'm standing on tiptoe and we're kissing again. My arms are around him, pulling him closer and his hands slide down my back, cupping my bottom and squeezing.

Soon I'm being swept away again, by an unstoppable tide of wanting and needing. . . I've definitely been magnetised and I just can't resist Seb's pull. I don't know if I'm in love or in heat.

But still there's the persistent murmur in my head, obstinately refusing to give in and telling me to stop. I might be ready to make the leap for someone like Seb but I still can't do casual sex. Not even for someone as divine as him. I haven't waited this long to give it up for nothing.

I pull back. It's possibly the hardest thing I've ever done.

Ever.

I take a deep breath. 'I think we have to stop, Seb.'

'Okay.' Seb exhales loudly as he lets me go. As though it's hurting him physically to let me go. I know how he feels, my own body is thrumming with protest and unfulfilled need. This is all so. . . complicated.

'I do. . . want you,' I whisper, gripped by fear that I'll never see him again. That he'll think I'm rejecting him.

'So what's the problem?' His fingers continue to caress mine where I'm gripping the rail, making it hard to keep my resolve.

'I don't do casual sex. I'm not into one-night stands.' I squeeze my eyes shut briefly, trying not to think about his seductive fingers and where else they might touch me. Maybe I'm also afraid to see his reaction.

'It doesn't have to be casual and we don't have to stand,' he murmurs gently, his words sending shivers down my spine.

This is bloody difficult. Seb is so very attractive. He's my sporting hero, everything I admire and yet. . . that still doesn't make him boyfriend material. He's impulse-driven. It's what makes him brilliant on the mountains, but I don't want to be tonight's impulse. Tonight's impulse is tomorrow's 'that Scottish girl I shagged'.

I'm smarter than that.

'But, being serious, I can't. . .' I break off. It actually pains me to say it, especially as unsatiated desire has me reeling.

'Can't do this ever or can't do this tonight?' Seb quirks a dark eyebrow.

'Can't do this tonight.' I bite my lip as I step out of reach. My body screams that I'm crazy. Who cares if he wants to use me and forget me the next morning? Seb would be mine for one glorious night.

But I do care and I can't do this. I'd despise myself afterwards for selling out for a few hours of pleasure.

'You are a very unusual girl, Lucy Lu.' Seb looks regretful but not annoyed, thank God. Any sense of irritation and I would've walked away. Permanently. 'Anyone else and I'd think you were playing hard to get but you're serious, aren't you?'

'I don't play games.' I make my way to the terrace steps, but each step away from Seb is a wrench.

'So, when can we make love, Lucy Lu?' Seb asks, a lot louder than I'm comfortable with.

I turn around to check the terrace is still clear and no one I know is listening. Then I turn back to face him.

'When I believe this is for real,' I smile regretfully, and make my way down the steps. When I look back, Seb salutes me and blows me a kiss.

'See you soon, Lucy Lu,' he grins. 'I feel it's only fair to warn you I plan to have a truly filthy dream about you tonight.'

I laugh as I walk away. I should go and find Tash or the others. It's rude to head off without saying goodbye to Sophie, but if I stay at the party any longer I'm scared I'll cave in and end up going home with Seb.

I barely notice the cold night air as I walk back to Chalet Repos. My skin is still flushed and warm, a heat that intensifies when I remember Seb's hands caressing me and how good it felt to kiss him.

He won't be the only one having a filthy dream tonight.

Oh crap, I'm in serious trouble.

Chapter 5

From: derektrent@gmail.com
To: sophietrent@hotmail.com
Re: MIA

Hello daughter. Could you drop your mother a quick line?

The thing is, if you don't reply soon, I won't be able to stop her reporting you missing again. We all know how embarrassing that was the last time!

So please email, unless you fancy a visit from Interpol.

Bye for now,

Dad

From: sandratrent@gmail.com
To: sophietrent@hotmail.com
Re: Wedding Plans (1 attachment)

Sophie darling, it was lovely to hear from you finally. It's good to know we don't have to send a search-and-rescue team out to Switzerland to find you after all. Ha ha.

However, I really can't agree there's 'no rush to decide things'. If we don't take the May slot at The Lodge I honestly don't think we'll be able to get in anywhere half decent.

Also, and you won't like me saying it, but you're not getting any younger. The trend may well be for women to have their babies later these days but the risks are so much greater the longer you leave it.

It might be old-fashioned of me, but I think it would be best if you marry before you get pregnant. You agree, don't you, darling? I know how much you want to be a mother. You always did love babies, even when you were a little girl. Do you remember when you were asked what you wanted to be when you grew up you said you wanted to be a mum?

I've attached an article from the *Daily Mail* with all the statistics about the risks for older mothers. I hope that will persuade you of the wisdom of getting on with things quickly.

Let us know if you want to reserve the May slot at The Lodge after all. It might not be too late to change your mind and it does have such lovely lakeshore gardens. Wouldn't they make a fantastic backdrop for the wedding photos?

Love,
Mum

SOPHIE

The Lodge Hotel, the Lake District and Mum all seem a million miles away as Luc negotiates the hairpin bends leading to his parents' mountain village. I wish I could pack up all my problems and ship them back to England.

Luc is gripping the steering wheel so tightly his knuckles are as white as the virgin snow blanketing the jagged peaks of the Alps. Other than that, and a tension around his jawline, there's no outward sign he's affected by the dreadful news we received this week.

The news I'm still reeling from.

I hug myself and stare fixedly at the view. Normally the combination of the picturesque scenery of the country I've adopted and being with Luc would lift my spirits but a black cloud has been trailing us since we left Verbier.

I don't know how to fix this. Or even if it can be fixed. By the time we reach Vex and Luc parks the car I'm grinding my teeth. I do my best to unclench my jaw and breathe.

We've agreed not to tell his parents, there's no point until we know for sure there's nothing that can be done. I want to go along with it, to help protect his parents from unnecessary worry. Especially given they've got their own stress to deal with. The problem is, I can't remember how to be normal. I'm rigid, wired for fight or flight. But there's no one to punch and no matter how far we run our problems would just come with us.

Luc guides me by the elbow across Vex's main square to the Café du Place. It's a gesture he means to be comforting but it makes me jittery. His awareness I'm struggling only highlights my awkwardness and makes the painful emotions harder to suppress.

Today was going to be difficult enough already, but now I have more than one minefield to navigate.

'Sophie, *ma chère*.' Thérèse, my future mother in law, greets me with an enthusiastic double kiss as soon as we've pushed our way through the café's heavy swing doors.

'Bonjour.' I attempt my 'everything's just fabulous' smile, but my face feels tight and strange.

It's only as I lean in to kiss Luc's dad that I see Thérèse is wearing a similar strained smile.

Oh crap.

We're all pretending, but we need the pretence, the familiar greeting rituals and fetching of drinks. Without this social framework we couldn't contain our feelings and today we need to.

The worried glance Luc shoots his mother and the brief swimming sadness in her eyes put all our less tangible problems into context.

Her eyes clear and she replaces her fake, bright smile for her husband, Olivier's, benefit but the slip tells me we're about to get more bad news.

I slip my hand into Luc's and squeeze. I don't want to ask the question but not to ask would be horribly rude.

'How did it go at the hospital?' I revert to English. This is too important to trust to my imperfect French.

Working at the bar hasn't exactly expanded my medical vocabulary. For the millionth time since I moved to Verbier

I wish they'd taught us useful French vocabulary at school. I remember being made to debate environmental issues for my oral exam. Nothing prepared me for when my car broke down in the middle of nowhere at three am and the mechanic I finally spoke to had no English. Beyond saying '*ma voiture est en panné*' I was totally lost. And I've never once debated environmental issues since I came here. More importantly I'm not sure I know the French phrases for triple bypass or likely prognosis either. I must get Luc to teach me some useful phrases when we get time.

'It wasn't good news.' Thérèse answers slowly and doesn't meet my eye.

'What did they say?' A muscle twitches in Luc's jaw.

'The doctors have said your father needs to take things much easier if we don't want another, more serious heart attack.' Thérèse sits back down next to her husband, eyes glistening. Her pose has an unnatural stiffness to it.

The dark shadows beneath her eyes make me wonder if she's shielding us from worse news. I have the feeling she's protecting us from the details. So she's protecting us and we're protecting her.

'I can help out more,' Luc offers straight away. I glance at him. We both know that won't be easy to manage.

'That would help, thank you, son. You know how your mother worries.' Olivier pats Thérèse on the arm, decades of affectionate ease and banter in the gesture.

Now I know it's serious. All previous offers of help over the years have had to hurdle almost endless barriers of resistance and pride. Immediate capitulation is unheard of.

This is very bad. The knowledge sends a chill down my spine.

'We should talk about happier things,' Thérèse declares, blinking hard and getting to her feet again. 'I need to check if the duck is ready, but when Paul and Marie get here we should talk about your wedding. I know you haven't set a date yet. I was thinking perhaps we ought to set a date for early Spring?

The glimmer of entreaty in her expression twists something in my chest. It's a conspiracy. If I didn't know for certain they've never met I'd swear Thérèse is in cahoots with Mum.

'Let's talk about it later.' I force a smile and ignore the growing tightness in my chest.

When she's out of the room I turn to face Luc and see my alarm about Olivier is mirrored in his eyes. I lace my fingers through his again and squeeze, holding on tight. I love Luc more than I ever knew it was possible to love someone. I want to marry him more than anything, but how on earth am I going to plan a wedding that will keep everyone happy? My chest feels tight, like I can't take a deep breath.

'How are your parents, Sophie? Are they well?' Olivier asks, his French accent far thicker than his wife's and the words more halting. I know he'd be insulted if I turned the conversation back to French. He says he likes practising his English with me.

'They're both okay, thank you.' I shove Mum's emails to the back of my mind, but it's like trying to stuff an armful of ping-pong balls into an already-full cupboard. They bounce back, refusing to stay put. 'Have you ever been to England?'

Luc and Olivier both laugh, as though I've asked if he's travelled to the moon.

'My parents rarely leave Valais. Isn't that right, Dad?'

'Why leave the most beautiful country in the world?' Olivier shrugs. 'I don't like cities either. I went to Geneva once but my heart is here in Valais.'

'You didn't like Geneva?' I ask.

'No. Too many cars and too many people. The mountains are in my blood, in my heart.' He puts a liver-spotted hand to his chest.

I bite my lip, trying not to think about how long that heart has left to beat. It's casting a second shadow over us, I can see it in Luc's eyes too. Only Olivier seems defiant in its presence.

The need to fill the silence presses in on me. 'You know the part of England I come from is called the Lake District? I think you'd like it. We have mountains too, just not as big as the Alps.'

Olivier shrugs. 'I am sure I would, cherie. Maybe if I were twenty years younger perhaps I could go and see. . . But I won't be travelling anywhere now. And I don't need to. I have everything and everyone I love right here.'

I blink hard and Olivier reaches over to take my free hand, squeezing it and smiling kindly at me. 'Don't look so sad, Sophie. I've had a good life and I'm glad I've lived to see Luc find a girl as lovely as you.'

There's a lump in my throat that won't go away. I wish I'd had longer to get to know Olivier. I wish I had a tenth of his courage. I wish a lot of things.

I stare down at the table. I feel as though I've been slapped in the face by death. I've been brought up short for daring to live as though it didn't exist.

'Papa,' Luc protests. 'You still have plenty more life to come and doctors can work wonders these days.'

'Luc, you need to face it, my travelling days are over.' The answer is gentle and resigned. Olivier's eyes shine with love tinged by pain and I have to look away again, my emotions are struggling to break through, but I can't be the one to crack when everyone else is being so stoical.

Luc tenses beside me and his lips compress into a hard line. I know he's not ready to accept this. He wants to fight it. I understand the feeling but instead of anger I feel a terrifying powerlessness. We've been dealt one piece of bad news after another recently and this feels like one hard thing too much to bear.

'Travelling? Who's travelling?' Thérèse comes back into the room, forehead creased.

'No one's going anywhere, Maman,' Luc reassures her. 'We were just talking about England, saying you'd like the Lake District, the region Sophie comes from in England.'

'It's a shame we'll never get to see it,' she tuts. 'But the doctors would never allow your father to travel now. Also we wouldn't get travel insurance with his heart condition and our age.'

Thérèse drops into her seat only to rise a second later when the café's swing doors open.

'Paul, Marie! *Bienvenue*.'

I join Thérèse at the door and go to kiss Luc's cousin and

his wife. Then I force myself to drop down to greet their two-year-old daughter Hélène.

'*Bonjour, ma petite*.' I stroke the toddler's cheek and smile up at Marie. 'Hélène is walking so well now.'

Hopefully I manage the exchange without too much emotional leakage. It's so hard to be around babies and small children at the minute. It doesn't help that Hélène is one of the cutest – all curls, dimples and giggles.

How do I keep a lid on the pain when a musical giggle or cheeky smile can wrench it wide open at any time and with no warning?

'*Bonjour*, Sophie. *Ça va?*' Marie crouches down next to me to unzip Hélène's coat and pull off her pink snow boots.

'Oui.' I nod and try to up the wattage of my smile. 'She's grown so much since I last saw her.'

Marie smiles that proud, contented-mother smile that has the same effect on me as salt on a red-raw wound. It excludes me and makes me feel less, somehow. Faulty and unwomanly. Unfulfilled.

I glance at Marie. Has Luc's mum has told her I'm infertile? I wish Luc and I hadn't agreed not to tell his parents about our adoption application problems. He doesn't want to worry them, which I get but. . . not talking about the thing tearing me apart isolates me even more. Like I'm trapped in a glass dome but forced to smile and pretend nothing's wrong.

I could think about the other elephant in the room, the one trumpeting loudly for my attention. How do I tell Mum she has to ditch all her plans, that the wedding has to be in

Switzerland? She'll understand with Luc's dad not being well, won't she?

Maybe if I open with that news, she'll suggest looking for Swiss venues herself? It's the wimpy way to do it, I know, but I can't face a big row. Not after the week Luc and I have had. I can't take the backlash of another emotional onslaught, not now.

I sit back down next to Luc and slip my hand into his as we wait for his mum to bring out her renowned confit of duck. She's a superb cook and it's one of my favourite dishes, but right now I'm not sure I'll be able to swallow anything. My chest feels too tight and my body too full of emotion to leave any room for food.

Chapter 6

From: debbie.johnson@gmail.com
To: beth.chapman@yahoo.com
Subject: Blind Date

I don't care what you say, you've got to be having more fun than me at the moment. So, as you replied to me I'll tell you how my date went. As soon as I got there he started showing me photos on his phone. Not willy shots like that other creep but photos of before, after and DURING his recent plastic surgery.

Can you imagine?

I think I should avoid internet dates and focus on work for a while. The men I find on the internet all seem to be either married or weird. Or both.

I've decided to actively not date in the hope the right man will come and find me. I figure I've tried everything else, so why not try not trying?

Did you hook up with someone at that party you went to? I can't believe you're partying in Verbier, you lucky cow :-)

Now I'm not dating I expect to live vicariously through you, so you have to stay in touch and give me all the goss.

Love,

Debbie

From: beth.chapman@yahoo.com
To: debbie.johnson@gmail.com
Subject: Blind Date

Your date sounds awful. I think you've got the right idea staying clear of Internet dating for a while.

I won't lie, the party at the chalet I went to was very glam, but I've not got much to report. Most of the men I'm meeting are ski instructors who aren't into anything long term or married men looking for a quick fumble behind their wives' backs!

So, it looks like it might be harder than I thought to meet someone.

I've got a skiing lesson tomorrow btw, wish me luck :-)

Love from

Beth

xx

BETH

So it turns out I'm a rubbish skier.

'I'm sorry, Lucy, I'm wasting your time.' I decide not to get up out of the snowdrift I just landed in. My salopettes are surprisingly warm and totally waterproof. I think I'll just stay here until I've recovered from the bruising to my pride and my bottom.

'Don't worry about it, it's only your first lesson after all.' Lucy parks her skis in the snow and sits down next to me. 'I learnt when I was a little girl in the Highlands. Trust me, it's much easier to learn as a kid because you're not so afraid of falling. Plus a child's centre of gravity is much lower anyway, so they're less likely to fall in the first place.'

As if to prove her point, a crocodile line of tiny tots makes their way down the nursery slope, zigzagging with perfect control. The two female instructors with them wave at Lucy and she waves back.

'Oh God, that's embarrassing.' I sink my head into my hands.

'It's because they're not afraid,' Lucy explains. 'They have no problem with shifting their weight to the front. You keep leaning back because you're afraid of falling forward. Which is why. . .'

'I keep ending up on my bottom,' I interrupt, groaning. 'I'm going to be sore tomorrow.'

'That's a given.' She shrugs. 'It'll be better when you get over your fear.'

Easier said than done. That might be difficult, given fear is my default setting.

'Shall we call it a day?' I unclip my skis. I've had quite enough of falling over for one day. 'I'm sure you'd rather be off skiing some black run or doing death-defying leaps at the snow park. I've taken up more than enough of your time.'

'Not at all, but it might be an idea to stop there for today.' She checks her phone. 'I think I'll head to the snow park, if you're sure you don't mind.'

'Of course not,' I reply hurriedly before she can change her mind. 'Thanks, Lucy, I appreciate you giving up your spare time to teach me.'

'No problem.' She smiles as she snaps her skis back on. 'I expect to see you here the same time tomorrow. No excuses.'

I groan.

'You'll thank me one day.' Lucy laughs and heads off at a speed that terrifies me.

It looks as if she plans to get me skiing if it kills her. Or me, which is much more likely. I make my way to the nearest cantine for a restorative hot chocolate and realise I haven't thought about anything unpleasant for the past hour other than staying upright and remembering Lucy's instructions. Maybe I will keep up the lessons after all.

The cantine isn't too crowded and I find a small table tucked away from the main terrace where I can sip my hot chocolate in peace. I'm already a bit in love with the snowy mountain peaks, fresh alpine air and warm winter sun. This certainly beats a London winter. I'd thought the others were having me on when they'd talked about sunbathing on the slopes but I'm far too hot in my ski jacket so I slip it off and drape it over the back of the chair.

I open up the kindle app on my phone and am about to start reading my book when a familiar voice carries across the terrace and interrupts my concentration.

'There are plenty of chalet-girl slags around here to choose from. In all the time I've been here I've never had to sleep with the same girl twice.'

I peek around the corner and then duck back, heart pounding. It's Thomas. How did I miss that arrogant tone to his voice when I first met him? I suppose he hid it along with his other less-appealing characteristics, beneath a charming veneer. The confidence I once admired now seems brash and tarnished.

What was I thinking?

I shudder and hunch down into my seat, my previous good mood evaporating on the chill air.

'What about that redhead you picked up at the party on Saturday?' Another guy I don't know asks.

I stiffen, the air sucked out of my chest.

'Her? She was a frigid cow.' Thomas dismisses me in six words.

Six words.

I could think of six hundred to describe what an utter tosspot he is. I start practising in my head. I should walk out there now. Make a scathing comment about his dire foreplay skills. I should say he never sleeps with any woman twice because I can't imagine anyone who's done it with him would ever want to repeat the experience. But, much as I want to my body is frozen to the chair, utterly incapable of movement. The rage that gave me strength to defend myself is absent now. It's best not to engage with him in any way. My teeth are clenched tightly together and the scathing retorts stay trapped in my head.

I'm frozen rigid.

It's just like that time when. . .

Why does my body do this? It shuts down. I check out. Like I'm no longer present in the situation. Eva did try to explain that freezing is a perfectly natural response to trauma. They even call it 'freeze'. Freeze and dissociation. I suppose it makes a change from the usual hyper-vigilance.

Despite the sun, I'm cold and shivering.

'He' said I was frigid too.

I close my eyes and focus on my breathing, as Eva taught me. In and out. In and out. At this precise moment all I need is oxygen. All I have to do is breathe, and anyone can breathe.

Next I concentrate on the warmth of the mug in my hands, trying to bring myself back to here, to now. Dissociation might be a coping mechanism. But knowing why I act the way I do doesn't always help.

I still can't manage raising the mug to my lips to drink. There's no way I could swallow. For twenty-four hours after I was raped I sat on the kitchen floor, immobile and wanting my mum. But even if she had still been alive, I don't know if she could've given me what I wanted.

When Eva came round and rescued me, persuading me to go to the police, staying with me and then taking me into her home, I couldn't eat, just drinking was hard enough. At first it was because my throat was sore, but after that my body simply refused. Instead of forcing me, she made smoothies and protein shakes and lots of creamy hot chocolate. . . I felt no need, no hunger. Eva wouldn't let Debbie or Mark comment on the untouched food on my plate. We all pretended it was perfectly normal. Mark never stopped trying to tempt me with chocolate, though. I think that's when my crush started. My belief I could survive alone had been dealt a shattering death blow and I was ready to cling to the first potential knight in shining armour to come my way.

I owe Eva so much. Thinking about her gives me a little strength. I want to be the remarkable woman she believes me to be.

I'm not sure how long I sit there at the cantine, but it's long enough for the lunchtime crowd to turn up and my chocolate to go cold.

Something clicks inside me. I'm past this kind of behaviour. This isn't me any more. I'm not sitting shivering and soaked to the skin on the sticky lino floor of a rented flat I'm about to get kicked out of. I had a bad experience with Thomas that brought back memories, that's all.

No biggie.

I give myself a mental shake and slip away, cautiously checking Thomas has left first.

'Hey.'

I turn to see Dan ambling towards me, a frown creasing his forehead.

'Beth, what's wrong?' His voice is gentle but it still makes me want to flinch away.

His eyes are filled with such concern I have to blink hard to avoid bursting into tears on the spot.

I feel utterly blank, incapable of speech. I stare back, helpless.

'Okay, different question.' His frown deepens. 'What can I do to help?'

'Somewhere quiet. I need somewhere quiet.' I manage to speak, but don't know what I expect him to do. Chalet Repos can be anything but peaceful, despite its name.

'Okay, follow me.'

It's a measure of how shaken I am that I follow him without question.

He chats to me about the lessons he taught this morning, not seeming to need my input, which is just as well. After a while I'm calmer.

'Where are we going?' I ask, not recognising our route.

His anecdotes about teaching bratty schoolchildren and lecherous yummy mummies have soothed me and left me feeling more myself again.

'My camper van.'

'Oh? You live in a camper van? Don't you get cold at night?'

'No, I'm hooked up to electric, so it's nice and toasty. And when the temperature drops lower than minus ten you get used to wearing several layers to bed.'

Once we're at the camper van I hesitate. I barely know Dan, so is getting into his van really a wise move? He feels okay, my intuition isn't sounding a mental klaxon. Although my supposed intuition didn't stop me going home with Thomas, did it?

Uneasiness stirs at the back of my mind that I didn't bother to listen to my instincts the night of the party. I was deliberately reckless, trying to prove a point to myself. I'm sure Eva could tell me why but having a trained psychotherapist as a surrogate mother doesn't help when you're deliberately ignoring the blindingly obvious.

'I'll give you the keys if you like,' he says lightly. 'If it makes you more comfortable.'

'Okay.'

If my acceptance surprises him he doesn't show it, just unlocks the van and hands the keys to me. It flashes through my mind that I could always use them between my knuckles as a weapon.

If I had to. If it turns out my instincts about Dan are wrong.

As quickly as the thought appears, I dismiss it. Isn't this why I came to Verbier? So I could live a life not governed by fear and hyper-vigilance and try to feel at least semi-normal again.

I slip the keys into my pocket and climb into the van after Dan.

'This is really nice.' I stare around at the brightly coloured cotton throws covering the seating area. It looks cosy.

'You sound surprised.' Dan grins.

'I wasn't expecting it to be so. . .'

'Clean? Tidy?' His grin widens, it's infectious.

'Well, yes, I suppose.' I smile back. 'Although I was going to say cosy.'

'What can I say? I'll let you into a secret.' He lowers his voice and whispers 'I like cleaning.'

'No,' I reply with mock horror. 'You are weird. Fancy swapping jobs? Do you cook too?'

'Yes, I love cooking. I haven't got much space here, but I try to avoid eating junk and cook all my meals from scratch.'

'Marry me,' I joke.

'Okay then.' He fixes his gaze on me in a way that turns the jokey atmosphere into something more serious.

My cheeks grow hot and I glance down at my hands.

'Fancy a cuppa?'

'Yes, thanks.' I sit down and lightly finger one of the cotton throws. It's a joyful swirling explosion of vibrant colours: blues and purples threaded with gold. I look down at my black salopettes and long-sleeved black t-shirt, remembering with a pang the brightly coloured clothes I used to wear. In particular, I miss the pretty summer dress I was wearing when I was attacked. I never saw it again, as it became a piece of evidence. Fat lot of good that did. 'This is gorgeous.'

'It's from India. And the rug on the floor is from Peru.'

'You're a traveler, then?'

'In that I like to travel, yes, I suppose so.' He puts the kettle on and sits opposite me. 'But I like to do a lot of things. It's an odd human obsession, wanting to label everything, don't you think? Label, classify and divide.'

'Um, I haven't really thought about it. I was just making conversation, really.'

He raises an eyebrow. 'So, if you were to think about it what label would you give yourself?'

'I'm just a chalet girl, I'm no one interesting.' I shrug.

'I find the people who think they are interesting are always dull and those who say they're not are nearly always wrong or lying.' He fixes me with a penetrating gaze that makes my skin tingle. Like I'm a jumbled-up jigsaw and he's looking for the edge pieces, working out where to start. The scrutiny makes me uncomfortable. Why can't he be superficial and boring, like the majority of the population?

But if he was, I wouldn't be here, would I? Maybe I want to be solved after all. I want him to put the pieces of me back together. If it's possible and the missing pieces aren't irretrievably lost.

'Can I ask you a question?' Dan leans forward and I tense mentally, waiting for the question that will penetrate my defences.

I nod.

'Do you take milk and sugar?' His lips quirk.

'Just milk, thanks.' I narrow my eyes. He's playing me.

Even worse, I'm enjoying it. Oh crap. I exhale slowly and try to relax. It's just a cup of tea, not an interrogation. It's not like he can really see inside me, it just feels like it.

When he hands me the tea our fingers brush briefly and a jolt of arousal stabs at me. Heat floods my cheeks.

'It's nice and warm in here,' I bite my lip.

'Yes, now are you going to tell me?'

'Tell you what?'

'What makes you so interesting?'

'I'm not.' I shake my head and take a sip of tea, even though it's really still too hot.

'So you want me to work it out? Okay.' Dan tilts his head to one side. 'Hmm. So tell me, Beth, what's your story?'

'I haven't got a story.' I roll my eyes.

'Okaaay. Most people like talking about themselves,' he replies equably.

'I'm not most people.' I take another sip of scorching tea. 'I'm just a. . .'

'Chalet girl, right,' Dan cuts in. 'So, what were your parents like?'

'Dan, I'm not talking about my childhood.' My jaw clenches. 'We could talk about you instead. Why don't we do your story?'

I don't know why I'm being such a bitch. The nicer he is the grouchier I feel. It's because he's probing, pressing at the painful abscess. I've noticed pain tends to make people grumpy, whether it's physical or emotional.

'Hmm, I sense a big secret.'

I scowl at him and sip more tea, it's more soothing now it's cooling.

'You were raised by the government to be a super spy and you can't talk because you're bound by the Official Secrets Act?' He quirks a brow.

I raise my eyes to the ceiling but the corners of my lips twitch.

'That's it, isn't it? You're on a secret mission right now, aren't you?'

'Yes, that's right, I've got to find the world's most annoying inhabitants and bump them off one by one,' I quip. 'I thought I'd start with you.'

'Ouch.' He places a hand on his chest. 'So how do you plan to do it? Please say you're going to seduce me first? Like a black-widow spider. I've always thought if you've got to go, that would be the way I'd choose.'

'Idiot.' I smile.

'Annoying and an idiot? You're just full of praise for me today. Are you this nice to everyone who makes you tea?' He shakes his head. 'Any more compliments, while you're at it?'

'Oh I don't know. I'm sure some more will spring to mind, the more time I spend with you. You just seem to inspire them.' I'm smiling, my bad mood receding finally. Something about Dan puts me at ease. 'I am grateful for the tea, though, thank you.'

'You're planning to spend more time with me, then?' He raises an eyebrow and his mouth curves into a smile.

'Maybe, maybe not.' I feel my own mouth twitching in response.

I'm mirroring him. Why on earth am I mirroring him? I don't want him to get the wrong idea and leap straight into another mistake. Next time, and no doubt there will be a next time, I'll be more careful about who I sleep with.

I look away, feeling a flush creeping up my neck. The camper van feels very cramped all of a sudden, the teasing atmosphere teetering on the edge of something far more complex.

'More tea? I think I've got some chocolate digestives somewhere.' Dan stands up suddenly and starts rummaging in an overhead locker, defusing the tension.

'Sure, why not? Where the heck did you get chocolate digestives? I haven't seen any in Migros.'

My appetite has returned. I think I might actually be able to swallow some food now.

'I have my sources,' Dan winks. 'You'll have to come to me for a fix when you need one.'

'We are talking about chocolate biscuits, aren't we?'

'Why? What else could we be talking about?' He opens the packet and hands it to me. 'Do you have other needs you'd like me to satisfy? Is there something else you fancy?'

He wiggles his eyebrows suggestively, making me laugh.

'Perhaps.' I take a bite of biscuit. 'Got any Ginger Nuts?'

'If you want to know the colour of my nuts you're going to have to buy me dinner first.'

'Dan, do you take anything seriously?' I laugh again and then cough, choking on a biscuit crumb.

'Sometimes, but right now I'd much rather see you smile. I like making you smile,' he says softly. 'Do you want to tell me what upset you so much earlier?'

I shake my head and cast my eyes down to my tea. My hands cradle the plastic mug.

'Would you like another biscuit?'

I look up and see only kindness. No pressure.

I nod. 'Thanks. So when were you in Peru?'

'I visit South America regularly. My parents are missionaries, and they work with a charity in Colombia.'

'Missionaries? Seriously?'

'Yes, seriously. Missionaries do still exist, you know. They take their skills where they're needed.'

'Oh, right.' I frown. Dan and I are clearly not from the same world. What on earth would they make of my background? And why the frick am I thinking about what the parents of a man I've met only twice might think of me? I stare down at the mug in my hands.

'I'm not going to try to save your soul, don't worry.' Dan watches me closely, misinterpreting my discomfort.

'So, is it your parents being nomadic that got you into travelling?' I glance curiously around at the van's interior and try to imagine fitting my life into a van and just driving away. The idea is strangely appealing. I'd have more space than I do now in the dorm room at Chalet Repos.

'Not really,' Dan replies. 'One day I'll tell you why I'm traveling. Maybe when you tell me what upset you so much today.'

'I guess we'll have to remain in ignorance, then,' I say lightly.

'I guess we will.'

'So you're a ski instructor, then? What do you do in summer?'

'I drive further south and pick up work. I'm going to try for yacht work this summer.'

'So you don't have any long-term plans?'

'Only to enjoy life and see as much of the world as possible. It's fun. You should try it.' Dan leans forward, his face serious.

So it's now, when he's talking about fun, that he chooses to be serious.

His world is so alien to mine I'm not sure we'd intersect in a Venn diagram.

'Thanks for the tea and biscuits. I probably ought to get back to Chalet Repos.' I stand up at the same time as Dan and am immediately aware of how close he is.

'Are you okay now?' He asks, taking my mug.

'Yes, I'm fine, thanks.' I fumble with the door handle and embarrassingly have to be helped. His fingers brush mine and I jump.

'Must be static from the handle,' I mumble.

'Must be.'

I hear the smile in his voice as I step down and walk swiftly away. My cheeks are burning as I zip up my ski jacket.

'Hey, Beth.'

I hear footsteps crunching in the snow behind me as Dan catches up with me.

'What?' I whip around to face him.

'You've still got my keys.'

Aargh. I hand them over, sure I must be crimson by now. My cheeks certainly feel like they're on fire.

'Thanks, Dan.'

'Any time. My kettle and biscuits are at your disposal.'

I sense him watching me as I walk away. I don't know why he's affecting me so much. I can't waste time chasing fun. Life is hard and I've been on my own for far too long. I need to keep to my plan. I need certainty and permanency. Someone who will stick around and take life seriously.

Commitment.

As for talking to Dan or anyone about the deep stuff, Mum's bipolar disorder, the memories that keep me awake at night or the fears that torment me during the day if I let them. . . Well, it's not going to happen. I told Eva everything once.

Once was enough.

She'd be worried if she knew I'd gone home with Thomas and am now taking risks like getting into a camper van with an almost-stranger.

What Eva doesn't seem to get is you're never safe. A stranger I'd never met before raped me in broad daylight in a park. I'd been caught in a thunderstorm and the park had rapidly emptied so there was no one around to help me. Or, at least, there was no one willing to answer my cries for help. And then there was that boyfriend of Mum's who liked to put the tip of a kitchen knife against my chest at night. I think he got off on seeing the fear in my eyes.

So, two situations where I should have been safe – my home and a park in broad daylight – both turned out to be utterly unsafe and the scenes of my greatest vulnerability.

In a weird way it frees me up. I know I'm not safe anywhere. Ever. At least when you know you're not safe it can't take you by surprise when someone turns on you. It's that initial shock I can't bear. That and the knowledge that someone really wants to hurt you, is going to take pleasure doing it and you can't stop them. You can shout and cry all you like but no one is coming to save you.

You've been to a few self-defence classes, but when it comes to it you freeze, forgetting everything, even your own name.

You're alone. Your world tilts and shifts to accommodate this new reality and. . . well, if you're lucky, you find a way to deal with it.

I don't know if there's a place in my new reality for a sexy ski instructor with laughing eyes who chases fun around the world. Fun feels like an almost totally alien concept to me. It's an irrelevance and a luxury I can't afford any more.

Chapter 7

LUCY

'Where are you off to?' I sit down on my bunk, glad I might get the room to myself this evening for a change.

'We're all invited to dinner at Chalet Amélie.' Rebecca smiles as she touches up her make-up. 'Emily's cooking and Jake's invited some of his friends. You never know, we might meet someone.'

'I was planning a quiet night in, given we're guest-free tonight,' I say.

'Oh come on, someone else is cooking for us, it'll be nice. Emily's a really good cook.'

'True, I only had plans for cheese on toast and I am starving,' I admit. I always am after a day on the slopes. All that exercise and fresh air makes me ravenous.

'So come, then. Oh and Emily said to bring our bikinis so we can use the spa.' Rebecca puts her lip gloss back in her make-up bag. 'The thing is, Lucy, I find dinner parties difficult. It would really help if you were there with me.'

'Um, okay, then.' I rummage in my bags for a clean top and

wonder if I've got time to shower and wash my hair. It's rare for Rebecca to admit that she's shy. Usually she covers it up with a bravado most people misinterpret as genuine confidence. I suppose I'd better get ready and keep her company. I wouldn't mind using the pool and steam room to relax my muscles after a day skiing. I could put my bikini on underneath my clothes.

It's Chalet Amélie, though. When I'm there I won't be able to stop thinking about Seb and what happened at the engagement party. Who am I kidding? I'll be thinking about Seb wherever I spend the evening, so what's the difference? I sigh and head for the shower. By the time we're ready to leave, my hair is at least clean and dry and I don't feel too shabby next to the others as we walk to Chalet Amélie. I've put a bit of lip gloss on, just in case.

I'm trying not to think about what I mean by that and am bombarded by memories of kissing Seb as we approach the chalet. I guess it was inevitable.

'Hi there.' Emily greets us at the door with a smile, her strawberry-blonde hair tied back in a ponytail. 'I'm glad you made it.'

When Rebecca goes in, Emily puts a hand on my arm to stop me following and leans in closer.

'I just want to give you the heads-up. You know a certain someone asked Jake to make this dinner happen. I think he's very keen to see you again.' Emily grins.

'Really?' I ask, startled. It has to be Seb. Please let it be Seb, my 'just in case'. My pulse races as I stare back at Emily and my cheeks grow hot.

'Yes, Seb and Jake are friends, they work together a lot. Seb must really like you. Go in, he's sitting over by the fire.' Emily gestures for me to go in before her, herding me in the right direction.

So, no pressure, then.

My stomach performs what feels like a triple back flip. She said he must really like me, is that true? Walking into the room feels like stepping off the edge of a cliff and then remembering that I don't know how to abseil and have forgotten to put a harness on.

Total free-fall.

'Salut, Lucy.' Seb gets up, his face lighting up when he sees me.

His reaction, his pleasure at seeing me just accelerates the fall. Am I really supposed to eat with all this going on?

'Hi.' I lean forward for the Seb three-kiss special. I'm aware everyone is watching us, but my spine stiffens. I don't give a flying snowball about the inevitable gossip.

We've been seated next to each other at dinner, unsurprisingly. Seb sits with his legs so wide apart his knee brushes mine. Touching him is all I can think about. I'm hyper-aware of the heat where our legs meet and the sharp jolt of sexual attraction coursing through me.

'So, what made you start big-mountain snowboarding?' I turn to Seb, my voice too bright and cheery, but I'm determined to make conversation. We need to connect on more than a sexual level if this thing developing between us is going to mean anything. I don't even know what name to give it. Relationship? That feels presumptuous.

'Ever since I started snowboarding as a young boy I looked

up at the mountains, the ones without resorts and ski lifts, and I dreamed of getting up there.' Seb fixes his gaze on me. 'Then one day my dream came true.'

I barely register that my wine glass has been filled up. What Seb says resonates with me.

'My gran always told me to dream big,' I say. 'She was the one who inspired me to come to Switzerland and see more of the world.'

'I'm glad she did.' Seb rests a hand on my knee and I almost jump out of my chair. 'Everywhere you go in life there will be people who try to limit and hold you back. We need to aim to live a life with no limits. How else are we to make progress?'

No limits. No restrictions like a pesky virginity issue? No restrictions like no commitment? I don't know if I'll ever have the courage to ask Seb those questions.

Seb makes me want to leap into the unknown with him, but that's scary. What if we need some limits to keep us safe in life? Isn't fear evolution's way of making us cautious and keeping us safe?

I feel my skin prickling to attention beneath Seb's hand. I don't believe in the religion that kept me a virgin any more, not my mother's version of it, anyhow. I don't believe sex is bad, but it's hard to shed twenty-odd years of indoctrination.

'Are you okay? You've barely eaten anything.' Seb strokes my knee and sexual electricity shoots straight to between my legs.

'I'm struggling to eat, my mind's kind of occupied at the moment,' I whisper back and surreptitiously put some of my bœuf bourguignon onto Seb's plate. I don't want to offend Emily and Seb seems to be having no problem eating.

Sod trying to keep it light and casual, I want Seb so much I think I might explode.

Seb's smile widens and his fingers dip to stroke the inside of my thigh.

I suppress a gasp.

'I think I know what's distracting you. Why don't we skip dessert and go down to the spa? Did you bring your bikini?'

'Yes.' I put my cutlery down, I can't eat another mouthful, even though it's delicious.

'Good, I look forward to taking it off you.' He murmurs in my ear and heat flares inside me like he's thrown a match onto a pile of kindling.

The Prosecco has been flowing liberally and most people seem wrapped up in their own conversations, not looking at us any more. Only Tash catches my eye and winks.

It must be the alcohol but I'm not as embarrassed about slipping away from the table as I thought I'd be. I probably should've eaten more to offset the Prosecco. Never mind, it's obviously giving me Dutch courage. I don't feel out of control, just nice and floaty.

Down in the spa I decide I don't want to go in the Jacuzzi. Something about Ben's chalet-girl joke puts me off the idea. What's happening with Seb doesn't feel tawdry and I don't want to tarnish it. There's nothing meaningless about what's happening between us. Whatever Seb's views are this means a lot to me. Maybe that's enough? Maybe it meaning something to me is the important component I've been waiting for. I've never felt like this before and I'm convinced the connection between me and Seb means something. To me, at least.

And that is enough.

'Steam room?' Seb suggests.

I strip off down to my bikini self-consciously, peeking at Seb as he undresses down to shorts. His chest is contoured with defined muscle and dark chest hair snakes down to his waistband. My fingers itch to touch, to stroke and explore this unfamiliar territory.

I feel Seb's darkening gaze on my body, lingering on my breasts and then down to my legs. Is he thinking the same?

Once in the steam room the wet heat hits us and water trickles down our bodies. Now there's nothing surreptitious about the way I'm eyeing up Seb in his trunks and admiring his muscled torso. I've met sporty, fit guys before but I've never had this kind of physical reaction to someone.

We sit and Seb presses up against me, his leg firm and muscular against mine. My pulse quickens and breath catches in my chest. It's dark in here, black-slate tiles and steam make it feel like a private cave. A safe place to let go.

I tilt my head so he can move in and kiss me. He dips his head down to meet me, his lips on mine, hungry. As his tongue probes and thrusts I feel the now-familiar, insistent need throbbing between my legs. Is this really happening?

Yes, it is. I want it, need it, have to have it. Now.

When Seb's hand strokes up my bare thigh and to the edge of my bikini bottoms I don't stop him. I part my legs for him, allowing him access and issuing an invitation.

Seb pulls back from the kiss. 'Don't worry, I know you want to take it slow, so I won't make love to you, not tonight. But maybe I could make you feel nice, what do you think?'

I nod, but there's no time to feel disappointed. I hiss with a sharp intake of breath as he stokes between my legs over the fabric of my bikini bottoms. Then his fingers dip beneath the edge of the fabric and plunge inside me. One, two, then three fingers thrust and tease. His thumb caresses my clit, spreading my wetness and massaging between my legs.

Will he be able to tell I'm a virgin? My anxiety melts away as a delicious pressure builds between my legs, a crescendo of sharp arousal that blots out all conscious thought.

All that's left is feeling. Raw, untamed arousal breaking through my defences. I'm gasping, writhing against Seb's hand with my limbs trembling.

'I want, I want you inside me. Please.' I crack. Why was I holding out against this? I can't even remember now. It certainly doesn't seem important or remotely sensible any more. I'd be happy to beg right now, the need is so insistent, demanding. With that hunger comes the knowledge that this is meant to happen. Nothing has ever felt more right than this, now, with Seb.

'I want you,' I repeat. 'Please.'

He stares at me through the steam, water running in rivulets down his chest. Then he manoeuvres me so I'm lying on the seat, knees up and legs apart. He tugs down my bikini bottoms and tosses them on the floor. Then he lowers his head between my legs. His lips and tongue caress and tease my clit and probe my sex until I'm shaking violently, a heavy pounding release racking my body and turning me into a writhing mess of screaming hormones. Anyone could walk in here, I suppose, but I don't even care. It even adds to the thrill. Okay, so I'm going straight to hell.

Once I'm spent and my sex is quivering against Seb's lips I'm still so sensitive that his final kiss makes me jerk against him one final time.

So that was. . . educational. I've tested the boundaries of no sex before marriage before. Most of the youth group seemed to decide almost anything short of full sex was okay. Teenage hormones only cared about the letter, not the spirit, of the law.

Seb exhales loudly.

I sit up and see the huge bulge in his shorts. What would it feel like to have him inside me? I can't wait to find out.

'Let me.' I slide my hand into Seb's swimming shorts, pulling them down so I can caress his thick, rock-hard erection. If I'm honest, I used to find hand jobs a bit of a 'your turn, my turn' obligation, but I really want to touch Seb, to know every inch of him.

'*Je bande pour toi*,' Seb groans. 'I am so hard for you.'

His words turn me on, quite ironic given I never know how to talk about sex.

He reaches out and pulls down my bikini top, so his hands can caress and squeeze my breasts, the palms running over my hard nipples. I've never felt so aroused in my life.

I slide down so he can rub his erection over my breasts. The sensation is so erotic I almost come again.

'*C'est bon. Tu m'excites*.'

'The feeling is mutual.' I stare up into his eyes.

Then he places my hand on his erection as he spurts hot semen over my breasts, rubbing it into them in hot, wet circles as he comes.

When he finishes we're both panting, dripping wet from the steam and naked.

'Let's shower.' He pulls me with him into the aroma showers. We're still alone down here. I can't believe what we just did. I am definitely going straight to Hell.

I really enjoyed it, though. The discovery of this sensual side of myself is a revelation. I want more. I've denied and suppressed my desires for so long and I've been missing out on something life-affirming and wonderful.

But first. . . Under the hot, scented massage-shower jets Seb rubs his hands over my breasts and down between my legs. I'm so turned on I'd do it right here in the shower but Seb takes me with him into the changing area and grabs two white robes for us. Then he gets a foil packet from his jeans and puts it in his robe's pocket.

He raises an enquiring brow. 'In case you change your mind. I know you wanted to go slow but I'm an optimist. Have you changed your mind? Can I make love to you, Lucy Lu?'

Abso-bloody-lutely.

'Yes please.' I nod, my small hand slipping into his larger one, trusting him.

We make our way into one of the downstairs guest rooms that's been finished. I'm gripped by a twinge of panic. Will I bleed? How much? Could I get sacked for this?

He locks the door, which reassures me a little. I grab a large towel from the en suite and put it on the bed. Then I lie on top and wait, undoing the tie on my gown. Seb lies next to me and runs his hands over my body, soothing away my nerves. He takes his time and the panic seeps away, replaced by growing, impatient desire.

When his hands dip between my legs I part them for him without hesitation, enjoying his confident, joyful exploration of my body and marvelling at his ability to arouse me again so soon.

When he thrusts at my entrance I'm so wet he slips in easily, but then I feel a tight pain and an unexpected shock as he breaches me. So this is what it feels like to have a man inside you. It's different from having his fingers inside. It feels. . . important, somehow.

I meet his dark eyes and am jolted by the connection I find there.

Then he begins to move. Back and forth and back and forth, stretching me. It feels amazing. It's more satisfying than I imagined, I feel complete. Seb inside me, joined to me, interlocking and sending me towards yet another orgasm. The soles of my feet tingle as Seb thrusts, rubbing against a sweet spot deep inside me.

His eyes are locked on mine as he moves, the connection is still startling. I had no idea sex would be like this. Sure, I'd guessed the physical sensations would be intensified and deliver on the promises of years of foreplay that never led to ‚after' play. What I hadn't prepared for was the emotional impact of being joined to another human being, of the incredible trust I'm placing in this man I barely know yet feel I've known forever.

'Lucy Lu.' Seb's breathing is ragged. 'I want you so much I don't know how much longer I can last, sorry. You're so beautiful.'

I wrap my arms around his muscular back, tracing my fingers over a couple of jagged scars and then dipping down to his firm bottom. On instinct, I squeeze his hard buttocks.

'*Merde*,' Seb groans.

I listen to my body and move with Seb, rising my hips to meet his thrusts, wanting him deeper and deeper. A throbbing orgasm grips me. On instinct I wrap my legs around Seb, pressing my heels against his bottom as I contract around him, needing him deeper still.

I cry out as I come, my body fizzing and tingling all over.

'Fuck,' Seb swears again and jerks inside me a second later, his face contorting into ecstasy. Then he collapses on top of me for a minute, still inside, just resting. I like the heavy weight of his body covering mine. When he rolls off he disposes of the condom and disappears into the en suite.

I roll off the towel. There is a little blood on it but I doubt Seb saw anything, given the room is in semi darkness and he was otherwise occupied. Quickly I wrap it up and stuff it into the room's laundry bin. I'll have to make an excuse to retrieve it so I can wash it somehow.

It suddenly seems really important Seb doesn't realise he took my virginity. I don't want him to feel pressured by this being a huge deal for me. I don't know why this is important, but I've been working on instinct all evening so I'm going with it.

I grab my robe and slip it on before Seb comes back into the room.

He eyes the robe quizzically. He's still completely naked and makes no move to cover himself up.

'I, um, need to go. I have to be up early.'

'You're loving me and leaving me?' Seb pulls a regretful face. 'Are you just using me for sex, Lucy Lu?'

I snort.

'No I'm, well, I wasn't sure. . .'

I don't know how to respond. I'm not equipped to deal with this kind of situation. Also the word 'loving' has thrown me.

'I thought you'd want me to go,' I add, fumbling with the robe's belt.

I want to tell him that I don't know what I'm doing. That I've never done this before. I don't know the etiquette.

'Stay.' Seb takes the end of my robe's belt and tugs me towards him. Then he opens the robe and pulls me onto his lap. 'If you give me five minutes or so we can go again and I'll last longer next time, I promise. I just wanted you so badly I couldn't hold back. Or if you'd rather, we can talk.'

'Do you think we ought to be in here, though?' I glance at the locked door.

'Jake won't mind.' A quiver of Seb's mouth arouses my suspicion.

'Did you ask him to host the dinner and invite me so we could. . . you know.'

'I do know and, yes, of course I did. I had to see you again. As for the 'you know', as I said earlier, I'm an optimist.'

'And if I'd said no?'

'I would have tried again another time.'

'And so now you have. . .' My heart lurches as I brave the truth. 'Is that it? I'll not see you again except on YouTube?'

'Ah, so you've been stalking me on YouTube?' He grins.

'That's what you're picking me up on out of what I said? No, not stalking. Admiring.' A flush creeps up my neck. 'I love what you do, it's amazing to watch. When you move it's like you're at one with the mountain. It's beautiful. It's art.'

'Of course I want to see you again.' Seb's dark eyes gleam. 'You get me. We're the same, you and I. We have this chemistry, it's like a connection. Plus I have many things I'd love to do with you. Naked things. It would be a crime to ignore this kind of chemistry.'

His mouth quirks as he runs his hands over my breasts. My nipples harden and so does Seb's erection beneath my bottom.

I shift a little, making him groan. 'I think the five minutes are over.'

'Do you want to go again? What do you like, Lucy Lu? Shall I take you from behind? Do you like to be on top? Or do you like it kinky? Have you ever been spanked or tied up?'

My eyes widen. 'I don't know. From behind maybe?'

Seb turns me over on the mattress, pulling my hips up over a pillow so I'm angled up, thighs splayed open for him. My pulse quickens. Should I admit I'm totally inexperienced?

But I'm quickly distracted, growing wet between my legs again and tensing with anticipation. Seb massages my bottom before drawing wetness out over my folds, circling my clit until I'm squirming beneath his fingers.

Then I hear a foil packet tear and after a brief, agonising, delay he's nudging at my entrance and thrusting in. I gasp again. It feels different from this angle, deeper still. Buried deep inside me, he begins to pump while his fingers continue to tease my clit. The sensation of him inside me while he brings me to climax is mind-blowing.

I thrust back against him, urging him on.

'*Plus forte*? Harder?' Seb asks breathlessly.

'Yes, harder.'

As he thrusts harder and deeper into me the swelling, arching pleasure erupts inside me and I contract around him, crying out and grasping the sheets in my fists.

Seb's hands are on my hips as he thrusts relentlessly on towards his own release. Sweat trickles down between my breasts and when Seb comes inside me I'm tingling all over. The soles of my feet, my nipples, between my legs. . . I'm one giant erogenous zone, I'm one with Seb. When he pulls out of me, I'm reeling.

I didn't expect to feel. . . what I'm feeling. It's intense and it's overwhelming.

I'm way out of my comfort zone. Where do we go from here? I've been swept along by a wave of endorphins. Am I honestly expecting Sebastien Laroche to be my boyfriend?

I squeeze my eyes tight shut. For now I'm not going to think about it. Doing this was right, I'm convinced of it. As for what comes next, I'll just have to wait and see.

Chapter 8

From: sandratrent@gmail.com
To: sophietrent@hotmail.com
Re: Wedding Plans

Sophie, darling, we were very sorry to hear about Luc's father. How sad that he won't be up to coming to England for the wedding. Does that mean his mother will be staying behind too? Such a shame we won't get to meet them. Although, as your dad and I don't speak French I'm not sure we would have had much to say to each other.

Your gran has had a touch of bronchitis and has been proclaiming her imminent demise. She says her dying wish is to see her only granddaughter marry, but you mustn't let that influence you, darling, not if you're really set on having a long engagement.

While I think about it, do you have any idea how many of Luc's relatives and your friends from Switzerland might be coming to England for the wedding? I know you're a long way off finalising a wedding list, but a rough idea would help your dad and I with the budgeting.

As you know, we've been setting aside money for your wedding ever since you were a little girl. The fund has been well invested and done quite nicely.

So money isn't a worry, if that's what's holding you and Luc back.

The WI ladies are longing for another project to get their teeth into and have all offered their help. You've always been such a favourite with them and they were thrilled when I announced you'd got engaged on Valentine's Day. So romantic. Joan and Daphne have already bought new hats, even though I did tell them you and Luc might prefer a more informal dress code. I don't want you to feel you can't have a say, just because we're paying for the wedding. If we can't get The Lodge after all we could always look at one of the Northern Lakes hotels. Joan says there's a lovely hotel with lake-shore gardens backing onto Ullswater.

I'd better go now, there's a new episode of *Sherlock* with that lovely Benedict Cumberbatch starting soon and I get very confused if I miss the beginning!

Love from

Mum

From: derektrent@gmail.com
To: sophietrent@hotmail.com
Re: Slight exaggeration

Hello daughter. Don't let your mum worry you. Gran has a bad cold, that's all. She's been predicting her 'imminent demise' (as your mum puts it) for at least ten years. She's as tough as old boots and will probably outlive us all!

Hope you're getting lots of skiing in – it's been very wet here.

Love, Dad

SOPHIE

As Luc and I tramp our way to the Appartements Belle Neige it's snowing. Thick white flakes swirl down from a heavy, silent sky. I love Swiss snow. It's nothing like the damp-squib snow of English winters.

The flakes form beautiful, intricate patterns, backlit by amber streetlights. Once on the ground they glitter like diamonds. It's apt, given the snow is as valuable as gems to the local economy.

As I slip my gloved hand into Luc's it's the beauty of the snow that soothes me rather than the thought of early snowfall increasing the numbers of skiers' bums on Café des Amis chairs.

'Okay?' He smiles down at me and pulls me closer.

I nod.

And it would be, if only we could stay like this. Just the two of us walking in the snow, hand in hand. No future and no past.

But all too soon we're at Holly and Scott's new home and Luc is pressing the intercom buzzer.

The indignant wail that greets us once we're through the front door tells me my goddaughter Maddie has no intention of going to bed and missing the party.

'Hi, Soph.' Holly leans in to hug me, her auburn hair hanging loose around her shoulders.

I hug back, holding her for a fraction longer than usual. I catch her concerned glance and look quickly away.

'Hey, Maddie, how's my little goddaughter?' Luc's face lights up as Scott walks towards us, an angry baby wailing and squirming in her father's arms.

'Crabby.' Scott raises his eyebrows. 'Our daughter is a night owl who objects to the concept of bedtime and rejects all the suggestions of the baby books.'

'Can I have a cuddle?' Luc asks, his brown eyes soften and his lips curl into a gentle smile that breaks my heart.

'I like you, mate, but that's taking things a bit far. Oh, you mean you want a cuddle with my daughter?' Scott grins. 'I'm wounded.'

He passes Maddie to Luc and I hastily place a muslin cloth over Luc's shoulder. Within minutes of being cuddled by Luc, Maddie stops crying and snuggles into him with a hiccup and a contented sigh.

I blink hard and hastily repair my defences. I can't watch them. Instead I follow Holly and Scott over to the L-shaped leather sofa.

'So, how's the work going on Chalet Amélie?' I choose the first non-baby subject that comes to mind. 'Are all the guest suites finished yet?'

'They're almost done. Some of the bathrooms need tiling and there's a little painting to be done, but Emily and Jake are supervising that.' Scott sinks gratefully onto the sofa. 'I'm on daddy paternity duty, officially banned from working on pain of death.'

'I'd torture you first. And it would be a painful lingering death.' Holly collapses next to him, gazing with evident relief at Luc and Maddie, who is now contentedly asleep in his arms.

I'm trying to block out the sweet little whiffly noises Maddie is making. Trying to crush the longing to hold her close and inhale her gorgeous new baby scent. I'm terrified. Afraid to love her, scared that along with the love I'll unlock a terrible grief for what I can never have.

'You know, Sophie, I might have to borrow your fiancé for whenever I can't settle Maddie,' Holly laughs. 'Hey, Luc, if you could just stay like that for a few hours you'd have my undying gratitude. She acts like I'm torturing her if I try to put her down in her crib. I can only get housework done if I'm carrying her in the baby sling.'

'Uh huh. No problem.' Luc doesn't look over but continues to murmur sweet baby nothings to a sleeping Maddie. I force myself to look away before the choking feeling can rise up again.

'So, how is the new chalet girl working out at Chalet Repos?' I ask, shoving my feelings down deep and slamming the door shut on them. There's too much crammed inside, giving me emotional indigestion. It feels like an overfull cupboard. The next time I open the door it'll all come spilling out.

'Beth seems to be fitting in just fine.' Holly pulls her legs up beneath her on the sofa. 'I've had to leave Matt and Amelia managing things at Chalet Repos. At least Tash, Rebecca and Lucy all know what's what.'

'How does Tash feel about Amelia being in charge?' I raise an eyebrow.

'Oh, about as well as you'd imagine.' Holly's mouth twitches with amusement. 'It may all end in ski poles at dawn, but I didn't have much choice with Tash running off to see Nate every five minutes. Luckily Nate seems to be keeping her happy, so maybe that'll keep the fireworks under control.'

'And the others like Beth?' I know only too well how hard living in a small dorm room can be if you don't get on with someone.

'I think so,' Holly yawns. 'When I interviewed her she seemed very reserved. Not prickly like Tash used to be but locked down and self contained somehow, you know? If I had more time I'd try and mentor her. You were always so good with the other chalet girls, Sophie. I'd have been lost without you when I arrived in Verbier.'

'I don't know about that, you didn't really need me. You certainly managed to impress the boss, given you ended up marrying him.' I smile at Scott.

'Don't put yourself down, Sophie, you've helped lots of people over the years. I knew I could always rely on you to look out for the homesick or lovesick,' Scott adds.

'Amelia is organised and efficient but she, well. . . lacks empathy,' Holly frowns.

'Organised efficiency will have to do. After all, you've got other priorities now.' I try to keep my tone light.

'How are things with you, Sophie?' Scott asks.

I glance over at Luc but he's still walking the room with Maddie and seems unaware of the conversation.

'Um, okay.' I bite my lip and think about what I can share. I haven't even mentioned Mum's emails to Luc yet so I can't open with her staggeringly tactless response to the news about his dad. 'But Luc's dad isn't too well.'

'Oh no, is it his heart again?' Holly's eyes fill with concern.

'Yes, and he really shouldn't be working, but he says the day he retires will be the day he dies.' I stare down at my lap. 'Luc is the only one who can make him rest but the second Luc leaves the Café du Place to come back to Verbier his dad is on his feet serving customers again.'

'I don't mind going over there,' Luc cuts into the conversation and walks over to us, gently lowering himself down onto the sofa next to me. Maddie is still clinging to him like a baby koala.

'It's just hard for us to manage both the Bar des Amis and the Café du Place, especially given it's almost an hour's drive between Verbier and Vex.' I lean into Luc, needing to recapture the intimacy of our walk over here. I don't add that we can't afford another full-time member of staff to replace him in Verbier and the Café du Place doesn't make enough to support more staff, either, even if his dad would allow it.

'We'll manage.' Luc rests the hand not supporting Maddie on my thigh. The crease on his forehead tells me he's worried, though.

'I'm sorry to hear he's not well again, Luc.' Holly sighs and stifles another yawn. 'Sorry, sleep deprivation. How are things going with the adoption process?'

'They're not.' Luc's jaw tightens and I feel him stiffen beside me.

'No, why not?' Holly asks, indignant.

'We're not suitable.' I control my voice to stop my bitterness leaking out.

'Not suitable? I don't know of a couple more suitable to

be parents than you two.' Holly's outraged tone makes Maddie stir in her sleep on Luc's chest.

'What reasons have they given?' Scott asks, frowning.

'They wouldn't be able to get an exact genetic match for us.' I shrug.

'What? I don't understand?' Holly leans forward in her seat.

'Neither did I to begin with. It didn't occur to me that Luc being Swiss and me being English-born would matter. After all, we'll be married soon and I'll have a Swiss passport, but it's not enough, apparently.'

'But they can't preclude you on those grounds alone, surely?' Scott leans forward too, his male brain clearly itching to fix this, to take action.

'There's also the fact that we run a bar and live over it,' Luc grimaces. 'It's not a suitable environment for a child, we've been told. It never did me any harm. They must have been more lax with the rules when I was adopted.'

'I suppose there were more babies available for adoption thirty years ago,' Holly replies thoughtfully.

'The final nail in the coffin was that I had counselling after the thing with the guy who, you know. . .' My cheeks redden and tears sting my eyes. 'My doctor referred me, so it was in my medical notes. They say it makes me emotionally unstable. So. . . it looks like we're not adopting.'

I can't look at Luc. It's all my fault. I'm the infertile one and I'm the foreigner whose language skills aren't up to scratch. Luc is properly bilingual and I'm just C-grade GCSE French and trying. At the interview the woman spoke so damn fast.

If she'd slowed down a little I might've caught ninety-five per cent of the conversation, but as it was I had to sit and grin like a gormless idiot while Luc tried to charm her.

But while Luc impressed, I certainly didn't. I know my medical records were the clincher. I'm sure of it. I've been on the online forums and found lots of other people who've been turned down as adoptive parents because they've had counselling.

Pain surges in my chest, rising into my throat and choking me.

Luc stirs uncomfortably beside me and Maddie opens her eyes. At the exact same moment both Maddie and I begin to cry.

Five minutes later and Luc and Scott have retreated to the nursery with Maddie, wisely deciding that two wailing females in one room are too much to cope with and Maddie will be the easiest to placate. At least her gripes can be fixed with action – like feeding, rocking, cuddles or changing a nappy.

Holly has replaced Luc by my side and is dispensing tissues, hugs and outrage in equal measure.

'It's just not fair,' she says, for about the hundredth time.

I shrug again. 'What can we do? It looks like I'm just not meant to be a mother, adoptive or otherwise.'

'Do they know what Thomas did to you? How he treated you and the fact he's the reason you're infertile?'

'If they bothered to read my notes in detail then, yes, they probably do. I had to agree access to my medical records as part of the application procedure.' I pull a face. 'It's not like you sit at the doctor's thinking about how what you're saying might be used against you in the future, but everything you say goes on record. Everything.'

'So they're basically saying you're not suitable to adopt because you had counselling to cope with the fact you couldn't have children. That's crazy.' Holly shakes her head. 'Presumably if you hadn't really cared about being a mother you wouldn't have needed help and would have been deemed suitable to adopt. It's nuts.'

I ball the tissue in my fist.

'It's all me, Holly. All my fault.' I can't keep the bleakness out of my voice. 'We both know if Luc had an infertile Swiss partner with no emotional problems then they'd let him adopt, bar or no bar.'

I don't add that given he's not the one who can't have children he could start over and choose a perfectly healthy Swiss wife to have a family with. There's only so much truth I can bear today. Speaking it aloud might be cathartic, but it still hurts like hell.

'I don't know anything of the sort.' Holly strokes my back like she does when she's trying to console Maddie.

I don't reply. I know it to be true deep in my gut. Luc hasn't been able to persuade me otherwise and neither will Holly.

'Luc adores you, Soph,' Holly speaks gently. 'It'll be okay.'

'Yes, I know,' I lie.

I close my eyes, thinking back to Valentine's Day, to the treasure hunt Luc set me for the second year in a row. The end proposal at the W hotel, also the scene of our first date, had been so romantic I'd floated for over a week, unable to keep the smile off my face.

Everything and anything seemed possible back then. We'd been determined to jump through whatever hoops we had to so we could adopt. I'd not given any thought to what country we would marry in, or how I'd keep everyone happy.

Now I need to find the words to tell Mum she can't plan the wedding she's dreamed of for me. That she and Dad have saved so hard for. That her WI friends won't get to pitch in and help with. Far worse, I still have to break the news to her that there'll be no grandchildren, not even of the adopted kind.

I have so much to be grateful for. I never dreamed a girl like me would end up with someone as fantastic as Luc. I'm living in a country I adore, with a man who loves me, so nothing else should matter, right? Yet I can't quite silence the voice whispering that if I truly loved Luc I'd set him free so he can start the family he's always dreamed of. He wants to be a parent as much as I do, maybe even more. Being adopted means Luc feels the absence of any blood relatives keenly. He always wanted to start his own family for that very reason. I can't help replaying the look on his face as he cuddled Maddie in his arms. By staying, I'm hurting him. It's me causing him this pain.

He'd get over me, I'm sure.

But I'm not so certain I'd get over losing him. I don't think I could bear a world without Luc in it.

Chapter 9

BETH

Lucy and I are collapsed on deckchairs, sipping cold drinks in the sun after another of my lessons. Well, I've collapsed, she's barely broken a sweat. I'm still not sure skiing is for me, but don't dare say as much to her. She lives to ski, as far as I can tell, and can't conceive of anyone not loving it as much as she does. Rebecca told me all Lucy cares about is sport and never dates but I'm not sure – after all, she did disappear off with that man at dinner.

While I appreciate the beauty of the Alps and love sitting out in the fresh mountain air I don't think I'm ever going to like the out-of-control feeling I get when I ski. To truly enjoy it I think you have to be willing to surrender yourself to speed or gravity or something. I just don't have it in me to let go like that. I close my eyes, revelling in the feel of warm sunshine on my skin. Whatever happens, I don't regret trading a London winter for this.

'Hi, Dan.' Lucy's voice makes me jump and my eyes jerk open.

'Lucy, Beth, working hard are you?' Dan sits down in an empty deckchair next to me. 'I don't know, you chalet girls have it easy.'

'Huh, it's the ski instructors who have an easy time of it,' Lucy retorts. 'You weren't up at dawn doing housework. Plus, once you're finished on the slopes you get the whole evening off.'

'Maybe you should teach next season, Lucy, instead of being a chalet girl,' Dan suggests.

'Perhaps.' Lucy shrugs.

'She's been teaching me.' I turn to Dan, glad the flush that springs to my cheeks can be put down to the warm sunshine. 'She's a good teacher. Any lack of progress is all down to me, I'm afraid.'

'You're doing fine,' Lucy protests. 'You just need to persevere.'

'I'm not going to be allowed to give up.' I grimace at Dan.

'I should hope not,' he smiles. 'Sometimes it takes a while and then one day it just clicks.'

'Hmm.' I shrug noncommittally. 'What if the clicking turns out to be a dislocated bone? I keep hearing the rescue helicopters overhead, off to fetch the injured. It's a bit off-putting.'

'You know what you need?' Dan grins.

'I'm sure you're going to tell me.' I can't help smiling back. He has such a nice smile, his whole face lights up and his eyes dance like they know a delicious secret.

Out of the corner of my eye I catch Lucy watching me speculatively. So what? I can appreciate a man's smile while acknowledging he's not right for me. A little flirting and teasing never hurt anyone and I'm not about to shut out a man who can make me smile this much.

'I think you need to have fun this afternoon.' His laughing eyes hold me, enticing, promising to share a delicious secret. 'I've had a cancelled lesson. Don't worry, I'm not talking about giving you another ski lesson. Instead I'm going to get you to really enjoy the snow and relax with it. I dare you. You'll find it's fun if you can get over your fear.'

How does he know it's the fear that's holding me back? And why does it feel like he knows me when we've only met twice before? I'm not sure spending time with an observant man is such a good idea. He's already convinced I'm hiding a secret. I don't want him digging. Some things are best left buried.

But really, for one afternoon, what harm can it do?

'Okay, I accept.' The rebellious part of me wins.

I ignore Lucy's smirk.

'Just make sure she's back at Chalet Repos in one piece later because we're on dinner duty tonight.' She drains her glass and stands up from her deckchair. 'See you later, Beth. Have fun.'

'So, what did you have in mind?' I try to ignore Dan's long outstretched legs, angled territorially towards me. It is nice to meet a man who's tall enough so I could wear heels if I wanted.

'You'll see.' He smiles.

'Do you know how annoying that patronising tone is?' I nudge one of his boots with the tip of my ski boot.

'Yes, I've a fair idea. Now come on, drink up, we need to pick something up first.'

'Chocolate digestives?' I reluctantly get up out of the comfy deckchair, unsure that Dan's idea of fun is going to be better than sunbathing.

'No, but you can have some chocolate biscuits afterwards, if you earn them.' He grins. 'If you're a very good girl.'

I roll my eyes. 'Why does it sound like it's going to be hard work?'

'It won't be,' he promises.

When we get to his camper van he unlocks the storage locker under the bed where he keeps his snowboard and boots and pulls out a sledge.

'You must've done this as a child?' Dan leads me to an off-piste stretch, where it'll be safe to sledge down without taking several skiers out at the same time.

A vague memory flashes into my mind of Mum pulling me along a snowy pavement, me sitting on a plastic sledge. That would've been one of her good days. When she was up, in one of her manic phases, we'd have days out and ice cream for dinner. It was fun, but I could never quite trust it, as there was always a part of me waiting for the inevitable slide back down into depression again.

When she died of a heart attack a year ago it wasn't a shock. She always drank a lot on top of her medication. They say that didn't cause her death but I'm not convinced. For years it felt like all Mum wanted was to check out and one day her body finally agreed with her.

She left me with a pile of debts and final-demand letters and a toxic mixture of grief and a guilty relief that I no longer had to ride the rollercoaster.

Thinking about happy times hurts even more than bad

memories, maybe because there are so few of them and now there'll never be any more.

Is Dan as laid back and even-tempered as he seems or is he hiding a rollercoaster temperament?

'Earth to Beth.' Dan stops and stares at me. 'Are you okay?'

'Um, yes. I'm fine.'

'You don't need to lie to me, you know.' Dan's voice is gentle and I know if I had the courage to meet his gaze I'd find kindness there.

'There's no need to lie? That's got to be the stupidest thing I've ever heard.' Irritation snaps me out of the past. I try to smile, but can't quite manage it. Why am I being such a bitch to him – again?

'Is that so? You must have spent your life surrounded by inordinately clever people,' Dan replies calmly. He doesn't seem offended at all.

'Ha.' I don't bother dignifying that with a proper reply.

Then it hits me. I'm testing him, I'm prodding Dan with a stick to see if he'll turn on me.

'Let's try again. Are you okay, Beth?'

'Not really,' I say, subdued, the fight abruptly seeping out of me.

'Want to talk about it?'

'Definitely not.' My lips tighten.

'Alright then.'

'Shall we get on with having fun?' My question is only slightly acerbic. If Dan wants honesty he can have it in spades. Full disclosure, now that's an entirely different matter.

I find I have no problem with speed or hurtling down a

snowy slope, so long as someone else more competent is in control. Dan sits behind me, legs either side of mine and his arms around me, so he can take control of the steering.

It's a fact that doesn't bear examination. Surely I should be more comfortable being in control of the sledge myself? Maybe it's the deep, three a.m. fear lurking inside me that I can't trust myself. What if Mum did pass on her bipolar genes to me?

On one run I swear Dan ploughs us into a snowdrift on purpose. We tumble into the drift in a tangle of limbs and, despite myself, I'm laughing. Dan's face is mere centimetres from mine, twinkly eyes dancing and laughing mouth so close, so kissable.

I blink and roll away. He's too nice for me. The thought flickers briefly in my mind. Eva would say it's more evidence that I don't respect myself.

After the Thomas incident I might have to agree with her.

'What next?' I determinedly switch off my inner-Eva. 'I'm tired of climbing back up that hill. You're much fitter than me.'

'Thanks, so you think I'm fit?' He grins.

'I mean, you have better stamina than me.' Frick, that sounds even worse.

'Women often comment on my stamina.'

'Really? So why aren't you spending time with your stamina-loving women instead of me. Why bother with me?'

'I like you, Beth, it's as simple as that.' He gets to his feet. 'You asked what next. I'm thinking we should have a snow-creature competition.'

He likes me? I feel a twinge of regret that this thing between us will never go anywhere or be serious. I feel strangely comfortable with Dan, but this isn't real life.

I learnt pretty young that ice cream for dinner can't be trusted.

Does Dan even do real life or commitment or the other basic requirements I need? After Thomas I need to be much more focused. Dan can be a good friend but I need to remember that one day soon he'll drive his campervan off into the sunset and leave me behind.

'Snow creatures?' I brush some powdery snow off my cheek.

'Yes, everyone does snowmen, it's so predictable. How about a snow rabbit or a snow marmot?'

'What's a marmot?'

'You've never seen a marmot? They're super-cute furry creatures – these mountains are teeming with them in summer.'

'So, where do they go in winter? Are you sure you're not making them up?'

'No, they really exist. I'll show you a photo on my phone later. I think they hibernate or something. Anyway, what are you going to do?'

'Snow cat.' I begin scooping handfuls of snow to build the body, hampered by my thick ski gloves. Still, at least they're waterproof and I'm not remotely cold. 'Did you ever get to do this as a kid? Were you always in hot countries with your parents?'

'Pretty much. I enjoyed the travel but I did miss out on snow. I'm all for making up for missed time. Who gets to arbitrarily put age limits on certain activities anyway?'

'True,' I agree. 'I miss ice cream and jelly. I haven't eaten jelly in years.'

'Jelly is underrated as a foodstuff.' Dan looks solemn as he sculpts a body out of snow.

'Also, I don't get all this putting adult covers onto children's books,' I say. 'A good story is a good story, so why should anyone feel ashamed to be reading it?'

'That's exactly what I think. I love A.A. Milne. Winnie the Pooh is my hero.' He places a hand on his heart.

'I always preferred Piglet because he was brave in spite of his fears,' I say, then I worry I've revealed too much of myself. It's been a long time since I read the books. Mum threw all my childhood books out one day in a manic de-cluttering frenzy.

'It's much friendlier with two.' Dan says quietly, then turns to face me, snow sculpture temporarily forgotten.

'I love that Winnie the Pooh quote.' I wish Dan wasn't quite so close, that his eyes weren't quite so dancy and I didn't feel the urge to kiss him.

I think for a second he's going to kiss me, but he pulls back and carries on with his snow creature, whatever it is.

'Okay, I've finished.' I rock back on my heels. I'm quite pleased with my snow cat, although the tail was tricky and looks a bit wonky.

'What's yours meant to be?' I frown.

'It's a marmot.'

I pull a face.

'What? You don't even know what a marmot looks like, so how do you know this isn't an extremely talented example?'

'Is it meant to only have three legs?' I ask.

'What, it has got four legs. Oh you're kidding me. Funny girl.' He grins. 'You do have a sense of humour after all. Right, you're going to pay for disparaging my masterpiece.'

He scoops up a handful of snow and advances, grabbing the back of my jacket and stuffing it down my neck.

'You sod,' I shriek.

I grab some snow and run after him, stuffing it down the front of his t-shirt. He hooks a leg around my ankles and pulls me off my feet, down onto him.

There's a moment of stillness when we stare at each other and wait, seeing if the other is going to pull away. Then the moment for extraction is over and my lips are on his. I can't honestly say if I'm kissing Dan or he's kissing me. We're just kissing and I don't want it to stop.

His hands snake around my back and pull me in closer, deepening the kiss. Surprisingly I don't feel remotely freaked out, but instead I'm relaxed and turned on. He's a good kisser, he tastes of mint and smells nice, all citrusy and fresh.

It's undeniably good, feeling Dan's solid body beneath mine. Not to mention his tongue in my mouth and this burgeoning feeling of connection. It's been a long time since I felt anything like this. It triggers a craving deep inside me, drawing me to him, making me want more. My thirst is both emotional and sexual. I'm parched for affection.

I feel safe enough to close my eyes, Dan's presence somehow makes it feel okay. Anyway, I'm more concerned with enjoying this kiss and being held. Some of the tension I hadn't realised I was carrying is seeping out of my tight muscles and almost permanently clenched jaw. No one has touched me for a very long time. This kiss is an oasis after a long, arduous trek in hostile territory.

Mmm. . . I could get lost in this kiss. The thought draws me up short. That can't happen. Dan's a distraction. A very nice distraction but. . . he's leaving at the end of the season. I shouldn't waste the opportunity I've got in Verbier. I can hang out with Dan and have fun but it can't be more than that. Not if I'm looking for security.

I was alone for far too long. I can't let myself get close to a self-confessed drifter who's going to leave me to go on to the next best thing. Life is serious and so I need to be too. I pull back.

'I need to make tracks,' I mutter, my cheeks flushed hot, and quickly get to my feet. 'I need to have a bath before I start dinner prep with Lucy.'

'Okay.'

'Thanks for. . . this afternoon.' I shake the snow out of my jacket.

'Did you have fun?' Dan props himself up on his elbows.

I feel a tug, deep inside me. Am I doing the right thing?

'Yes,' I finally admit. 'I had fun. Thanks.'

'It's good to see you smiling. You have a lovely smile.'

I turn away, flustered.

Dan's lack of resistance to my leaving bothers me. Doesn't he want me to stay? I need to bear in mind he doesn't do subtext. If I say something he takes me at my word. Also I've got to remember this might be fun but he's not going to take care of me, provide for me, keep the bailiffs from the door and nightmares from my sleep.

There I've said it.

From the first time I had to look after Mum, run the flat and take care of myself I dreamt of a rich man swooping in to take care of us and love Mum. I'd hoped maybe he'd be able to keep her happy because I was certainly failing to.

When Mum died I wanted it for myself. Wanted the luxury of not handing over my bank card afraid it's going to be refused. Wanted to just once go into a supermarket and be able to buy whatever I fancied. It's complicated. It's not so much about wanting material things as about craving the absence of the fear, of stomach-clenching, gut-gnawing anxiety.

More than that, I want a man who cares what happens to me and wants to take care of me. I don't want to do life on my own any more. I want someone to hold me at night and look out for me.

Eva thinks I'm yearning for the father who abandoned me and left me to deal with Mum's illness alone. But why would I want that waste of space? He's clearly incapable of looking after anyone.

She also thinks my approach is anti-feminist and dysfunctional. But then she also says I'm remarkable and strong. Can I be both?

I know I'm not strong. I don't think I've known a genuinely fear-free moment since the rape. Since before that, really, if I'm going to be truly honest. Even while I was mucking about with Dan it was there in the background, pulsing through me. Never safe. . . Never safe. . .

I want someone who at least makes me feel safe. Though

deep down I'm afraid real safety is out of my reach. Out of anyone's reach, not just mine. Life is fragile and uncontrollable. Nevertheless, I'd like a relationship that at least helps me forget it.

From: debbie.johnson@gmail.com
To: beth.chapman@yahoo.com
Subject: skiing lessons

Hi there. We need to have a serious word! Don't you know it's positively your duty to hook up with a sexy ski instructor? Accepting free lessons from a fellow chalet girl is such a waste! You said you're starting to get good tips from the Chalet Repos guests, so why don't you splash out for one-on-one tuition with the sexiest male instructor you can find? Maybe it could progress to one-on-one tuition of another kind? ;-)

Oh, you'll never guess, Mark said the funniest thing the other day. We were talking about you and he said he thought you'd had a crush on him while you were living with us, that it might be one of the reasons you decided to go to Switzerland. I told him he was full of himself and you were way out of his league. Anyway, I had to pass it on because I knew it would make you laugh. You and Mark, imagine!

I've not been on any internet dates since I last emailed so it's your positive duty to have hot sex with a ski instructor and email me all the details.

Email soon.

Love, Debbie

Chapter 10

From: sandratrent@gmail.com
To: sophietrent@hotmail.com
Re: The Lodge Hotel

Hello, Sophie darling. Now, you mustn't be cross, but Rita's daughter needed a final answer regarding the May slot at The Lodge, so I made an executive decision and asked them to reserve it. We haven't paid the deposit yet – your Dad won't let me until we have the go-ahead from you and Luc.

I know Christmas and New Year are your busiest times of year, but if you were able to come home just for a few days it would be lovely to sit down with you and start planning things properly. I've been saving up lots of ideas to show you. Your dad says I could use our printer to scan things in and then email them to you, but you know what I'm like with technology. It would be so much more fun doing it face to face.

So, what do you think? I'm sure Luc could spare you for just a couple of days.

Love from Mum.

SOPHIE

'Oh fuckitty fuck.' I chew my lower lip.

Max lifts his head from my knee and quirks a furry ear, doggy concern shining in his dark, soulful eyes.

'Sorry Max, it's okay. My phone made me cross, not you. You're not in trouble, I promise.'

It takes a few behind the ear scratches to reassure him. Luc rescued Max a few years ago and though he's much more confident than he used to be, he still can't shake the fear he's in trouble whenever he picks up on human anger.

What is Mum thinking? I told her in no uncertain terms not to reserve The Lodge booking. Does she have a kind of textual blindness? If so, it's selective. Just as with everything else in life, she ignores anything she doesn't want to hear and just steamrollers ahead.

At least Dad stopped her putting a deposit down. I hate to think what Mum would be like without him to restrain her. She'd probably have the wedding planned, my dress bought and flights booked back to the UK for me and Luc.

I have to put a stop to this now.

From: sophietrent@hotmail.com
To: sandratrent@gmail.com
Cc: derektrent@gmail.com
Re: The Lodge Hotel

Hi Mum (and Dad!). I really appreciate you wanting to help plan the wedding but you're going to have to cancel the booking for The Lodge Hotel.

It's far too soon to make concrete plans and with Luc's dad ill things are a bit up in the air.

Also there's no way I can leave Luc at our busiest time of the year, it wouldn't be fair on him, sorry Mum.

Maybe you could come out to us instead? You still haven't seen where we live. I'd love to show you around and help you to understand why I love Switzerland so much.

Love Sophie

From: sandratrent@gmail.com
To: sophietrent@hotmail.com
Re: Wedding plans

Sophie, darling, you know we never go abroad nowadays. We couldn't possibly leave Toby. Having a diabetic dog is a big responsibility. I couldn't trust a dog-sitter to do the injections properly and you know we never put him in kennels.

Are you really sure about The Lodge? I'd be happy to

take care of all of the details for you. We really would love to see you. It feels like so long since you were back in the summer.

Love, Mum

From: sophietrent@hotmail.com
To: sandratrent@gmail.com
Cc: derektrent@gmail.com
Re: Wedding plans

Yes, Mum, I'm sure about The Lodge. I'm sorry if you had your heart set on it.

Re: Toby you know you can get pet passports now? That would mean you could drive over and bring Toby with you, maybe have a few stops in France on the way to break the driving up. Your route would take you through the Champagne region and you could add a day or two and detour to Burgundy for wine-tasting. Remember, you and Dad were always saying you'd love to do that one day?

Love, Sophie

Aargh.

Wedding bossiness aside, it really irks that I'm being made to feel guilty about not going home to England. Why does it never occur to Mum that it's exactly the same distance for us to go there as it is for them to come to us? Plus, since Dad took early retirement it's much easier for them to take time out. Yet they haven't been out here once. When I took Luc home to meet them last June we had to close up the bar for a week. I don't think they appreciated that. Not that Luc complained, but still.

I don't get a reply back. Either Mum has switched their computer off or she's in a huff because I didn't capitulate as usual.

I idly open the Facebook app on my phone to kill time while I wait for Luc to finish up downstairs. An update from Katie, a Lake District friend, makes me pause. It's a photo of a smiling Katie clutching a sonogram of an unborn baby.

Her unborn baby.

Breath catches in my chest.

It hurts she didn't tell me first, privately, though I know why. She's the only person back home who knows about what happened with Thomas – the STD, the pelvic inflammatory disease and my scarred ovaries. I went home that summer and she helped me pick up the pieces. It was Katie who packed me off to the doctor to get a counselling referral.

If only I'd known what that would cost me.

'CONGRATS :-) xxxx' I type into the comments box and then scroll down through the other comments.

A comment from Vanessa catches my eye.'Totes fantastic news! Now our babies can be playmates :-)'

Before I can stop myself I've clicked on her profile. There's no way stalking the wife of my first boyfriend Steven can help, but, just like reaching for a second doughnut it's irresistible.

I scroll through photos of Steven and Vanessa's beautiful, blonde-haired, blue-eyed toddler twins. Then, to further punish myself I go on to read the news that they're expecting another baby.

My chest constricts again.

It feels as if a black hole has opened up inside me and is sucking at my soul. As though I'm in danger of losing myself. I can still see the cute twins when I close my eyes. Dimples, blonde curls and cute grins.

If. . . If. . .

I ignore the klaxon sounding in my head, telling me not to go there but I'm mired too deep in boggy territory. I'm already there, in the land of 'If'.

If I'd said 'yes' when Steven asked me to marry him, before I came to Switzerland then I never would have met Thomas. If my self esteem hadn't been so low that I'd been flattered by that charming bastard I wouldn't have gone home with him. I wouldn't have caught the STD Thomas so generously shared with me, refusing to use protection when I asked him.

If I'd stopped him. If I hadn't been weak.

I wouldn't be infertile.

Max shifts on my lap, turning soulful brown eyes on me. It feels like a reproach.

Luc.

I can't imagine a world without Luc. Not one I'd want to live in. I cuddle Max tightly, his warm fur comforting beneath my fingers. He snuggles into me contentedly, with an audible sigh.

I really should stay away from Facebook when I'm feeling fragile.

Luc finds me curled up on the sofa with Max stretched out happily on top of me while I stare at the ceiling.

When he hears Luc, Max leaps off me to greet him and I miss the comforting warmth of his furry body, his unquestioning loyalty and love.

'Can I take Max's place?' Luc quirks an eyebrow at me, lips twisting into a smile that transforms his tired face.

'Sure.' I make myself smile back.

Luc sits on the sofa and pulls me onto his lap. Peace ripples through me. I might dream of building a chalet one day, but I'm perfectly happy here in our little flat above the Bar des Amis. It's small but cosy. I love retreating to it at the end of the day and finally getting Luc all to myself.

I sigh, letting my body fit into his and welcoming the feel of his hands on my body. It might be familiar, but his touch still triggers darts of arousal beneath my skin and makes desire stir and curl deep in the pit of my stomach.

When he kisses me my body sings, aching to be one with him again. I'll forget about Mum, the wedding and adoption stuff, just for tonight.

Live in the moment. Isn't that what's popular nowadays, with the trend for mindfulness?

I ignore the voice in my head that says I'm storing up trouble. Luc has been so stressed about his dad I can't add to that, not tonight.

'I love you Luc,' I say, once my lips are free.

'I love you too, Sophie. *Toujours*.' He cups one of my breasts through my top and my nipple hardens to his touch. I help him undress me, lifting my arms so he can pull my top over my head.

Once my bra's discarded, he lowers his mouth to my breasts, kissing and teasing them, sucking hard on my nipples.

I shiver in delight and grind against the growing bulge of Luc's erection, seized by a growing impatience to have him inside me. Wanting. Needing the reassurance of his desire for me.

I unbutton his shirt, needing to feel him skin on skin. His breath quickens when I lean forward, purposely grazing my nipples against his bare chest. In the way I know turns him on. He groans and rises from the sofa, taking me with him to the rug in front of the wood-burning stove.

His lips are on my skin as he tugs down my jeans and knickers with practised ease. I lie bare and exposed to him as he strips off. I'm his and my body delights in the knowledge.

When he lowers his head between my thighs my stomach flips with anticipation. He's such a generous lover, taking pleasure in making me come. His tongue teases my clit and I buck beneath his mouth, squirming with growing need.

Oh boy, Luc really is very good at this. He says he loves watching me come, which is fine by me, I'm happy to oblige. I have no inhibitions in front of him and love how comfortable I am in his company.

I lose myself in the swelling tide of arousal building in my sex and tightening nipples. I give myself over to sensations that wipe my brain of thought and sweep the emotional pain to one side. When I feel the wave of arousal washing over me, taking me with it, I cry out, welcoming the much-needed release.

While I'm still tingling and super-sensitive, Luc parts my thighs and enters me, his thrusts prolonging the pleasure and making me moan. I clutch at his back, needing to hold onto him, to keep him closer, deeper. . .

Making us one.

'Sophie,' he cries out my name as he jerks and comes inside me. I'll never tire of the musical inflection Luc's accent gives my name. Making love with him could never get old. Familiarity has only brought us greater intimacy and deeper unity. We know each other's bodies and exactly how to turn each other on.

Once recovered, he rolls off me and lies by my side. I know not talking to him about my concerns potentially threatens that closeness, but when I see the weariness etched onto his brow and the dark shadows beneath his eyes I can't bear to add to his problems. Surely love means to protect?

I'll just have to deal with it on my own.

'Come to bed, you look like you're ready to drop.' I slip my hand into his.

He blinks sleepily and nods.

I should be grateful for what I have. I love Luc more than I ever believed it possible to love someone. My world lights up when he smiles at me. His love has done a hell of a lot more for me than counselling ever did.

So why is the other stuff so hard? I can cope with a childless future, I think. Even though I always wanted to be a mother. When I was a little girl I used to beg neighbours with babies to let me have a cuddle with them.

Once I was old enough to babysit I was in great demand. Children seemed to like me as much as I liked them. I loved reading children's books and watching Disney and Pixar DVDs.

Well, okay, I still do. Luc watches them with me and pretends not to enjoy them, but secretly he does. I always catch him watching instead of reading his book.

Something in me lights up with joy when I connect with a small child or a baby clamps a tiny fist around one of my fingers. I love that special baby smell, the peachy soft skin, the big eyes and the tiny toes. . .

I even have wide, child-bearing hips and large, full breasts.

All of which makes infertility horribly cruel, but I could learn to deal with it, I think, if it was just me.

But it's not just me and the guilt that I'm imposing this agony on Luc too is killing me. As we climb into bed I try to ignore the voice that says he doesn't have to cope with it. There's nothing wrong with him. It's all my fault.

I close my eyes against the surging emotion and try to lock down the bleak thoughts.

They're too scary, too much. A deep, gaping chasm I could lose myself in.

Instead I'll live in the moment. This moment is lying with my fiancé and a hot-water bottle of a terrier who's jumped onto the bed to settle on my feet.

* * *

'I really need this.' Holly is smiling as we walk to Chalet Repos the next day, through powdery snow freshly fallen overnight. Verbier is basking in glorious sunshine today.

'Need what? Some time with the girls?' I ask, determined to make the most of the afternoon. I need this too, if I'm honest. With the extra shifts to cover Luc's absences and all the stressing, I could really use some downtime.

'More like some child-free time,' Holly says, seemingly oblivious that her words feel like a slap to me. 'I love Maddie to bits, but if I don't get some baby-free time I might go stark-raving mad, forget who I am and turn into a zombie milking machine.'

'Lovely image.' I crack a smile. 'Should we set a password so I can tell if you're the real Holly?'

'Who is that again?'

'Hmm, let me think.' I link arms with her. 'You're Holly, a super-cool mum, and a smoking-hot wife. Not to mention a really lovely friend.'

'You always make me feel good about myself, Sophie.' Holly grins. 'I need to keep you on call for whenever I need an ego boost.'

'I thought I already was on call for that.' I raise an eyebrow.

'True.' She smiles. 'Well, hopefully we'll both have a nice afternoon. You can chat weddings with Amelia.'

The W word. My heart plummets. I was doing okay not thinking about it. Why does life insist on interfering with my living-in-the-moment policy?

'Hmm, maybe.' I don't look at her.

'How's your Mary Berry impression?'

'Er, what?'

'Or Paul Hollywood, either would do.'

'Are you suffering from baby brain, Holly?' I pause before we enter Chalet Repos.

'No, you dope. We're judging a Great Chalet Repos Verbier Bake-Off, ' Holly says, as though she's making perfect sense and I'm being particularly slow on the uptake.

'Okaaay. . . Mind backing up a few steps?'

'Well, we've got a few days before the Christmas and New Year guests arrive, so the girls are doing a Bake-Off-themed contest to try out some new recipes,' Holly explains. 'And we get to taste and judge them.'

'That does sound like fun.' My spirits lighten. 'I'd prefer if we were Mel and Sue, though.'

'I think Tash and Amelia are taking it pretty seriously,' Holly adds.

'Rolling pins at dawn?'

'Exactly.'

Once we're through the door we're greeted by delicious cakey aromas and a chorus of welcomes. My stomach rumbles, reminding me I forgot to eat breakfast.

'Where's Matt?' Holly asks, flopping down onto a sofa.

'He and Jake have made themselves scarce, but they want us to save them plenty of cake,' Amelia says, taking off her apron and draping it over the back of a chair.

On the dining table there's an array of cakes – chocolate cake, carrot cake and sponges. There are even a couple of giant cup cakes and two three-dimensional chalets. I look more closely, impressed. One of them even has a hot tub with whipped-cream bubbles.

Behind each plate is a lolly stick with a card circle glued to it, presumably with names or photos facing away from us.

So Holly was right, someone is taking this very seriously. Not so much so that we can't have fun, I hope.

'It all looks amazing,' I nod over at the table. 'I can't wait to taste them.'

'Who would like some tea or coffee? Or we have a couple of bottles of Prosecco if you'd rather.' Amelia plays the part of hostess very well. I wonder if Holly feels odd, ceding her role to Amelia.

'I'd better stick to tea, given I'm breastfeeding,' Holly says.

'Prosecco please,' I add quickly, not sure I can bear it if the talk turns to babies. Guilt floods me. I'm a terrible friend and a bad godmother, not to mention a faulty fiancée and a disappointing daughter.

Bloody hell. I really need that drink. And to lighten up.

The thing is, I've always been a people-pleaser. I often hear the aphorism that you 'can't please all the people all the time', but what's so wrong about trying to do just that? The better you are at it, the happier you can make the people around you.

All I want is to help make the people I love happy. When did that suddenly get so difficult?

I blink hard and take a large sip from the glass of Prosecco Amelia hands to me.

'Thanks. Those cakes look amazing,' I say.

Amelia smiles smugly. She thinks she's going to win.

I gaze over at the cakes again. I bet hers is the chalet with gingerbread walls, butter-cream icing snow and hot tub with whipped-cream bubbles.

With the looks Tash is shooting at the creation, I guess hers is the other chalet. Awkward. I wish I wasn't judging.

At least I'm no longer living in a dorm room and coping with all the tensions and petty jealousies that enforced proximity creates.

Twenty minutes later I'm full of cake and Amelia is looking even more pleased with herself than before, if that were possible. Unfortunately her creation had the edge both in taste and presentation, so Holly and I had no choice but to place her first. Hopefully Tash will forgive us.

I bet the competition was Amelia's idea in the first place.

'Well, that was kind of intense.' Rebecca sits down next to me. I've always had a soft spot for her. She can't help coming from a privileged background. Her father is a high-court judge and she grew up with the big house, a private school and a pony. But I get the impression money is the only thing she ever got from her parents, and I know she's not happy. I think she's lonely, never feeling like she fits in here and certainly not accepted at home.

I used to be bullied at school, so I know that kind of loneliness. I smile at her and budge up to make more room for her.

'How's the wedding planning going, Sophie?' she asks and I resist the urge to grind my teeth.

Why does everyone assume I'm just dying to talk about my wedding plans? It's as though now I'm engaged, nothing else matters.

I restrain my sigh. Rebecca's only being polite.

'Um, well it's still early days. I'm not sure. . .' I break off as the rest of the room falls silent to listen to me. 'Luc's dad isn't well at the moment, so things are a bit up in the air.'

I catch Amelia shooting a knowing look at Emily. So, they're assuming something's wrong between me and Luc and I've got cold feet. Or that he has. Great.

'What about your parents, are they the get-involved kind?' Lucy asks from where she's perched on the edge of the sofa.

'I told my mum she had to stay well out of it. After all, it's my wedding, not hers,' Amelia says.

Why doesn't that surprise me? I briefly consider what would happen if I did the same. The universe would implode. Not to mention that I'd seriously hurt Mum's feelings. I can't flick a switch and suddenly stop caring.

'Mum does seem to want to take over. She's been planning things behind my back,' I say. I can't mention about her nagging me for grandchildren because Holly and Tash would realise that means I haven't told Mum about being infertile. It's all so complicated.

'It's really nice she wants to be involved,' Holly says quietly. She doesn't add any more, but the look in her eyes tells me she'd give anything for a mother who loves her so much she wants to plan her wedding.

I glance along the sofa to Tash, a refugee from the care system, and feel even worse. I should be grateful and I am thankful to have a mother who loves me but. . .

'How about you, Beth? Do you have the kind of mum who wants to organise every detail of your life?' Holly turns her gaze on Beth.

'My mum's dead,' Beth replies, staring down at the floor, meeting no one's eye.

A silence follows in which I now know for definite that I'm the most ungrateful person in the universe.

'Sorry, way to kill a conversation,' Beth adds and looks up with a self-deprecating smile. 'Anyone for more Prosecco?'

It's painful to watch her attempt at bravado. I wish I knew Beth better so I could reach out to her. But while I feel awful for her and Tash and Holly a tiny voice screams inside me with frustration that the attempt to voice my own stress has been shot down. I love Mum, but she doesn't listen. She can also be kind of scary when crossed and I hate confrontation. Defying Mum has never ended well.

And now I can't talk to either of my two closest friends about it without feeling like an ungrateful brat because they'd do anything to have a mother who loved them.

I sigh. Then, I look at Holly's tired face and it occurs to me she might feel like she can't complain about any aspect of motherhood to me, for exactly the same sort of reason.

That stings. I don't want Holly to have any problems she can't talk to me about. Yet, if I'm being totally honest, I know I find it hard to hear Holly's complaints. A part of me always wants to tell her how lucky she is. I also know my belief that if I had a baby I wouldn't care about sleepless nights and mastitis is stupid and unrealistic. Of course I would mind them because I'm human and so is Holly.

When did it all get so bloody complicated? A rush of loneliness sweeps over me. I feel more detached from my friends than ever. I don't know how to retrace my steps to recapture the time when there were no barriers between us.

It seems there are some problems even Prosecco and cake can't make better.

Chapter 11

LUCY

Hi Lucy, lunch today at my place? I've got someone I want you to meet. Apartement 16 at Belle Neige, I'm two floors up from Holly and Scott. C u at 1.

I stare at the text. I've been waiting, agonising to see if Seb would want to see me again. I know Jake passed on my mobile number to him because Emily checked it was okay with me first. Even so, I've had a bad case of the jitters and sleep has been virtually impossible.

I hadn't expected to feel so different after sex. To feel changed. But I do and it scares me rigid. Sex is a huge deal to me, but probably not to Seb. I'm sure it means no more to him than a need, like eating or drinking. It's just scratching an itch.

The casual assumption we're seeing each other again, that I'll come, both reassures and confuses me. And who on earth does he want me to meet? He's not talking about a threesome, is he? I know I'm naïve, but you wouldn't spring it on a new girlfriend, surely? Or friend who happens to be a girl, or. . . whatever.

Oh crap. Please don't let it be a sex thing.

I plug my phone on to charge and sit down on my bunk, my lips pursed and my forehead creased. I feel like I'm a beginner skier who should really be on a nursery slope, but instead has taken a wrong turn and is hurtling down a black run. This whole territory is off-piste for me anyway. It's thrilling and exciting, but possibly catastrophically dangerous.

Hmm.

'Not skiing today?' Tash is changing out of jeans and into her salopettes.

The new guests who arrived yesterday are all heading out too. It's a perfect day for the slopes, with clear, blue skies and fresh powdery snow from an overnight snowfall.

'No, I don't think so.' I bite my lip. 'Not today.'

'Are you okay? You've been really quiet the last couple of days. Quiet even for you, I mean.' Tash fastens her salopettes and sits cross-legged on the floor in front of me, examining my face closely.

'I'm. . . okay.' It sounds false, even to me. I stare at Tash uncertainly. She's used to skiing off-piste, so to speak, when it comes to sex. But is she really someone I want to advise me?

'Fuck me, you actually did it, didn't you?' She raises a perfectly plucked eyebrow.

'Did what?' I wish I could stop the flush flooding my cheeks. My body seems determined to give me away. Can she tell? Do I look different somehow?

'You had sex with Sebastien Laroche. Finally.' Tash declares triumphantly.

'Could you announce it a little louder? I'm not sure all our guests heard you.' I glance anxiously towards the door.

Tash grins. 'How was it?'

The desire to confide in someone overcomes me.

'It was much better than you made me think my first time would be.'

'Lucky girl, not everyone's first time is that great. Although, that's probably because they start earlier and sleep with boys who don't know what they're doing rather than men with experience,' she says, thoughtfully. 'So what's the problem?'

I bite my lip again and stare down at my hands.

'Do I have to torture the information out of you, Lucy?'

I manage a smile. 'I don't know what happens next. He's not the kind of guy I thought it would happen with. I don't know if I've done the right thing.'

'You imagined it'd be with Mr Perfect Boyfriend material, didn't you? Well he doesn't exist and even if he did, he'd be bloody boring.' Tash eyes me quizzically. 'Did you tell Seb you were a virgin?'

'No and it wasn't obvious, I mean he didn't see . . .' My cheeks burn even hotter. It will take a long time before I'm comfortable talking about sex.

'Hmm. I think you should tell him.'

'Why? Won't he feel pressured?' I stare at her.

Tash shrugs. 'Trust me. I've discovered it's best to be upfront in relationships. Tell the truth and if he can't handle it, he's not the man for you. It's a hard truth but generally applicable.'

I pull a face.

Tash pats my arm. 'If he's not the right man for you there'll be another one along.'

'Like buses?' I laugh.

'That's how it works until you meet the right one.' Tash shrugs her response. 'Problem is, it doesn't work to our timetable. It happens when it's meant to.'

'Hmm. Like it did for you and Nate?'

'Yes. Trust me, I had to kiss a hell of a lot of frogs until I met my prince. This might feel like a big deal to you at the moment but it won't always feel this way, I promise.'

I nod. 'Okay, I'll tell him. I'm going over to his place for lunch, that's why I'm not coming with you today.'

At the moment I've no idea whether I'll tell him or not, but I know Tash won't leave it alone. She might have slightly feline features, but she has a terrier's obstinacy.

'You'll be okay. Let me know how it goes.' Tash heads out.

I take a deep breath and try to find something to wear that isn't too crumpled. Lack of wardrobe space doesn't do much for your clothes. I've never bothered with dressing to impress so I don't have many options. I opt for dark-indigo jeans and a black crewneck jumper.

At one o'clock I press the buzzer to Seb's apartment and he releases the door to let me in.

'Hi.' I try in vain not to blush. Heat sears my cheeks and a remembered intimacy lingers in the air, tinged with expectation.

Seb greets me with a kiss on both cheeks but not on the mouth. Is he taking a step back now? Have we morphed from lovers to friends so quickly?

'Salut, Lucy Lu.' Seb gestures for me to enter the apartment.

'Who do you want me to meet?' I look around the open-plan living area but it's empty. I then peer down the corridor.

At that moment a young girl with wild, dark curls hurtles into the room. She looks around six or seven years old.

'My daughter, Estelle.' Seb pulls the girl to him. The resemblance is obvious. 'Estelle, say hello to my new friend Lucy.'

'Hello, Lucy.' The girl beams. 'I helped make lunch.'

'Did you? I'm sure it will be yummy. Your English is very good.'

I raise an eyebrow at Seb. I can honestly say I wasn't expecting this. In none of his bios on the internet is there any mention of a daughter.

'Estelle speaks German and English as well as she does French,' Seb boasts proudly. 'Her stepfather is English.'

I want to ask a million questions, most of them about Estelle's mother, but I can hardly do that in front of Estelle.

'I didn't know you had a daughter,' I say quietly as Estelle runs off back to her room to fetch her colouring books. 'She's lovely.'

'You want to know if what we have is for real?' Seb eyes me gravely. 'This is my way of showing you that it is. I don't introduce my daughter to anyone. . . casual. I think we're at the start of something special.'

My heart races. The intense way he looks at me ignites feelings I shouldn't have with a child present.

'So, er, what's for lunch, then?'

'Some poached salmon and salad.'

'Sounds good.' I follow Seb towards the laid table in the

kitchen area of the open-plan living space. 'Does Estelle live with you?'

'No, she lives with her mother in Geneva. My schedule is very hectic. I travel a lot, but I see her whenever I can. It's easier in the school holidays.' Seb opens a large bottle of mineral water and pours it out into three empty glasses.

I sit down at the table. I really do want to know about Seb's relationship with Estelle's mother, but I'll have to try and contain my curiosity.

'Estelle looks a lot like you.' I turn to look at her dark, wild curls and animated face creased in fierce concentration as she colours.

'Yes, but she's much prettier.' Seb smiles fondly. 'She has her mother's eyes, though. You'll see when she comes to pick her up.'

Excuse me?

'What, here, now?' My muscles tense and I wonder if I should do something with my hair. I just washed it and let it dry naturally this morning. Why didn't I make more effort? Aargh. Come to that, why didn't Seb warn me I'd be meeting his daughter and his ex? Talk about an ambush.

'After lunch.' Seb seems oblivious to my discomfort. Maybe it just never occurred to him I might find this difficult.

'Is she your ex-wife?' I whisper, glancing furtively at Estelle.

'No, we never married.' Seb puts fresh bread on the table and fetches plates. 'We were only together for a few months and by the time we realised we weren't right for each other Gabriella was already pregnant.'

'Right.' I take a sip of water, feeling hopelessly out of my depth again for the second time this week.

'We are good friends now. She'll like you, I'm sure.'

I stare at him.

'Like I said, you wanted to know that what I feel for you means something to me, so I'm proving it, Lucy Lu.' Seb takes my hand and squeezes it. 'I'm proving it by letting you into my life. It's what you want, yes?'

'Yes, I do. I just feel a bit . . .' I want to say 'ambushed', but that sounds too combative. 'It's taken me by surprise, that's all.'

'After Estelle goes back to her mother, I was hoping we could spend some time together.' Seb lets go of my hand but lightly circles a finger on the back of my hand, leaving delicious sensation in its wake.

I nod. 'That would be nice.'

'Better than nice, I hope.' Seb whispers, his lips brushing my ear. He retreats when he sees his daughter coming towards us. 'Estelle, come to the table, let's eat.'

'Do you ski, Estelle?' I ask once we're seated and helping ourselves to salad and salmon fillets.

She shoots me the 'adults are silly' look, universally perfected by children everywhere.

'Of course,' she replies, politely nonetheless.

'Ever since she could stand she has been on the slopes,' Seb says proudly.

'Are you going to do what your dad does when you're older, then?'

'No, Mum says Dad is crazy and if I ever decide to compete

or do anything dangerous she'll move us to a desert where there's no snow.' Estelle's eyes are wide. 'Can you imagine having no snow?'

I smile. 'Where I come from we don't have as much snow as you do here.'

'Is that why you're here in Switzerland?' She asks. 'Dad says we get some of the best snow in Europe here. And the best slopes.'

'That's the main reason, yes. I love the snow and I'd really hate it if I couldn't ski.' I pick up a forkful of salmon.

'Me too. Do you like my dad?' She fixes her dark eyes on me. They're so much like Seb's.

I almost choke on the salmon.

'We haven't known each other very long, but yes, I do, very much.' I don't meet Seb's gaze but focus instead on Estelle.

'Good.' Estelle beams. 'Then you can look after him when I have to be with Mum. I look after him when I'm here, but he needs a good woman to keep him grounded.' She sounds so serious that my lips twitch and Seb barks with laughter.

'Is that what your mum said, Estelle?' He pats his daughter on the head.

'Don't do that, Dad. You'll mess up my hair.' She giggles and pulls away. 'Yes, I heard Mum say you need a good woman. She also said she worries about you. Why does she worry, Dad?'

Seb raises his eyebrows. 'Your mum worries too much. I'm fine, Estelle.'

I keep quiet, but my brain is churning.

Later the intercom buzzes and Seb gets up to let Gabriella

in. Estelle runs up to my chair and puts her mouth close to my ear, covering it with her hands.

'Don't forget to look after my Dad, Lucy, it's very important.'

Her idea of a whisper isn't all that discreet and I'm sure both Gabriella and Seb hear.

I stand up and air-kiss Gabriella, trying not to squirm too much.

'Ciao, Lucy.' She smiles.

She's petite, like me, but maybe five years older. She has the same straight, nut-brown hair as me but she's much glossier, her clothes designer and stylish and her make-up perfect.

I really wish I'd made more effort. Clean jeans and a not-too-crumpled jumper don't quite cut it.

'Hello, it's nice to meet you.' I smile back at her and try to hide my nerves.

'You are right, she is very pretty.' Gabriella turns to Seb. 'I approve.'

This is bizarre, I've just been vetted and approved by Seb's daughter and ex-partner, neither of whom I even knew existed before I came to lunch.

Thinking about it, I've never seen anything about either of them in the press. Which must mean Seb really is letting me into his private life.

Perhaps he really does feel the same connection I do?

When they've gone, Seb walks up to me and draws me close to him.

'Did you enjoy lunch?'

'It was . . . interesting. Your daughter is lovely.'

'She is.' Seb beams proudly.

'Why does she worry about you so much?' I ask curiously.

Seb frowns. 'It's Gabriella. She doesn't like what I do. She worries I'll get myself killed. She worries all the time and I'm concerned she's passing on her anxieties to Estelle.'

'Is that likely?' I stare at Seb as he pulls me down onto the sofa with him. 'The getting killed part, I mean.'

Seb shrugs. 'Who knows. There are younger, hungrier guys coming up all the time, willing to cut corners and take chances that are dangerous, just to get the edge on you.'

I stare at him. We're talking about a possible risk of death and he's shrugging it off?

'Oh.' I wish he hadn't told me that. I knew that what he did was risky; it's not called an extreme sport for nothing. But the idea of him being pushed harder in order to take even riskier chances makes me feel sick. I'm beginning to feel some sympathy with Gabriella.

'It's okay, I'll be okay.' Seb lifts my chin and kisses me, long and deep, drawing me in and driving my fears away.

I'll have to think more about this when I'm not being distracted by Seb's seductive touch and kisses. For now I'll shove my niggles aside.

'So, what would you like to do this afternoon, Lucy Lu? I have been longing to make love to you. Tell me what turns you on.'

Seb skims his hands over my arms, my breasts and my thighs and the delicious fizzing sensation that's been buzzing constantly in the background since we made love erupts with a vengeance. It's as if he's flipped a switch to turn me on. It's positively embarrassing how responsive I am.

There's one hovering anxiety I can't swat away. It's buzzing in my ear, whispering insidiously, asking what I'll do if he asks me to do something sexual that I'm totally ignorant of.

'I um, need to tell you something, Seb.' I swallow hard.

'Sure, go ahead.' He doesn't halt his caressing reacquaintance with my body.

'Could you stop touching me for a minute? I can't think when you do that.' I take a deep breath.

He stops, examining me quizzically.

'What do you need to tell me?'

'I was a virgin before we slept together.' I blurt it out, my cheeks flushing again like emotional traffic lights.

Seb's eyes widen.

'A virgin?' He tilts his head to one side. 'Really?'

'Why does everyone say that like it's as rare as an alien?' I huff at the note of incredulity in his voice.

'I think it might be.' Seb raises his eyebrows. 'I knew you were pretty inexperienced, but I didn't guess you were a virgin. I wish you'd told me.'

'Why?' My pulse quickens and I tense. Is this where he dumps me?

'I could've been more gentle with you, maybe.'

'You were great, it was all, you know . . . good.' I stare down at my hands. 'I didn't want to make a big deal out of it.'

'So why?' Seb's gaze is focused on me, a gleam of intense curiosity shining in his eyes.

'Why what? Why was I a virgin?' I shift awkwardly in my seat.

'Sure, let's start with that.'

'Well, I suppose you could say I come from a religious family. I had a long- term boyfriend back home but we met at the church youth group. At the youth group there was a big deal about saving yourself for marriage, you know? Then, when I left home and came out here everyone seemed so casual about relationships. I didn't want to have sex with just anyone, I didn't want it to mean nothing.' I sigh. 'I still believe in God, I just don't believe sex is wrong outside of marriage.'

'I'm glad to hear that.' Seb puts a hand on my knee. 'Now we've dealt with why, how about why me?'

'Let's just say you were kind of irresistible.' My cheeks heat up.

He grins. 'And now we get to find out what you like. I can catch you up on all you've been missing, if you want to.'

'I definitely want to.' The words escape me like a sigh. He still wants me. Relief courses through me, releasing a weight I hadn't realised I was carrying.

Seb runs a hand up my thigh, his large fingers spanning my thighs and dancing with unexpected grace between my legs. Even through the denim of my jeans I'm super-sensitive, my body embarrassingly responsive.

I exhale slowly, trying to keep my cool. I just wish I knew what a normal response should be on the date after sex.

Things have changed between us. I feel a deeper pull, a belonging of sorts, but can't tell if that's real or just my social conditioning. They taught us in the youth group that if you had sex you were basically married. After all, in the Old Testament you were joined by sex, that's what they told us.

But a modern application of that never made sense to me, after all what if only one of you was a virgin?

I need to stop thinking like this. I've been away from the critical kirk culture for a few years now. I learnt to think for myself. I haven't thrown away my heritage, I just dared to question a few things. For a religion supposedly based on love I've never understood why I saw so little love growing up.

Aargh, and now I've really stressed myself out.

'Are you okay?' Seb pulls me closer and lifts me onto his lap. He strokes my cheek.

'I'm okay, I just feel like. . .' I take a deep breath and decide to stop second-guessing what I should be feeling and tell the truth. 'I don't know what I'm doing.'

'That's okay, I can show you, a lot of it is instinct but some of it is simply working out what turns you on.' He strokes my denim-clad thigh. 'So, what do you like that we've already done?'

'I liked it when you put your fingers inside me,' I answer, feeling a little shy, but not as awkward as I expected, talking about sex with Seb. Now I've told him my secret, most of my fear has been dispelled.

Silently he undoes the button and zip at my waistband and pulls my jeans down. I help him by wriggling out of them. Then he positions me so I'm leaning back against his chest and both my legs are hooked over his thighs, stretching me wide. Breath hitches in my chest as he runs his fingers over the top of my knickers. I lean back to allow him better access. I gasp when he pulls my knickers aside and thrusts two fingers inside me.

'Do you like this?' His thumb traces circles on my clit while his fingers massage me inside, making me writhe on his lap. 'That's better, you're nice and wet for me now. Can you feel what you're doing to me?'

I rub my bottom over his growing erection. 'You mean that?'

I smile when he groans, taking pleasure from the knowledge I have some power in this relationship, that it's not all one-sided.

He pulls my knickers down and spins me round so I'm straddling him. He spreads the wetness from his fingers onto my top lip. He then licks it off.

I didn't even know that was a thing. I'm surprised to find it turns me on, to know he likes the taste of me.

'You taste delicious. *Je veux te lécher des hanches jusqu'aux pieds*.' He grins, a wicked gleam in his darkening eyes.

'What does that mean?'

'Something very naughty.' Seb grins, then whispers in my ear. 'I want to lick you from your hips to your toes.'

A fierce jolt of sexual electricity shakes me.

'Say something else in French.' I grind against him, desperately seeking release. That he is still in his jeans and I'm naked from the waist down makes me feel exposed, but I find I like it.

It looks like my time with Seb is going to be very educational indeed.

'*Ta voix sexy me fait bander comme un porc*.' Seb grins. 'That means your sexy voice gives me a hard-on.'

'Sexy?' I push against his erection, pleased to feel a pulse in response.

'Very.' He cups my bottom and squeezes, getting his revenge.

We're both breathing hard now. I might even be panting, but I'm too far gone to care. I think Seb's as turned on as I am as we both strip off the rest of our clothes with indecent haste. I fumble with the buttons on his shirt, my hands shaking a little.

I've no room for thoughts about Seb's suitability, only the insistent urge consuming me. I have to have him inside me. It's an imperative. Somehow it feels like the most important thing I should be doing, which sounds crazy, I know.

Crazy or not, it's happening. Now. I need him. I run my hands over his muscular chest, trying not to think about how he got the jagged scars.

I'm not sure how it got there, but my bra is lying on the floor and Seb's lips are on my breasts, sucking and teasing my nipples. Then he presses me back down onto the sofa and trails kisses down my stomach to between my legs. Now he's sucking my sensitive clit, his tongue lapping and tasting me. I come almost instantly in a burst of fiery sparks, jerking against his lips, my body quivering with the intensity.

'Can I do the same for you?' I ask, once I've stopped shaking. I can feel Seb's rock-hard erection pressing against my thigh. 'I've never done it before, so I might get it wrong, but I'd like to try.'

'That would be wonderful,' Seb exhales loudly. 'You can't really get it wrong. Just don't use your teeth.'

I take Seb's erection in my mouth, licking and exploring, instinct taking over. I then brush my tongue over the hard tip, tasting the drop of salty liquid and then moving my mouth up and down, taking him deeper in.

I like the intimacy of it. I love how powerful it makes me feel, seeing Seb's face contort in pleasure and knowing I'm the one who's making that happen. I look up and our eyes meet, intimacy deepening and connection forging.

'I. . . thought. . . you said. . . you hadn't done this before.' Seb's breathing is ragged.

I pull away and crawl up beside him. 'I want you inside me.'

Seb retrieves a condom and shows me how to sheathe him. Then he guides me on top of him.

I straddle him and let him position me, lowering myself down until the tip of his erection breaches me. I'm wet and ready for him, so I sit down hard, hungry for friction, for the sensation of him moving inside me. Seb groans and I move instinctively, my body guiding me as I rock back and forth, a delicious throbbing warmth building inside me. I rest my hands on his chest and lean forward so my nipples graze his chest.

'*Merde*. Fuck that's good, Lucy Lu,' Seb groans again.

I pick up the pace as he grabs my hips and then my buttocks, urging me to move faster. Ah, so that's why they call it 'riding'. It makes sense now. Suddenly I begin to spasm, my body shuddering with the onslaught of another orgasm. I contract around Seb, squeezing him hard. He jerks inside me, face contorted as he comes.

'Fuck me, Lucy Lu, you're a natural,' he gasps, and we lie panting, me collapsed on top of him. 'Did you like that?'

'Yes, I liked it very much.' I can't stop smiling. I rest my cheek against his chest, my body still tingling. I had no idea orgasms could be like that. My own attempts never had anything like that result.

'Good. I look forward to continuing your education,' Seb laughs and lightly trails his fingers down my bare back, tickling me.

'Me too,' I agree and find a ticklish spot under his ribs to exact my revenge.

'Good afternoon?' Tash looks up from her magazine.

'Bloody fantastic,' I beam.

Tash raises her eyebrows.

'You swore! For you to swear it must've been good. It was months before you stopped flinching every time I said fuck, the first season we worked together.' She stares at me, curiosity gleaming in her eyes. Being with Nate is definitely changing her, she never used to show this much interest in other people.

'I told you, my parents are very religious. My mother would kill me if she heard me swear.' I shrug, some of the shine has gone out of my mood just thinking about home and how much of a disappointment I am to Mum. She'd be horrified if she knew what I'd been up to this afternoon.

'Did they beat you or something? You know, the more you tell me about it, the more your set-up at home is sounding like a cult.'

'It's not a cult, Tash, just Scottish Presbyterianism, the Highlands' version. My parents are very active in the church, and my grandfather was a minister.' I shrug. 'They didn't beat me for swearing, but my mum would make me clean the range cooker, sometimes the toilets too. She said I was lucky, because her mother used to wash her mouth out with soap if she didn't like her language.'

It wasn't really the punishment I minded but the look of irritated contempt on Mum's face. I was always disappointing her, it seemed. She was far harder on me than my brothers. They could rarely do any wrong, but I was always accountable to a higher standard, for some reason.

'Range cooker?' Tash frowns. 'Just what century are you from, Lucy?'

'The same one as you, Tash. It gets very cold in the Highlands, and lots of people have range cookers that help heat the house as well as cooking the food.'

'Hmm, it sounds a bit like the Amish. I saw a film about them. Did you have to wear a headscarf? Were you allowed to use a computer or watch TV?'

'My family aren't Amish, Tash, and they're not backward,' I pause. 'Although we were never allowed to watch television on a Sunday.'

'Well, if you say so. No wonder you don't go back home much.' Tash stares at me.

I daren't say there's a danger Mum would lock me in the barn and refuse to let me leave again, after having read what supposedly goes on in a ski resort. Although, after what I've been up to with Seb . . . well, I don't think she'd ever look me in the eye again.

'Anyway, you're getting me off the point.' Tash narrows her eyes. 'How's it going with Sebastien, then?'

'Good, I think he wants a relationship.'

'That's great. Just be careful, okay?' Tash's forehead creases with concern. 'You're so green I feel like I need to protect you. If I had a pound for every time a man made me a false promise or lied to me, let's just say I'd be as rich as Nate.'

'I don't know, I think Seb's being straight with me.' I bite my lip. Am I being too naïve?

'Just promise you'll be careful, okay?'

I nod. Things have been moving really fast. He's not the kind of man I imagined finally doing the deed with. He's got a daughter, for a start, not that it puts me off him, but I can just imagine what Mum would say – that in God's eyes Seb is still married to Estelle's mother and I'm helping him commit adultery. That I'm probably going to Hell.

Why do I still care what she thinks? I don't believe it any more, so why is it still so powerful and hard to shake off? I thought I'd given up caring what they thought of me. That I'd grown out of my desire to please my parents. I guess it's not that easy. They might be hundreds of miles away but their influence and a childish longing for their approval is harder to leave behind.

Tash goes back to her magazine and I head off for a shower. I can't help thinking about how judgemental I've been, waiting for my future partner to be perfect. Tash is right, no one is perfect.

Have I been just as guilty of the rigid thinking I left home to get away from? Maybe Tash isn't the only chalet girl to come to Verbier needing sharp edges smoothed away.

Chapter 12

From: eva.johnson@gmail.com
To: beth.chapman@yahoo.com
Subject: News

Hello Beth,

I hope you're okay? The photos you emailed me are gorgeous. Living and working in such a beautiful place must be a real blessing.

Darling, I've got some news. I've been debating whether or not to tell you this, but decided on balance that you'd want to know. I think I'd want to know in your position.

Okay, here goes – two more victims have come forward and Michael Robson has been charged with two counts of rape. At least we know that if they had enough evidence to charge him there's more chance of a successful prosecution this time. Fingers crossed.

I know this will stir up some incredibly painful memories for you. Please Skype me to talk about this or at the very least talk to someone you trust in Verbier. You mustn't bottle up your feelings again, we both know how unhealthy that can be for you.

I wish you weren't so far away. I want to give you a big hug right now.

Lots of love,

Eva

BETH

When I read the email bile rises in my throat. I'm hot, so hot I can't breathe. The room blurs before my eyes. I click my phone into standby and slide it back into my pocket.

'I have to go. Please can you cover for me?' I turn away from the unstacked plates next to the dishwasher to face Rebecca. 'I'll do the same for you when you need me to, I promise.'

I try to take a deep breath in and can't. Panic courses through me, stress flooding my body and constricting my chest.

'No problem. Are you okay, Beth?' Rebecca's tone is hesitant.

'I'm fine.' I force a smile to my lips and probably look completely nuts. And why not? Crazy mother, crazy daughter. 'I've just got a bad headache coming on and really need some fresh air.'

'Okay, well I hope you feel better soon.' Rebecca takes my place at the dishwasher.

I turn and walk swiftly out of the chalet before she can ask me anything else. I dismiss the pinpricks of guilt as pain throbs at my temples. I really do have a headache coming on. After a few minutes I realise two things.

One – I've forgotten my jacket. Not necessarily disastrous as it's sunny. Hopefully it'll stay that way and I won't freeze. Although today I'm not sure I care all that much.

Two – I'm halfway to Dan's campervan, hoping he'll be in.

I hesitate. Is he really the right person to go to?

Yes. My inner voice is emphatic. I need to get to Dan. If I can get to Dan I'll be okay. By the time I'm knocking at the van door I can barely feel my fingers. It must be colder than I realised.

A new panic assails me. What if he's not in? He has to be. Otherwise I don't know where to go.

When Dan opens the door, a welcoming, easy smile on his face, palpable relief courses through me.

'Hi, Beth, do you want to come in?' Dan's wearing salopettes and a long sleeved t-shirt that skims his muscled torso. He doesn't seem surprised to see me, just pleased, but his reaction barely registers.

I stamp the snow off my boots and scrape them on the steps before climbing up into the van. It's not just my hands that are numb now, all of me is.

The numbness is protecting me from all the questions crowding in, bombarding me like ill-mannered paparazzi. Will they get him this time? Why wasn't he punished for raping me? Is it because I don't matter? What if he walks free and he does it again?

The knowledge he's already done it again at least twice makes me want to throw up. The idea that he'll probably go free turns my heart to ice. What do you do when even the police and justice system fail to protect you?

'What's happened, Beth?' Dan's eyes take in my appearance and the relaxed smile vanishes from his face. He keeps hold of my hands. 'You're freezing. Where's your coat? Here, put this on and I'll make some tea.'

He hands me a thick navy hoodie and I slip it on, but

there's a chill inside me I don't think the van heater is capable of touching.

'What happened? Has someone hurt you?' He thrusts a mug of tea into my hands and I cradle it. 'Sit down.'

I slump down onto the day bed.

'No, well yes. . . but not recently.' I rub the mug handle with my thumb.

The silence in the van grows heavy as Dan waits, patiently, for my answer. He sits down next to me, not touching me but protecting my personal space. Strangely I don't feel pressured to answer. Instead Dan's easy-going peace is permeating my frost, thawing me, along with the van heater.

'I. . . was. . . attacked a few years back now.' I take a deep breath. 'It was rape.'

I stare down at the tea, relieved to have got the word out, but unable to bear direct eye contact. Eva would be proud of me. It was months before I could say ‚raped' instead of ‚attacked' when talking about what happened. Dan is silent, calmly waiting, inviting more detail. He won't get it. The words simply aren't there. They are knotted up in a painful lump in my throat. I can only cope with this if I don't feel, if I stay detached from the bald facts, as though they have nothing whatever to do with me.

'I guessed.'

Dan's reply shocks me into looking up. I'd expected a platitude or the standard 'I'm sorry' response.

'You guessed?' I eye him sharply, my hand gripping the mug handle so tightly my knuckles grow white.

'Yes,' he replies simply.

'Oh.' I try to relax my grip on the mug handle and bite my lower lip. Is it obvious to everyone, then? Do men look at me and see a potential victim?

I've often wondered if I looked especially vulnerable the day it happened. Bereavement had dulled my instincts and left me in a fog. With Mum's death the knowledge I was all alone, with no family to turn to, had overwhelmed me.

'What happened today?' He asks gently.

I blink hard and then wordlessly I open up Eva's email on my phone and pass it to Dan to read.

I watch his face as he reads it, but his expression remains inscrutable. When he's finished reading he hands me back the phone. His silence infuriates me for a reason I can't understand. The coldness in me is fragmenting, splintering into something much more dangerous and far more terrifying.

'So you see the man who. . . who raped me, he's on trial for raping another two women.' My chest heaves as I fight the panic.

'It's okay, Beth. It'll be okay.' Dan's gentle tone makes me feel like punching something.

'Really? Did you know one in five women are victims of sexual violence? And something like thirty per cent of women say they were victims of sexual abuse as children?' I feel like roaring, anger finally flaring to life. The statistics I know by heart are spewing out of me. 'That's a hell of a lot of not okay.'

A scream is building up in my throat. I desperately try to damp it down. I can't misdirect this anger at Dan. It's not his fault. But still it rises, choking me, vile in its ugliness.

'If the world was okay I'd be happy to spend the rest of my life building snow marmots and kissing, but it's not. We can't all run away and treat the world like a playground.' My tone is scathing.

Dan watches me silently. Calmly.

'You know, I did the maths, I worked it out.' Bitterness streams out of the dark place inside me. 'Eighty-five thousand women are raped every year in the UK. Only fifteen per cent of those rapes are reported to the police. Only six per cent of those reported rapes end in a conviction.'

I glare at Dan, as though he is personally responsible for those appalling statistics. I know it's unfair, but this rage, this living monster I've let out of its cage, wants blood. He asked for more from me and he's getting it. Probably far more than he wanted.

In his eyes I see only compassion, knowledge and something more, an empathic connection I can't bear. He's patiently sitting, waiting for me to get past this, to meet him on safe ground once I get past the crazy.

I look down at my hands. I must've put the mug down somewhere, it's nowhere to be seen. My nails are digging so hard into the palms red ridges are appearing.

I don't know what I expected to get from researching the conviction rates for rape. If I'd hoped knowing I wasn't the only victim to be denied justice would leave me feeling less alone I was disappointed. All I got was a growing sense of fury and nowhere for it to go.

'That means out of eighty-five thousand rapists only seven hundred are punished.' I grit my teeth. 'Each year. And that's just in the UK, Dan. He'll get off again, I know it. It's not safe, the world is a fucking awful place, so don't try to tell me life isn't serious.'

I'm shaking. With fear? With fury? Maybe a mixture of the two. Rage and terror are out of control, adrenalin pumping through my body.

'Hit me.' Dan walks up to me and holds his arms outstretched. 'You want to hit someone. So hit me.'

'I don't want to hit you.' The monster inside me disagrees, it writhes and spits.

'This anger is good, Beth.'

It's official; Dan's a moron. Suddenly I do want to hit him, badly. But I control the urge.

'It's not good,' I grind out between clenched teeth. 'Why do you think I work so hard to contain it?'

'At least it's real. Pushing anger down isn't healthy. I can show you the scientific studies online if you like. It has a real physiological effect on the body.'

'Well, what am I supposed to do with it?' I glare at him, annoyed he's said something that actually makes sense.

'Let it out, use it to make yourself stronger. When you're angry you're not giving up and that's a good thing. You have energy to propel yourself forward.

I stare at him. What kind of drifter understands about the physiological effects of anger?

'Why do you know this, Dan? Who are you? You're always trying to find out my secrets, but I think you've got your own.'

'Okay.' Dan reaches out, crossing the boundaries of personal space to take my hand. 'I'll tell you how I ended up travelling.'

I hold on tight to his hand, the fight seeping out of my bones and leaving me weak.

'So tell me, Mr 'Wherever I park my camper there's my home'.'

'They call me 'Dan the Van' but I like your nickname too.' He answers, as though he hasn't heard the acerbic edge to my tone.

I fix my gaze on him. Dan the ski instructor, the free-spirited traveller.

Right.

When I told him the rape statistics there was no spark of surprise, only recognition. He either couldn't give a flying snowball or the figures are no great surprise to him. I wait silently for his answer, half afraid of what he might share.

'I trained as a barrister. I was idealistic and I thought providing a defence to people who needed someone to speak up for them would be a noble way to spend my life.' Dan's tone is self-deprecating. 'I wasn't really that naïve, not entirely. I knew some of my clients would be guilty, but I still believed everyone was entitled to a defence. As a pupil and a junior you have to take the work you're given. You don't get to pick and choose.'

I glance sharply at him.

'You were a criminal barrister? Is this leading up to you confessing you defended rapists? If so, is the offer to hit you still open?' I feel a tightening, a hardening deep inside me. Like ice re-freezing after a thaw, creating a treacherous inner landscape. One wrong footing and I'll slide away.

Dan eyes me warily. Even I'm not sure if I'm joking or not.

'I'm not sure I like the word 'confess'. At the risk of sounding like a complete dick there is a sound principle behind everyone getting a fair defence.'

The atmosphere feels taut between us, stretched so tight it could break. Or I could let up a little and ease it out. I could try to meet Dan halfway. He has been good to me. That day at the café he gave me a lifeline. I pause and try to get my breathing under control.

'In my head I know that,' I admit. 'But my emotions . . . they don't agree, they're kind of stuck on the six per cent conviction statistic and they want someone to blame.'

Dan sighs heavily. 'I get that, Beth, I do. Ideals and reality diverge, and some degree of cynicism is justified. Anyone who starts out their law career idealistic loses their illusions pretty quickly.'

'Is that what happened with you?' I ask, my anger damped down, curiosity temporarily putting it on hold.

'Yes, to some degree, but it was more than that,' he shrugs. 'The competition is fierce for tenancy. There aren't enough places in chambers for everyone called to the Bar. I was fortunate to get a pupillage and then tenancy, but the job demands your life and to some degree your soul. After five years something happened and I had an epiphany. I couldn't see myself doing it for the rest of my life. I'd fought tooth and nail for the life I had but I didn't want it any more.

'So, did you defend rapists?' I hear the edge to my voice, although I didn't mean to put it there.

'Yes,' Dan sighs again. 'You don't exactly get a choice. You take the work you're given and everyone is . . .'

'Entitled to a defence, I know,' I reply flatly, staring down at my hands, tightly knotted together in my lap.

'I want to tell you about the thing that happened, the event five years ago that acted as a catalyst,' Dan replies slowly.

'Oh?' I look up from my lap.

'My sister Kate was raped. I know she wouldn't mind me telling you. The CPS couldn't get enough evidence to secure a conviction and the bastard went free.'

'I'm sorry.' I'm so thrown I utter the expected platitude, but it's not an empty response. I really am full of sorrow for his sister. Of course I am. I know how it feels, after all.

'I saw what it did to her.' Dan's voice is tight, there's nothing easy-going about his tone now. 'There was no professional barrier in place at that time. I couldn't hide from the impact or protect myself with distance. I still believe everyone is entitled to a defence, but I'm not the man to do it any more. I bought the campervan, did it up and I have different priorities now. I'm not hung up about acquiring wealth and stuff I don't need.'

'How is your sister now?' I ask, genuinely curious.

I went to a support group once, at Eva's suggestion. I couldn't go back, because I found all the negative emotions too much to handle, but it taught me one important thing – everyone copes differently. Some women stay victims their whole lives, and the rape defines them. Others grab the coat tails of their anger and cling to a lifelong hatred of all men.

I realised pretty quickly I didn't want to belong to either group. The rape was just one part of my life and it wasn't going to rob me of my identity or my sexuality. Even if that meant I secretly cried in the bathroom after every attempt at post-rape sex.

I grew up coping with Mum's illness. After the rape I had to step up my coping skills, with Eva's help.

'She's coping.' Dan's eyes display a bleakness I hadn't expected to see. 'She had a nervous breakdown and it took her a while to pick herself up again. She's living with my parents now, and I think she'll be with them for a while. It's because of her I knew something similar had happened to you.'

'Oh?'

'There's this shut-down look Kate gets when she's struggling. I saw the exact same look in your eyes that day at the cantine.'

I stare at the floor. I don't like this. It's like discovering I've been branded. V for victim. V for vulnerable. Permanently scarred by the memories I thought I'd left behind. Rapists seek out the vulnerable. Will I ever escape this?

I like to think if I'm ever attacked again I'll fight tooth and fingernail. I'll spit and bite and go for my attacker's eye sockets. Yes, fighting back might get me killed, but the sensible, freezing-until-it's-over and disappearing-into-my-mind option isn't one I can ever choose again.

What no one tells you is that both options get you killed. The freezing option just kills you more slowly. At least death would be quick.

'Is that the reason why you've been so nice to me?' I keep my eyes on the floor. 'Because I'm a victim?'

I imbue the word victim with a whole world of bitterness.

'No, I've been nice to you because I like you. A lot. And you are not a victim, you're a survivor. You're you. You're Beth and no one and nothing can rob you of your identity.' His hand spans the distance between us and he lightly nudges my little finger with his.

It's the gentlest of touches, an overture and, possibly, an offer.

I stretch out my hand and accept the interlinking of his fingers with mine. This tentative connection feels powerful and intimate. The camper interior is our micro universe and we are its only inhabitants.

I exhale the breath I hadn't realised I was holding. My anger has morphed into a tension of a different kind. I want the comfort of his touch. Maybe instead of hitting him I need release of a different kind. It's tempting. I know Dan would be gentle, maybe too gentle. His awareness of my past makes it hard for me to keep it locked away. And it has to be locked away, far from conscious thought, or sex would be unbearable, tainted by the ghost of the rape.

'Can I stay?' My heart thumps in my chest. I know the overture has to be made by me.

'Are you sure?' His thumb caresses my palm.

I don't think he meant the gesture to be sexual, but it triggers a corresponding dart of desire between my legs. What can I say? That I honestly don't know. Anything. I never stop second-guessing myself. Dan isn't what I thought I wanted, but he's what I need, now, today.

How do I explain all that when I barely understand myself?

I won't even try. I'll go with what I need today. Tomorrow can wait.

I turn to Dan, to the man who sees me.

'Yes. I'm sure.' I inch towards him.

Dan stares back, then leans forward to kiss me. My mouth opens for him, my tongue welcoming his, my body hungry.

My body says yes, but my mind is panicking because this feels like real intimacy. Why was it easier to go home with Thomas? How can the thought of sex with someone who doesn't like me be less frightening than intimacy with someone who cares about me, who sees me?

Eva would no doubt have a lot to say on the subject. She was so sure I wasn't ready for this. Maybe she was right after all.

Dan pulls out of the kiss and rests his forehead against mine. 'If you want we'll stop. It's important that this is your decision.'

Sod it, I'm doing this. Why do I have to overthink everything?

He likes me and I like him. We both want sex and I really need the release. I still like sex. That bastard rapist doesn't get the right to shut me down sexually. It would've been easy to avoid sex completely after the rape, but then he would've won.

There's no way I'm letting him win.

I've been so tense, so tightly coiled since I read the email. This feels like the right way to survive, to release the tension.

I need this.

I slide onto his lap and put my arms around his neck. There's a sharp intake of breath from him as I wriggle on his lap and feel his growing erection under my bottom.

'I want this, I want you,' I say, and mean it. The urge to continually overwrite the space the rape used to occupy is urgent. The past won't control me; it won't ruin sex for me.

I close my eyes and press my breasts against his chest.

Dan pulls back from the kiss. 'Hey, Beth.'

'Hmm?' I reluctantly open my eyes.

'Don't disappear on me.'

'What do you mean, I'm right here, I'm not planning on going anywhere.' I frown.

'I mean up here.' Dan touches the side of my forehead. 'Stay with me.'

I stare into his eyes. There's that connection again. So tempting.

And so terrifying. I learnt to cope with sex again by disappearing. Dan is the first guy who actually seems to notice and care.

'I'll try.' I swallow hard.

'That's all I'm asking. Let it be about us. Just us.'

I nod and pull my top up over my head. Dan undoes my bra clasp, letting the bra fall onto the floor. He exhales heavily as he takes my bare breasts into his hands. My nipples harden against his palms. My whole body aches for him, driven by an urgency I can't understand. It's as though I need to act fast before my mind can catch up and decide this is a mistake.

I pull Dan's t-shirt up over his head and press my breasts against his bare chest. His muscles are firm against my softer, more rounded, flesh. I shiver.

He lowers his mouth to mine again and I lose myself in

the kiss, in the intimacy of tongue on tongue. His fingers run through my long red hair, letting it trail over my breasts.

'You are so sexy, Beth.' He groans and clasps me to him.

'You're not so bad yourself.' I smile and shift position so I'm straddling him, my knees resting either side of his thighs.

He cups my denim-clad bottom and squeezes, then reaches in front of me to undo my jeans zip. He pulls my jeans down and I lie back to wriggle out of them.

'Relax,' Dan whispers. He pulls my knickers to one side and slides a finger inside me. 'You're wet, but I bet I can get you wetter.'

I exhale and lean back, trusting him, the tension seeping out of me as his fingers stroke and tease my clit before thrusting inside me. I part my thighs for him, pulling my knees up towards my chest and he kneels between my legs, kissing down my stomach and placing a kiss on top of the wet cotton between my legs.

I groan and wriggle my hips. He interprets correctly, pulling my knickers down, then lowering his mouth between my legs and licking at my bare sex.

After a minute of exquisite torture he pulls back and plunges two fingers inside me. When he draws them out they're dripping wet. 'That's much better.'

I moan, feeling an almost unbearable heavy ache in my sex as the wetness drips between my legs.

'What do you want me to do to you, Beth?' Dan asks softly. 'What do you need?'

'I want you to fuck me. I need you to fuck me,' I gasp. 'Please.'

'You want to go on top?'

I know what he's asking. Do I need to take control?

'No,' I groan the emphatic answer. I don't want him to be tender, or to do anything that reminds me of the past, giving room for the ghosts to appear. 'I need you to fuck me. Don't you dare be gentle.' My tone is fierce.

I am not a victim and I won't be treated like one.

I reach out and squeeze the huge erection straining at Dan's jeans.

'Fuck,' he swears, breathing heavily.

'Yes, fuck. As in do. Me.' My breath is coming fast now, my chest heaving, nipples tightening and my sex clenching at air. 'Now. Please.'

Dan pulls off his jeans and sheathes his straining erection with a condom. Then he pulls me to the edge of the mattress, spreads my thighs wide apart and plunges into me.

I contract around him and meet his thrusts with an urgency that pulses through me – anger, need, desire and hope all intertwined in the arching of my hips as I push up against him.

Then he flips me over onto all-fours on the mattress and caresses my breasts as he positions himself behind me and thrusts back inside me. His hands move from my hardened nipples to my clit, where he strokes the tip of a finger round and round, lightly increasing the pressure with each thrust.

Heat is building up inside me, an unbearable intensity swelling to bursting point between my thighs.

Then I'm tipping over the edge into a screaming, roaring orgasm, the likes of which I've never felt before.

I feel Dan coming with me, tensing and jerking deep inside me as my hips buck and my thighs shake.

Eventually we collapse onto the bed together, gasping.

'Feel better?' he asks, once we've got our breath back. 'Was that okay?'

'Yes thank you.' My response feels oddly prim considering what we've just been doing. Laughter rises up in my chest and I give into the giggles. 'That was a much better idea than hitting you.'

'I can't help but agree.' Dan grins. 'You win, your idea was better than mine.'

He strokes the side of my face, his expression growing more serious.

'If you ever want to talk, I'm here for you, okay?'

'Hmm. I ought to get back to the chalet.' I sigh and roll away, wishing he'd stop asking if I'm okay.

'Will you be alright, Beth?' Dan sits up.

'I'll be fine.' The automatic response slips out. I hesitate, unable to locate a better, more honest, response. I suppose the most accurate answer is 'I'll be'. I'll exist and I'll carry on. What other choice is there?

We often think we can't cope or that events are unbearable and yet we endure them. We carry on breathing in and out and the days keep rolling on regardless of personal tragedy.

I will be okay, someday. It's the only certainty I can be sure of for now.

'If you're not and you need someone, you know where to find me. Any time, including the middle of the night.' Dan pulls his jeans back on. 'Or you can come over even if you just fancy my company. Okay?'

Okay. That bloody word again. Why is there this insistence that we all have to be okay all the time? I'm convinced most of us are carrying loss, hiding secrets, nursing heartbreak or chronically anxious a lot of the time. Scratch a little below the surface and you'll find a huge tangled jumble of wires, knotted so deep they'll always be a part of us. Or maybe it's just me who feels this way, but somehow I don't think so. Still we skate over the surface with words – I'm okay, I'm alright, I'm fine – even when we're so tangled up inside we're afraid we'll never be free.

'Okay,' I nod, wondering if I ever will be.

Chapter 13

From: sandratrent@gmail.com
To: sophietrent@hotmail.com
Re: Christmas!

Hello, Sophie. I put up our Christmas tree today and it brought back such happy memories. Do you remember our little ritual? You were always such a perfectionist, insisting the glass angels had to go together otherwise they'd be lonely. I still put the fairy you made at school at the top of the tree, even though it's looking a little worse for wear nowadays. I must admit, it made me a tad teary. You'll understand when you have children of your own, darling. I just hope when that day comes you'll bring them back home to their English grandparents for plenty of visits. I could teach them how to make decorated gingerbread houses and bake mince pies with them. Do you have mince pies in Switzerland?

I suppose I should get off the computer and get on with the last-minute Christmas cards. Would you believe the snobbish Robinsons at number 22 sent us a card?

After they accused Dad of bribing a council official to get that last allotment too! I'll send them one of the boring cards with the robins on. I only bought them because they were charity cards.

Speak soon, darling, and see you on Christmas morning too if your dad gets that Skype thingie to work. I know Luc sent him instructions.

Love, Mum

SOPHIE

I'm not going to let the W word affect Christmas. It's going to be hard enough with Luc convinced it'll be his dad's last Christmas. Never mind the fact we've been rushed off our feet coping with both the Bar des Amis and the Café du Place and half our staff being stricken by a flu bug. I've barely had time to wash my hair, never mind think about things. Just how I like it.

Despite all the hard work, I usually love Christmas. The Bar des Amis isn't one of the trendiest in Verbier but we attract business owners and locals as well as tourists. It means there's a nice, extended-family feel on Christmas Eve, which is a bigger deal here than Christmas Day itself.

It also means we know some of our regulars are happy to stand in and help man the bar in return for free drinks if it gets busy while we're in Vex visiting Luc's parents.

Last week I spent half a night decorating the bar, with Tash's help. It was fun, but putting up decorations made me think of Mum decorating the tree back home without me, even before I got her email. We always used to do it together and I loved it. We'd have carols playing in the background and gingerbread baking in the oven. Christmas Eve for Mum and Dad means drinks and mince pies with the neighbours and a midnight service at the local church.

They have traditions I always thought I'd carry on with my own family.

That I'll never get to decorate a Christmas tree with my

own daughter or son hurts like crazy but I have to push those thoughts down. It's that or drown in them.

I used to think you could only grieve for things you'd actually lost. Now I know the pain and loss you feel for things that will never be bad enough to leave you doubled over and gasping with grief.

Growing up I assumed I'd get married, have children, take them round to see Grandma and Grandad and have big family Christmases. Back then I believed everything was possible. I suppose, in a way, it was.

Maybe living in Switzerland will help me forget that other ghost life – the ghost of Christmases that will never be. Will that ghost haunt me every year in my very own version of *A Christmas Carol*?

At least as long as we have Bar des Amis we'll have to work for most of the Christmas break. Also there are new, different traditions here. Father Christmas walks through the mountain villages on Christmas Eve dispensing gifts to children. There's also the snow. I always longed for snow on Christmas Eve back in England. Sleet or hail just doesn't create the same ambience.

There's no danger of that here. I watch the thick snowflakes falling outside the window on Christmas morning. It's cosy in the flat. I'm sitting on the sofa in front of the wood-burning stove with my legs draped over Luc's lap. Max is pressed as close to the stove as he can get without burning his nose. Maybe making new traditions, just the two of us, isn't so bad.

Once we've drunk our Kir Royales we Skype my parents to wish them a Happy Christmas. Thankfully Dad is more technically competent than Mum when it comes to the computer. I've worn the silk jersey-mix dress Mum and Dad gave me as a present and I'm wearing the silver dog pendant Luc gave me too. I'm feeling pretty chilled.

Mum beams out of the laptop screen, Dad hovering slightly behind her wearing his obligatory reindeer Christmas jumper.

'We both love our presents, darling. Your dad has been glued to his Kindle since he opened it this morning and I love the cookbooks you bought for me.' Mum hesitates and then adds. 'Wouldn't it be wonderful if next Christmas there was a grandchild to buy presents for?'

Luc stiffens beside me, his jaw tensing.

'I don't think that's very likely, Sandra,' Dad interrupts, putting a hand on Mum's arm. 'You're expecting them to move pretty fast. They'd have to get quite a move on to get married, pregnant and have the baby by next Christmas.'

Luc smiles, but it's the kind of smile he reserves for patrons who've outstayed their welcome. It's automatic and polite, but it's not genuine. He makes conversation about what books Dad has loaded onto his Kindle and which recipes Mum is going to try from her new cookbooks.

I'm glad he's talking because I can't think of a word to say. I should've known my earlier peace wouldn't last long. I bite the inside of my lip to keep from crying.

At last it seems we've exhausted any conversation about gifts or plans for the day.

'Anyway, it's been great seeing you both,' Mum beams, seemingly oblivious to the fact I've said very little. 'We should probably be going now, though. We've got friends coming over for lunch.'

I exhale with relief when the call ends, but the relief is short-lived when Luc turns and looks at me sternly.

'You have to tell your parents, Sophie. It isn't right to keep them in the dark. I had no idea they didn't know about us, about us not being able to. . .'

He can't even say the words.

There's a lump in my throat and I don't feel very Christmassy any more.

'I know,' I reply, my voice barely a whisper. 'It's just she's going to be so. . . so. . . disappointed.'

The sob catches in my throat and Luc presses me to his chest, his expression softening.

He's right. I need to tell her. Just get it over with, like ripping off a plaster. I just have to rehearse in my head what to say.

'Mum, I can't have children, so all your dreams of grandchildren are over. Oh, and, by the way, I'm infertile because I caught an STD from a jerk called Thomas who slept with me once and then humiliated me.'

So, that's not going to happen. I don't think Mum would ever speak to me again. Every time I looked at her I'd see the disappointment and disgust in her eyes. Not to mention Dad. I couldn't bear for him to know the details. It's so sordid.

Shame shudders through me. I was so easily flattered by the charming, handsome Thomas. He was my first and only one-night stand and I paid dearly for it.

Maybe I'll just go with the infertility and leave out any details. That'll be quite enough truth for Mum to deal with in one go. If I email instead of telling her on the phone at least I can be sure of it coming out exactly how I want it to.

I'll also have time to think about how to answer any questions she asks – because she will.

Thank God for email and the ability to keep your relatives one step removed. I sense an email buffer is going to be needed for the train wreck about to hit it.

From: sandratrent@gmail.com
To: sophietrent@hotmail.com
Re: Bad news

Sophie darling, your Dad and I are both very sorry to hear your news. This is why I was so worried about you leaving things so late. Can you tell me exactly what the doctors said?

Have you considered fertility treatment? They can work wonders these days. I know they have excellent specialists at Manchester. If you came home we'd be happy to take you to any appointments.

In the meantime, we'll just have to be brave and focus on the wedding. I've found a hotel further north with gardens on the banks of Ullswater. Do you remember you used to love going on the Ullswater steamer when you were little? It seems fitting for you to have your reception somewhere you used to be so happy.

Chin up, darling. You can rely on me to plan the wedding of your dreams to help cheer you up.

Lots of love

Mum

'What's wrong?' Holly opens the door to me and immediately wraps me in a big hug.

'Can't . . . can't . . . do it.' I sob, struggling to voice what brought me here. I'm incapacitated by an unbearable sadness. It's an unstoppable tide, sweeping me away with it to some unknown destination.

'Sit down and try to . . . you know, breathe. In and out, nice and slow. It helps.' She guides me towards the sofa and then rushes off to fetch tissues.

'Where's Maddie?' I hiccup, once I'm more in control.

When the tsunami first hit me I instinctively stumbled my way to Holly, my three a.m. friend. The one I know is always there for me. It's a relief to discover Holly becoming a mum hasn't changed that dynamic between us.

'She's asleep. Amazingly.' Holly sits next to me. 'I was going to take advantage and do the washing and dishwasher but I'd much rather be talking to you. Although, ideally, you'd not be leaking quite so much.'

She hands me a wad of tissues.

'Sorry,' I half-laugh, half-sniff. 'I seem to be making a habit of this lately.'

'It's payback for all the times you've done the same for me.' She puts an arm around my shoulders. 'I'm relieved, frankly. I've always been the needy one in our relationship and this helps redress the balance.'

'Happy to oblige.' I blow my nose on a tissue and manage a crooked smile.

'So . . .' Holly eyes me speculatively.

'So,' I reply and then reluctantly give in to the need to fill the silence. 'I finally told Mum about me not being able to have children. I edited Thomas and the cause of it out, though.'

'I don't blame you.' Holly pulls a face. 'If only it were so easy to edit Thomas out of real life. I'd write him out with a particularly painful skiing accident.'

'Don't give Luc ideas.' I snort with laughter, the image of Thomas encased in a plaster cast providing a much-needed mood boost. 'In his current state of mind he might see that as a constructive suggestion rather than a joke.'

'Who's joking?' Holly arches her eyebrows.

I bite my lip. 'Luc still doesn't know the name of the man responsible and I need to keep it that way. He's. . . struggling at the moment, with his dad and the adoption issue. He wouldn't want me to tell you that. You know what men are like.'

'I know, Scott's the same,' Holly sighs. 'Like depression is a weakness. I think it's because they don't talk about the same things we do. They assume everyone is coping fine and if they're not it's an epic fail.'

'I think everyone struggles at one time or another, that's just being human. Not being weak.' My heart contracts at the thought of Luc struggling with long hours at both cafés, trying to be the supportive fiancé to me and deal with his own pain and impending loss.

'I had no idea your mum didn't know about you not being able to have children,' Holly adds, her tone gentle.

'I'm a coward,' I admit. 'She's been nagging me for grand-children for years now. Maybe she's worried she'll be slung out of the WI for not having any grand-offspring photos to show at coffee mornings. I think it's a bit like not having cool trainers at school. She'll be a social outcast.'

'Did she take it very badly, then?' Holly pulls a sympathetic face.

'Oddly she took it better than I thought she would.' I shrug. 'Well, apart from wanting to ship me home for medical tests and second opinions, but I expected that. It was the fact she was so nice about it that did for me. She wants to make it up to me by planning the wedding of her dreams.'

'Don't you mean the wedding of *your* dreams?'

'No.'

'Oh.' Holly grimaces sympathetically.

'I'm not sure my involvement or desires are important beyond turning up on the day with a bridegroom.' I sigh.

'Have you tried talking to her?'

'I've just crushed her dreams for grandchildren and now I need to tell her to shelve her dreams for her only child's wedding too? I can't do it.'

Holly frowns. 'Am I missing something? I know it's not ideal, but can't you just go through with your Mum's wedding plans if you really want to make her happy? I'm not saying you should, by the way. I think you should press for the wedding you and Luc want.'

I resist the temptation to laugh hysterically and try to explain the tangled mess in my head.

'Luc's dad isn't well enough to travel. Not unreasonably he wants to see his son married before he dies. So his family have assumed we're getting married in Switzerland. I think they might have started making plans. Again, without actually consulting either of us. Getting married in Switzerland is fine by me but Mum and Dad won't travel.'

'Why not?'

'They won't leave their diabetic dog. They don't do kennels or dog-sitters. Mum swears he'd die in anyone else's care. It's why they've never been out here to visit, even though I've told them countless times about the pet passport scheme.' I throw my hands up in the air. 'Mum's just like a steamroller when she gets going. Anything you say she doesn't want to hear it's like she's got her hands over her ears and is singing la la la. Seriously, it's that bad. Every time I come up with a solution she finds another insurmountable problem.

'Have you tried talking to Luc about it?'

'The thing is, Holly, like I said, Luc's so stressed about his dad at the moment. With running both Bar des Amis and Café du Place, along with all the extra driving between Verbier and Vex, he's permanently knackered. When he's really low I don't want to make things worse, but then, when he's actually in a better mood, I don't want to spoil it and bring him down again.'

'You're going to have to at some point. You know that, right?' A sympathetic quirk of her lips acknowledges it's not going to be easy.

I nod and grimace. 'I suppose. I just don't want us starting out our marriage with him thinking my mum's a heartless cow for expecting us to marry without his parents present. I'll have to find a way of talking her round. If I can work out a solution Luc will never need to know.'

'That doesn't sound like the greatest plan, Soph.'

I shrug. 'It's the only plan I've got. Coming on top of the adoption nightmare it's all been a bit much.'

I close my eyes and try to take a deep breath. Looping round and round in my mind are the thoughts – I'm with the man I love, who loves me and wants to marry me. So why is life so complicated?

If our story were a film it would've ended on Valentine's Day with the treasure hunt and romantic proposal at the W hotel. There would've been a montage of kisses beneath cloudless blue skies and playful snowball fights with a soft focus lens applied to all life's hard edges.

Why is living happily ever after in the real world so damn difficult?

'I think you could do with some tea to go with your sympathy.' Holly pats my knee.

I open my eyes and struggle to bring myself back from the edge of something very dark indeed. 'Thanks, Holly.'

She scrutinises me. 'Chocolate too, you look like you need it. I've got some hidden away from Scott.'

'I thought he got wise to you hiding chocolate behind the vegetables?' I smile, remembering the chocolate bars Holly used to hide from Scott when we were all living together at Chalet Repos.

'I've got a new hiding place. It's in the hall cupboard behind the vacuum cleaner. Scott claims not to know where that lives so I think I'm safe.' She grins as she gets up from the sofa. 'I think you could do with a boost to your serotonin levels. It's scientifically proven, you know, chocolate is good for you.'

'Thanks, Holly.' I smile back, more grateful than I can express for our friendship and her willingness to drop everything for me. I stare around at the piles of dishes and dirty laundry loads. 'Why don't I help with the dishwasher while the kettle's boiling. It'll be quicker with the two of us doing it.'

'That would be great, if you don't mind, thanks. You're going to be okay, aren't you, Soph? You and Luc are so great together.'

I avoid her direct gaze and turn away to stack plates, wishing I could reassure her.

Wishing I could reassure myself.

Holly would smack me if she thought I'd been entertaining 'Should I give up Luc so he can have the family he's always dreamed of?' thoughts. I'd probably smack me too if I were her.

Truth is, even if I should give him up, I don't think I can. I'm not cut out to be a martyr. The idea that Luc might be having second thoughts about marrying me and willingly giving up his chance for a family fills me with gut-wrenching terror. Who knows what he's thinking? He's keeping all his emotions locked up at the moment. We both are.

I dread what might happen if we both decide to turn the keys and let the truths spill out.

It's so much safer to carry on as we are. I'll find a way to sort things out. I have to, both to protect the people I love and to keep my own heart from breaking.

In my mind I play the ending of our rom com film – the version of my love story with Luc that ends after a Valentine's

Day treasure hunt and proposal. In that version Thomas would have the hideously painful skiing accident Holly suggested and I'd magically become pregnant, despite all the doctors telling me it's impossible.

If only I were in that film or a heroine in my own romance novel. Then someone could write me out of this mess and hit the delete key on this sadness so heavy I can't bear to carry it any more.

But this is real life. This is what happens after the credits stop rolling or the last page of the romance novel has been read. There's no script and no soft-focus lens.

It's all down to me.

I just wish I felt up to the job of being the author and producer of my own life.

'Don't worry. It'll all work out.' I keep my eyes averted so Holly can't use her best-friend telepathy skills to read my mind.

It'll either work out or it'll all go hideously wrong.

One of the two.

Chapter 14

From: jake@yahoo.com
To: emily@hotmail.com
Subject: Ring me!

Hi Emily,

Have you accidentally switched the ringer on your phone off again? I've been trying to get hold of you. Something happened during filming. There's been an accident. Don't worry, I'm okay, but I need to talk to you and see if you can get hold of Lucy.

Speak ASAP.

Jake

LUCY

I'm in Bar des Amis having coffee with Sophie, Holly, Tash and Rebecca when Emily rushes in, her face white as snow.

'What's up, Emily?' Sophie pulls out a spare chair.

'Lucy, have you heard?' Emily sits down, breathing hard and turns to stare at me, her eyes wide.

For a second my mind goes blank, but there's a lurching sensation in my stomach that suggests my body is quicker on the uptake.

'Heard what?' My pulse quickens.

Emily takes my hand and the lurching upgrades to a full-on plummeting-to-the-bottom-of-a-lift-shaft experience.

'Jake was on Seb's team today for the shoot.' She pauses. 'I . . . er . . . don't know how to tell you this. I know you're seeing Seb. He told Jake he wanted you to know if anything happened to him.'

'What's happened?' I stiffen, and it feels like ice is trickling down my spine.

'There was an avalanche.' She squeezes my hand.

'An avalanche?' I repeat, my brain still struggling to compute what my body already fears. 'Is he okay?'

My mouth is dry. I can't lose Seb; I've only just found him.

'We're not sure yet. His ABS Avalanche airbag meant the helicopter found him fairly quickly. He's been taken to hospital, but he's still unconscious.'

I stand up from my chair, as though my action, any action, can help in any way. Why on earth did I ever care that Seb wasn't what I expected? That he has a history and baggage? I don't give a flying snowball that my parents won't approve of him. I only want Seb. I need him and I can't bear to lose him.

'Do you want to go to the hospital, Lucy? I can take you, if you like?' Sophie stands up and gently takes my other hand.

I blink hard. 'Yes please.'

I'm deaf to what the others are saying as Sophie gets her bag and keys, the words have receded to background noise. They're irrelevant. All I can think about is a whiteout, being buried alive beneath several tonnes of snow. How must that feel? My chest is tight and my jaw clenched. Have the mountains taken Seb from me when I've only just found him?

'Please God, don't let Seb die. Please.' I whisper a prayer as we start the journey by car down to the hospital on the valley floor. I don't know if Sophie hears me pray. If she does she doesn't comment on it.

I knew what Seb did was dangerous, but somehow I fell for the fantasy that he was bullet-proof. He's done stupid, crazy things and got away with them for years. You don't get awarded a Biggest Guts award at The Reels festival or acquire numerous Freeride World Tour Champion titles for doing the sensible, safe thing.

I let Sophie do the talking at the hospital reception. I'm still in a daze, half unbelieving, half feeling as though I want to vomit. That I feel this bad confirms the awful truth. I'm in love with Seb. The fear of losing him has crystallised this knowledge. It's a physical ache, spreading through me, gripping my body in a way I didn't know emotions could.

It's an awful truth because it exposes me, makes me vulnerable. I'm no longer in control and it's scaring me shitless.

'I've said you're his fiancée so you could get in to see him,' Sophie whispers in my ear as we're ushered into one of the curtained cubicles in the emergency ward.

'Thanks, Sophie, you're a star.' I follow her gratefully, wondering what on earth I would've done without her help today. She underplays her French-language skills but she's done far better than I could've managed today. I miss having her in the bunk above me at Chalet Repos since she moved in with Luc. She's one of those rare people who are both kinder and lovelier than they will ever believe themselves.

When all this is over I'll find a way to let her know how grateful I am, but for now all I can think of is Seb.

Please God, let him be okay. Please.

My urgent prayer is silent but heartfelt. My relationship with God is complicated, but I still believe He's there, whatever name we give Him or whatever He communicates through imperfect, human filters.

When I see Seb lying in bed, eyes open and conscious, I almost crumple under the weight of the surge of relief that hits me. Apart from looking groggy, he seems absolutely fine. I exhale with relief and then take my first proper breath since I heard the news.

'You're okay?' I resist the urge to hug him in case he's got broken ribs or something similar.

'Yes, I got off pretty lightly. Just a mild concussion.' His face is a little grey and less animated than usual, but otherwise he looks alright.

'Really? Thank God. I was so worried.' I sit in the plastic chair next to the hospital bed and barely register Sophie squeezing my shoulder and muttering something about going off to fetch coffee.

'I'm okay, Lucy Lu. No need to worry about me.' Seb's attempt at a grin slips into a grimace of pain.

I blink hard, my hands gripping the edge of the plastic chair. No need to worry? Seriously? If this thing with Seb is going to last, then this will be my future – hospital corridors reeking of disinfectant and anxiety where I'll have to sit and wait for news.

I search Seb's face, looking behind the bravado, seeking out the fear I'm hoping to find. Because if there's only recklessness there I don't know if I can do this. I think I can see the truth in his eyes, the knowledge that he was damned lucky this time.

'What was it like?' I whisper. 'Being in the avalanche?'

'At first I thought I could outrun it, this monstrosity breathing down my neck.' Seb shakes his head and then winces at the pain the motion triggers. 'I tried to outrun it, going faster and faster, until I was tearing down the slope at breakneck pace. That was when I noticed the cracks all around me. It was like being on top of a rollercoaster.'

'Scary stuff.' I stare at Seb. The picture he's painted in my mind is so vivid I can practically feel the cracks forming around me. It's every skier or boarder's worst nightmare – the day your luck runs out.

'Yes, as you say, scary stuff.' Seb fixes his dark eyes on me and I know I'm seeing the truth. 'Then the entire hillside crumbled away from me in a fraction of a second. It was so quick. You forget how things can change in a split second. It was like the mountain broke up around me and swallowed me whole. It reminded me how small we are, how fragile our lives are.'

He sighs and my heart lurches as I imagine Seb buried beneath several tonnes of snow. Just thinking about it makes me feel panicky.

'What did you do then?' I reach out to grip the hand not hooked up to a cannula.

Seb squeezes his eyes shut and lets out a shuddering sigh. 'I must've activated my avalanche airbag instinctively. I don't even remember doing it. After that, it was the waiting that was hard. I couldn't move under the weight of all the snow. Up until then I was acting, responding. . . waiting I don't do so well. It kind of drives me crazy.'

'Yes, I think I can testify to that.' I smile, but my cheeks flush and feel strangely tight. I hadn't realised how tense my body was; all my muscles are rigid and I'm leaning forwards, on the edge of my chair. 'How did you cope with the wait?'

'I don't remember, I must've lost consciousness. Next thing I know I'm waking up here.' He pulls a face.

'You're lucky your team found you so quickly. Thank God for your ABS airbag.' I mean it, my thanks are heartfelt. That Seb escaped with only a few minor injuries seems like nothing short of a miracle to me.

Out of the corner of my eye I catch a flash of movement and see Gabriella entering the ward. Her face is ashen. She acknowledges me with a nod and then turns to face Seb, hands on hips and a hard edge to her expression.

'The hospital phoned me. Sebastien, you could've been killed.' She narrows her eyes, glaring at him with a ferocity that reveals her barely contained fury.

I'm processing the fury at the same time as absorbing the fact that Gabriella is still down as Seb's next of kin. I suppose that makes sense with his daughter in the picture.

Seb grimaces back at Gabriella. 'I'm fine, thanks for asking.'

I feel as though I shouldn't be here, that I'm intruding on something private.

'I'd better go.' I let go of Seb's hand.

'No, please don't, there's really no need for you to go,' he protests, but I've already pushed back the plastic chair and backed away.

'No, really. I ought to,' I babble. 'Sophie gave me a lift and she needs to get back to Bar des Amis. Take care, okay? I'll be in touch.'

I attempt a small smile and then nod quickly at Gabriella without meeting her eye. Then I leave the ward as quickly as I can. Combined with the intensity of Gabriella's emotion the next-of-kin issue niggles at me. There's any number of reasons why Gabriella might be listed as Seb's next of kin. His family are in France. He didn't get around to changing it when they split up. He wants Estelle to know first if something happens to him.

Estelle.

I think about Estelle's solemn eyes and wild, dark curls and her request that I look after her daddy when she's not around.

And I get why Gabriella is so furious.

I text Sophie to say I'm ready to leave, then head to the loos, mind reeling and emotions churning. I'm washing my hands when Gabriella stalks in. In the mirror I see her stare at me appraisingly, eyes thoughtful and serious and carefully plucked eyebrows arched. I tense, I don't want this, whatever she's about to impart, my head is already too full.

It doesn't look like I'm going to get a choice, though.

'Be careful, Lucy. Seb is great and I want to see him settled and happy more than anyone, but you need to know something. He'll always love the mountains more than he loves anyone else.' Gabriella shrugs and smiles wryly. 'I should know.'

I stare into the mirror. It's odd, staring at her reflection instead of facing her head on. It's easier absorbing the intensity of her honesty while I'm one step removed and can focus on the process of washing my hands. I prolong the process by adding more lurid pink liquid soap to my palms, but can't spin this out forever or she'll think I'm OCD.

I take a deep breath and turn around to grab a paper towel from the dispenser.

'Right.' I dry my hands and find the courage to make eye contact.

I don't know what to say. Nothing in my life so far has prepared me for a heart to heart with the mother of my boyfriend's child.

Why does everyone keep warning me about Seb?

The silence stretches between us, broken only by a dripping tap.

When my phone beeps to alert me to a new text I'm pathetically grateful.

'Sorry, I just need to check this.' I pull out my phone and glance at the screen, expecting it to be from Sophie, but instead it's from my brother, Ben.

Lucy call me. URGENT.

What now? My pulse races as I lean back against the sinks, reassured by the solidity of the hard enamel ridge holding me upright.

'Sorry, Gabriella, I really need to make a call. Family emergency.'

'I understand.' She smiles weakly, but there's a resigned grimace that indicates she thinks I'm just trying to escape, that I don't want to hear what she has to say.

I hurry out, phone clamped to my ear, adrenalin and stress coursing through my body for the second time today. Each second I hear the phone ring at Ben's end and it's not answered the panic builds, twisting my stomach into gnarly knots. Surely there ought to be a limit to the amount of bad news one person can get in one day?

Finally Ben answers.

'Lucy.' The tone of his voice makes my stomach clench.

'What's up, Ben?'

'It's Dad. He's had a massive stroke. Tess wouldn't stop barking until I followed her to the barn, where I found him . . . and . . .' His voice cracks and it's like I've been punched.

'Is . . . is he going to be okay?' I lean against the nearest wall, winded and physically weak. I had no idea before today that my usually athletic body could be so easily defeated by emotion. I take care of myself, I eat healthily and do yoga every day as well as skiing in winter and mountain-hiking in summer. But all of that can be wiped out in an instant by a text or a phone call.

There's a pause, a pause in which I think my heart might actually have stopped beating and I really might throw up this time.

'He didn't make it, Lucy,' Ben's tone is flat. 'He died before the air ambulance could get here.'

'Oh, Ben. . . I. . .' A bizarre sense of unreality creeps over me and I feel dazed. This can't be happening. If I close my eyes and then open them again I can wake up and start the day afresh.

'You need to come home – the next flight you can get. Mum wants you back. She needs you, Lucy.'

'Right,' I repeat blankly. 'Are you okay, Ben? I mean, obviously not but. . .'

I try to imagine the horror of watching someone die, of being helpless to save them.

Someone. It's not just anyone, though, is it? It's Dad. It's my dad.

My throat contracts and for a moment I'm sure I can't breathe.

'Just come home. I want you back too.' Ben sounds as close to tears as I've ever heard him. Our family doesn't really do emotion. His plea tugs at my heart.

Somehow I make my legs obey me and I head back to Seb's ward to say goodbye. I don't know when I'll see him next.

'He's asleep,' Gabriella says quietly. 'I don't think we should wake him up.'

'I suppose not.' I suppress the pang of disappointment. My natural instinct is to turn to him, although maybe that's selfish, given what he's just gone through.

If I were alone with him I would kiss him on the cheek or squeeze his hand, craving the reassurance of some kind of physical contact before I leave to go home.

'Goodbye, Gabriella.' I try to keep my voice steady, but needn't worry as she's preoccupied with Seb.

'Goodbye, Lucy. Don't worry, he'll be fine.' Gabriella says, turning and smiling briefly.

I head to the hospital main entrance in a haze of unreality, torn between my new life and my old one. There's no choice to make, though. I have to go home. I'll send Seb a text explaining. He's going to be okay, Dad's . . . not. Not ever going to be okay again.

Never.

I'm never going to see him again. The thought hits me like a punch and I'm reeling again, bumping into lines of plastic chairs bolted to the floor.

'Are you alright, Lucy?' Sophie walks towards me, eyes wide with concern.

It's the compassion that does it. For the first time in years, I burst into tears. Messy, noisy, out-of-control sobs that wrack my body. Sophie puts her arm around me and guides me to a chair.

'What's wrong? Is it Seb?' She frowns. 'I thought he wasn't badly injured?'

'It's not him. Seb's okay, nothing major anyway.' I sniff noisily and take the tissue Sophie hands me. Bless her, she always seems to have what you need on her. 'I, I just heard that my dad died.'

Saying the words aloud feels surreal.

A blizzard of thoughts swirls around in my head. I never got to say goodbye to Dad. He died thinking very little of me. . . I never got to make him proud and now I never will.

I barely hear Sophie's words of comfort as she rubs my back, but I'm not sure the actual words matter, it's the soothing tone that works. The torrent of tears takes me by surprise. For so many years I hardened my heart against Dad's crushing disparagement and rejection, training myself to expect nothing from him. I knew he was never going to turn into the kind of tactile dad who hugged me or expressed affection.

I thought I'd come to terms with it.

Apparently not. It appears I never stopped hoping.

I think he probably did love me, in his own buttoned-up way. Probably in the same way as he loved his best milking cows, but almost certainly less than he cared for Tess, our working collie dog. The big surprise is that until this moment I didn't realise how much I loved him. Now my control is shattered, the emotion spills out in an ugly mess of childish longing and the searing pain of rejection that grew in intensity with every look of disgust or dismissal.

Oh God. Fresh pain assaults me and I have to clench my teeth to keep from howling. My hands form tight fists, nails digging into flesh, as though I can claw the feelings back and squash them down inside me.

'What can I do to help you?' Sophie squeezes my arm and the action tethers me.

I breathe in slowly, gathering myself together. Stepping back from the brink of something unbearable.

'I need to speak to Holly,' I say. 'I need to go to Scotland for a week or two and I have to check if that's going to be okay.'

'It will definitely be okay. There's no doubt about that, so don't worry. I can speak to Holly for you if you like,' Sophie reassures me, continuing to stroke my back. 'So you're going to need to go to Chalet Repos first and pack a few things. Tell you what, I'll drive you there and then you can use your phone to book a flight to Scotland during the trip to the chalet. Does that sound like a plan?'

'Thanks, Sophie.' I pull myself together and stand up, needing to move and take action.

Once we're in Sophie's car I use my phone to book a flight for the next morning before we've even exited the hospital car park. At least it's ski season, so there are direct flights from Geneva to Inverness. The journey home in summer involves a lot more hassle.

'Are you close to your dad, Sophie?' I ask. I rest my head back against the headrest, exhausted by the tension of the day. My whole body aches as if I've got flu. It's an effort to talk, but I need to. It's preferable to the other option – being left to the mercy of my own thoughts.

'Yes, I get on better with Dad than Mum.' Sophie indicates and exits the automatic barrier, driving the car out towards the autoroute. 'He's got a sense of humour, which is a good start.'

'I didn't get on that well with mine. It sounds so awful to

say that now he's dead.' I stare bleakly at the trail of red brake lights stretching out in front of us. 'Now I'll never get the chance to put that right.'

I pinch the bridge of my nose and squeeze my eyes shut, willing the full weight of grief to keep its distance for a little longer.

Sophie is quiet for a minute before she replies.

'I think you're probably grieving for the father he wasn't, as well as for the father he was.' Her soft, thoughtful words pierce me with their truth.

Grief for the father he wasn't and the father he will never be now.

'I think you're right.' I continue to stare out the window, wondering about the occupants of all the other cars around us. Are they happy? Is there such a thing as a normal, happy family? I honestly have no idea. I suppose the other drivers are probably concerned about getting home, what they'll eat for tea, problems at work or credit-card debt. . .

Today, with Seb's accident and Dad's stroke, life feels incredibly fragile. All those other concerns we normally give such weight to seem trivial by comparison. So much of what we worry about is irrelevant. Death feels close, haunting me and taunting me with its power to rip away those I love in a split second. It sneers at our complacency, at our delusional belief that we're in control of our destinies. The ground can crack around us and swallow us whole. Quite literally, in Seb's case.

I wonder what time Dad died. Before or after Seb's accident? I'm suddenly seized with the bizarre notion that Dad died because Seb lived. I had to lose someone today. It's nonsense, I know it is. I have to stop these thoughts from taking root.

It hits me full force what Estelle nearly losing her father today means. I get Gabriella's fury. Can I really be with a man who willingly cheats death for a living? Or do I choose to live with my nerves in shreds every time he competes or is filming? There's a possibility that surviving the avalanche will make Seb even more reckless. He might believe he really is invincible.

'Talk to me, Sophie. Talk about anything except death. I need distracting,' I murmur.

'Okay, um, what did you want to talk about?'

'Tell me about your wedding. I need to think about something nice.'

I glance over to see a pained look flash across Sophie's face.

'I'd rather not, if you don't mind.'

'Oh, okay.' I frown, confused.

I do hope nothing is wrong with Sophie and Luc. They're so perfect together. Sophie deserves to be loved the way Luc loves her. Why is their wedding a sore subject?

'We could talk about the inside gossip from Chalet Repos and Chalet Amélie?' She suggests. 'Is it true Tash threatened Amelia with a bread knife the other day?'

'Not quite.' I smile, but it feels stiff, my face locked in grief. 'Amelia blew it way out of proportion. To be fair to Tash, Amelia has been getting a little. . .'

'Up herself?' Sophie suggests.

'That's one way of putting it.' A ghost of a smile twitches at my lips.

I settle in for a gossip session, anything to forget the numbness creeping through me. Trying not to think about how hard going back to Scotland will be and how I don't want to leave Seb.

Trying not to think about death.

Chapter 15

SOPHIE

By the time I get back from the hospital, Luc is locking up the bar. His forehead is creased and his face drawn with exhaustion. I get the impression we're both guilty of lying by omission, to avoid hurting each other. It's creating a barrier between us and I hate that. Maybe I should take the plunge and talk to him, properly talk to him. The idea terrifies me. I feel like our life together is a precariously balanced tower of Jenga pieces. Telling the truth about what's going on might mean pulling out that one crucial wooden block that is keeping the others up. If all those wooden building blocks of our life together come tumbling down, I don't know what I'll do or how we'll ever rebuild.

When Luc catches sight of me he smiles and the frown lines disappear.

For my benefit.

Something twists inside me. We can't keep doing this. Lying to protect each other is still lying. Even if it's for all the best reasons.

'How is Lucy? Is Seb going to be okay?' He wraps his arms around me and some of the tension of the day seeps away. I cuddle into him, reassured by his solidity. I don't think I could ever get tired of this feeling, this instant warmth and knowledge that Luc is on my side. We're a 'we' and I love it.

I think of the avalanche and how precarious life can be and hug Luc even tighter.

'Seb's got a bad concussion but he'll be okay.' I sigh, my head on his chest, reassured by his solid heartbeat. 'Lucy isn't doing so well, though. While we were at the hospital she got the news from home that her dad had just died from a stroke. It came out of the blue – no warning at all – so she's in shock. I suppose even if she'd had any warning it would still be a lot to cope with all in one day. The avalanche, Seb's near-miss and her dad dying. It's terrible timing.'

'Poor girl.' Luc reacts to my firm grip by tightening his hold on me too, as though he's afraid to let me go. I wonder if he's thinking about the day he'll get the news about his own father. 'Her dad can't have been that old, surely?'

'No, he was only fifty-five.' I leave my head resting against Luc's chest, still gleaning comfort from the steady, reassuring thrum of his heartbeat.

How can something so real, so solid, at the same time be so fragile? Hearts get diseased, arteries clogged or valves leaking. One day all our hearts will fail to beat, but we don't think of it happening to us.

When we're young, dying is something other people do. It's so distant in our future we pretend we don't need to think about it yet.

With Luc's Dad's prognosis we can't pretend any more. Death is closer tonight. I shiver and hold on to Luc, trying to ignore the fear that has crept into the shadows.

'Sophie, I've been thinking we should get married sooner rather than later,' Luc says, then kisses me on the forehead.

'What, why?' I pull away and look up at his face, the shiver of fear transforming into full-on panic.

I don't want to do this now, when we're both so tired. Big conversations shouldn't be allowed to happen when you're too shattered to form coherent sentences.

'Dad wants to see us marry,' Luc says. 'Mum hasn't said anything because she doesn't want to pressure you, Sophie, but we really need to start making concrete plans soon if that's going to happen.'

His frown lines make a reappearance and my chest constricts as panic grips me. Several answers rise to my lips and fall away again unspoken.

Frick. Frick. Frick. What do I do?

'Sophie?' Luc's frown deepens.

'Yes?' I stall for time.

'Is something wrong?'

'Hmm, it's been a draining day.' I close my eyes and inhale his familiar scent. 'Believe me, Luc, there's nothing in the world I want more than to marry you, but it's complicated.'

'What's complicated?' Luc leads me to a table and puts two chairs back down on the floor. 'Sit, let's talk.'

'Now? But we're both really tired.'

'If not now, then when? We're always tired at the moment. What's so complicated, Sophie?' He ignores my pathetic attempt at deflection. 'You say you want to marry me and I want to marry you, so what's so difficult about that?'

He holds my hand and massages the palm with his thumb, teasing away my reticence and reminding me we're connected.

'There's too many people to keep happy.' My voice catches and I blink back hot tears, but they trickle down my cheeks despite my best efforts.

'All that matters to me right now is that you're happy, Sophie.' He pulls me onto his lap and strokes my back.

'I. . . don't. . . deserve. . . you,' I choke out. 'I don't want to add to your stress at the moment, but it's really not that simple.'

'So talk to me now. I can handle it and you know I won't take no for an answer. Besides, you know I have ways of making you talk.'

His hands skim my breasts and run over my thighs. I sigh with pleasure, more tension leeching away with each caress. With his fingers he reminds me I'm his, his touch challenging and melting the barriers between us.

'That could be fun.' I manage a smile.

'Please tell me what's wrong, chère Sophie. I can't help fix it if I don't know what the problem is.' His lips tighten with frustration. 'And it doesn't matter how tired or stressed I am, you can always talk to me. Always.'

'Okay, so to start with I told Mum,' I whisper. 'Like you told me to. About not being able to have children.'

'How did she take it?' Luc kisses me tenderly on the top of my head.

'Um, Mum was upset but, and this is why I'm stressed. . .'

I pause. 'She wants to plan us the wedding she's always dreamed of for me. Back home in England, I mean. She and Dad have been saving for years. She's been hoarding wedding magazines and fabric swatches. I've just robbed her of her dreams for grandchildren. I didn't have the heart to reject her wedding plans too. Not at the same time.'

I haven't explained it properly. I'm too tired to describe the complex and precarious mother-daughter dynamic and how much a Lake District wedding, with all Mum's WI friends, means to her. I don't want to say I feel my loyalties are torn because that sounds unsupportive to Luc and yet he means the world to me.

This is why you don't have these discussions late at night. It's so much easier by email when you can edit what you've written. If only speech had a delete button, so many arguments could be avoided.

'She knows about my father being ill, right?' Luc frowns and I know he doesn't understand.

I take a deep breath and try to assemble the right words, the ones that will enable me to walk the loyalty tightrope and reach the other side without falling.

'Yes,' I say slowly. 'But I don't think she's connected all the dots. I don't know if it's the same in Switzerland but in England it's traditional for the parents of the bride to pay for the wedding or at least help pay for it and the bride's mother is usually heavily involved in the planning. I think Mum's got her mother-of-the-bride blinkers on.'

And in Mum's case it's not so much get involved in the planning as steamroller her own plans ahead regardless of anyone else! How do I explain that there's often the emotional blackmail of being the bankroller attached, if the parents of the bride are so inclined? Probably best not to add this. I'm fairly sure Mum wouldn't do anything like that in a calculating way.

At least, I do hope not. Hmm.

Luc's frowns deepens. 'But my parents must be at our wedding, Sophie. That's non-negotiable.'

'I know, of course I want them there and I'd far rather have a much simpler ceremony over here.' I sigh, a hot pressure at the back of my eyes issuing an imminent tears warning. I blink them back. Yet another reason not to do these conversations when you're tired. I bite the inside of my lip and manage not to lose it.

'I also don't want the next six months to be about choosing napkin colours or working out how to accommodate the wishes of relatives I haven't seen for ten years,' I add. 'But how am I going to break Mum's heart for the second time in quick succession, Luc? What if she never speaks to me again?'

I battle the unshed tears while I wait for Luc's response. He regards me silently, his expression inscrutable. I have no idea what's going on in his head. A wave of panic surges up inside me. My chest feels so tight I don't know how my lungs are still working.

The cupboard I've squashed all my feelings into – all my failure, my inadequacies, my inability to give Luc what he needs, come crashing out, overflowing in a tide of messy, painful emotion. I open my mouth and am speaking before I know it, the words carried along on that dark tidal wave.

'Also, Luc, I've been thinking maybe we shouldn't rush things because of. . . you know, the adoption stalemate. No, please don't say anything.' I place a hand on his chest. Now the dam is breached, this can't be stopped. 'When you proposed to me you knew we couldn't have our own biological children, but we both assumed we'd be able to adopt. Now that's not going to be an option, I think you ought to take some time to be sure you really want a future with no children in it.'

My voice catches and I squeeze my eyes so tightly shut it hurts to keep the tears back. There's some initial relief that I've let the words escape, but now they're out there I'm terrified of the damage they might do.

What have I done? The thought starts as an internal whisper and quickly grows in intensity to a berating wail. I don't care if it was the right thing to do, I already want to claw the words back.

I need that fricking delete key.

'Sophie, I want a future with *you*.' The violence of Luc's tone takes me aback and I open my eyes. 'We will work things out.'

'But. . .' The words wither and die on my lips.

Why can't I just shut the hell up? It's Luc's decision. I've given him the choice. That's enough.

'Shush.' Luc places a finger on my lips, clearly agreeing with me. Then he silences me with his mouth. The long, lingering kiss is delivered with a passionate intensity that leaves me breathless.

I feel weak, exhausted by the emotional rollercoaster of the day. So I don't protest when Luc stands up, scooping me into his arms and carrying me up the stairs to our little flat. He heads straight for the bedroom. Once he's deposited me on the bed he tugs and pulls at my clothing, stripping me naked with a fierce urgency. Lowering his mouth to my body he covers my skin with kisses. He strokes my thighs, my stomach and my chest and then follows with his mouth where his fingers laid the trail.

He caresses my breasts reverentially, making me feel treasured and wanted.

Luc wants me. It's going to be okay. I can scarcely dare to believe it.

After licking and teasing my erect nipples he kisses down my stomach and then presses his lips to my sex. I moan when his tongue makes contact with my clit. As he sucks and teases the delicate nub of nerve endings with practised ease he thrusts first one and then two fingers inside me. I contract around his fingers, wanting more and arching my hips up to meet his tongue.

I silence the voice that says we should be talking. Luc's always been good at speaking through actions. I'm not such a masochist that I want to force this issue. I need this physical reassurance of his desire for me, of his love. It heals and restores me.

Pulsing pleasure throbs and builds between my legs. Luc holds my hips to keep me still and I cry out his name as he tips me over the edge into a shattering orgasm. Before I've recovered from the aftershock he's stripped off and his hard erection presses at my entrance. He enters me with one hard thrust, a perfect fit. He knows I love him doing that while I'm still sensitive.

Although I'm expecting the friction, I still gasp. He pauses, staring down at me, piercing me with his gaze as well as his erection.

'Sophie. *Je t'adore. Toujours.*' His words unlock something deep inside me and I wrap my legs around his back, pressing the soles of my feet against his buttocks and pulling him inside me, deeper still. The hard thrusts go some way to obliterating my fear and insecurity. My fingers grip his back, pulling him in, needing to take his love into the darkest, deepest parts of me.

This feels more raw, more primal than usual. It's more like fucking instead of our usual love-making, but no less emotional for that. He's using his body to drive his words home.

'*Je t'adore. Toujours.*' He pierces me with every syllable, imprinting me with his thrusts and with his tongue in a physical act of reassurance.

He pauses only to seize my ankles. He hooks them up over his shoulders so he can go deeper still. The different angle means he rubs against the sensitive spot inside me that we spent weeks discovering together.

Aching need builds up inside me again, morphing into an intense explosion of pleasure, another orgasm rocking my body. I fist the sheets at my sides and cry out just before Luc climaxes. I feel the rigid tension in his frame, the sudden jerk inside me and the hot, wet feel of him emptying his seed deep inside me.

When he rolls off me we lie still, drained both physically and emotionally.

Luc is asleep within minutes. I creep to the bathroom quietly so as not to wake him. Max pads after me, his claws clacking on the tiled floor.

He sits watching as I cleanse my face with a baby wipe. I stare at my image in the mirror. I'm nothing special, just an ordinary girl with fair hair, full breasts and curvy hips. Luc says I'm far from ordinary, that as well as my very obvious physical charms my kindness has a beauty all of its own. He loves me, enough to sacrifice the family he's always wanted. But will he feel the same in ten years' time or just end up resenting me? Everyone seems to be giving things up because of me. Mum's had to give up dreams of grandchildren. Now it's her plans for my wedding. Just because of one mistake I'll be punished for the rest of my life, the consequences of one stupid action rippling out around me and causing pain in endless concentric circles.

I'm doing a really crap job of making those I love happy. I shiver, pulling an oversized clean navy t-shirt out of the airing cupboard and over my head. Max moves forward, sensing my distress and rubs himself against my legs.

'You're a muppet, Max. Don't you know you're a dog, not a cat?' I reach down to scratch him behind his ear. 'If only everyone was as easy to please as you, eh?'

I wonder how Luc is going to help sort things out. It's a relief to have shared the problem with him, though. I'm going to try to trust him.

By the next morning some of the edge has been taken off the pressure cooker of emotions building up inside me. Last night and the events of yesterday have left me subdued and a little low, exhausted by the maelstrom of feelings. At eleven-thirty I come into the café from the stockroom to find Holly and Amelia at a table, Maddie in a car seat at their feet.

'Hey, Soph, take a break and come and join us,' Holly calls over. 'It's okay, I've cleared it with the boss.'

I glance at Luc and he smiles. 'Go ahead, I'm not going over to Vex for another hour.'

Suspiciously fortuitous timing. I bet Luc called Holly and asked her to come over.

'Hi, Holly.' I force a smile to my lips. 'Hi, Amelia, congrats on your Bake-Off win, by the way.'

'Thanks, I'm thinking of making my own wedding cake, a ski-resort theme.' Amelia smiles.

And we've hit the 'W' word within the first minute of conversation. I raise my eyebrows a fraction at Holly. We have a running joke about how often Amelia uses the 'W' word in every conversation. She can turn pretty much any topic around to herself and her forthcoming nuptials with impressive but scary ease.

'That sounds like fun.' I sink into a seat next to Holly and reach down to very gently stroke a sleeping Maddie's cheek. Her skin is oh-so soft. I blink hard and look back up, aware Amelia and Holly are waiting for my attention.

'I hope you don't mind me tagging along,' Amelia says and hesitates. I get the sense she's psyching herself up to ask something. 'Holly said she was coming over and it occurred to me you might be able to help me out with a problem.'

'Oh?' I eye her warily, worried I'm going to be press-ganged into cutting metres of white ribbon into precise ten-centimetre segments or other similar bridezilla- imposed activities.

'Our wedding reception venue has fallen through. The hotel had a fire in its function room,' Amelia says. 'Given it's such short notice, I'm not sure it'll be possible to find anywhere else and we have about a hundred people coming over from the UK.'

'I'm sorry to hear that, but I'm not sure what I can do to help.' I frown. 'Don't you have wedding insurance?'

'We do, but it doesn't solve the problem of lots of our guests who've already paid for their non-refundable flights and booked annual leave. Matt and I were wondering if we could hold the reception here. The main café is smaller than the hotel function room, but you've got room to erect a marquee out back, so we could use that space and the main café.' Amelia gazes at me hopefully. 'Please consider it, Sophie. Everything else is booked for March. You'd be a total lifesaver.'

She knows me too well. Via email I might have found a way to say no, but face to face I find it impossible to refuse someone needing help. Holly says my empathy is both one of my best character traits and also my greatest weakness because it leaves me unable to say no to anyone.

'Okay, I'll ask Luc, but we have closed the café for private dos before.' I ignore the sinking feeling that I'm going to regret this. Amelia will no doubt email me every day between now and the wedding and I'll end up having to repress the desire to strangle her with flower-arranging wire on a regular basis. Oh well, what's a bit of murderous repression between friends? I can't see Amelia's wedding ruined, not when it's the only thing she's talked about in living memory and I might be able to help.

'So are you marrying at the mountain chapel where Scott and I married?' Holly smiles. 'It was fun skiing down afterwards.'

'I think I'm going to snowboard down in my wedding dress. Look, I found this place in Canada that does great winter weddings. I'm using it for inspiration.' Amelia takes out her phone and opens up her Pinterest board to show us photos of brides in voluminous white dresses and grooms in full morning dress snowboarding down a mountain. 'We're going for a winter-wonderland theme for the reception. Snowball cocktails, ice sculptures, silver cake pops. The colours will be blue, white and silver. What do you think?'

'I think it'll be wonderful.' I stare at images of smiling brides and grooms walking hand and hand in the snow and reception rooms turned into glittering ice palaces with frost-laden trees decked out with lanterns.

I hate to admit it, but I'm jealous.

It's the kind of wedding I'd have if I were free to choose. Free from all the expectations of the people I love and want to make happy. I'm sure Luc's mother would prefer her own village church and priest in Vex to a mountain chapel on this side of the valley. Mum, on the other hand, wants a string quartet, a Church of England service and my second cousin's children for my bridesmaids, even though I barely know them. Not to mention having every relative and WI member she wants to show off to in attendance at a swanky hotel.

Luc's only stipulation is that his parents are present, which is pretty undemanding, comparatively speaking.

I've been ducking questions about wedding plans because I haven't even let myself think about what I want. I even kidded myself I really didn't mind about any of the details, but now I know that's not true.

I want Amelia's wedding.

Chapter 16

LUCY

Inverness airport is tiny compared to the international terminal at Geneva. It feels like I'm stepping back in time when I collect my bag and walk through to the exit. The sky is dark grey and threatening rain. I'm home. Verbier may as well belong to another universe.

I scan the faces of those watching for relatives and am pleased to catch sight of Ben waiting for me. I might not be thrilled to be back in the Highlands but I'm happy to see Ben at least. Genuine affection pierces the layer of numbness that's covered me since the Avalanche of Bad News Day, as Tash dubbed it.

I reach up and hug Ben tight. At six foot two and broadly built he's practically a giant compared to me and today that feels like a comfort. We hold onto each other for longer than we normally would. I think we both feel a little adrift. The stubble on Ben's face tells me he hasn't shaved today, which is definitely unusual. I peer up at him more closely. His eyes are bloodshot.

What was it like for him to find Dad collapsed in the barn and have to watch him die? I briefly imagine the horror of it and blanch.

'Have Tom and John stayed home with Mum?'

My other brothers are a lot older than me and we've never been close. They took their cue from Dad and basically ignored me. It was Ben, just two years older than me, who taught me to ride and fish and skim stones on the loch.

The riding and the stone-skimming I loved. The fishing not so much, but I didn't care, I got to spend blissful time alone with Ben and away from the constant disapproval of Mum. He's basically the only member of my family I've ever felt genuinely loved by. The thought makes my eyes burn hot and I squeeze them tight shut.

I knew coming back to Scotland would be hard. I just need to get through the next two weeks. I can do it. If I survived twenty years here I can do a measly two weeks now and offer Mum my support, whether she wants it or not.

Ben nods. 'Yes. They're both at the croft. Aunty Sylvia is staying too. Mum put her in your old bedroom, so you'll be sleeping on the sofa, sorry.'

'No need to be sorry, it's not your fault.' I nudge his elbow.

'You could have my room,' he offers.

'Do you still have engine parts all over the floor and your clothes in piles graded by how dirty they are?' I ask.

'Um, maybe.' He shrugs apologetically.

'Thanks for the offer, but the sofa will be fine.'

I recognise the move to the sofa as the punishment it's meant to be. Mum is still angry that I dared to leave the croft and go to Switzerland. I'm lucky she's not put me out in the barn.

We pay for Ben's parking and then walk towards his jeep. As we head out of the airport carpark and drive south to Drumnadrochit the threatening grey clouds deliver on their promise – a cold misty, drizzle of a rain shower. The kind that gets under your skin and into your mood, pulling you down with it. In Verbier this precipitation would be falling as snow.

I'll return to Switzerland once this is over. No matter what Mum says.

Home at the croft I get the sensation of travelling back in time again. This is the world of another Lucy, one who doesn't exist any more. It certainly doesn't belong to me and I don't belong to it. I step on the creaky floorboard in the hallway, a noise that takes me back to all the times I'd try to sneak into the house without Mum hearing me. I'm sure she keeps it that way on purpose. It triggers a familiar anxiety in me, one I try to squash down.

Mum is sitting by the range, Aunty Sylvia next to her. I pause in the doorway, shocked by Mum's appearance. She seems to have aged ten years since I last saw her. There's a fragility in her eyes I've never seen before. Mum is never frail. Ever.

My instinct is to hug her, but when she sees me her mouth purses in disapproval. It's a look I'm very familiar with. One that never fails to make my stomach clench in a muscle-memory sort of way.

'So, you finally made it,' she sniffs.

Great, I've been home for two minutes and already I'm in trouble.

'I got the first flight I could book.' I hate the defensive tone that creeps into my voice.

She eyes me coldly and tension ratchets up a notch in my gut. I have to crush the part of me that wants to sob in her arms, to ask Mum to make it all better.

That's never going to happen. I'm not sure it ever has. When my first pet kitten died I was seven years old. Mum stared at me coldly and told me to toughen up, that as a crofter's daughter I had no business crying over a mere animal, especially one that had no monetary value. She only let me bring the kitten into the house in the first place because it could grow up to be a mouser. The outside barn cats hadn't been doing their job well enough and some brave rodents had dared to break into Mum's kitchen.

I stare at her now and feel an immense sadness creeping over me. Too much has passed between us. Too many misunderstandings and too many words that were, sadly, all too easy to understand. A gulf has opened up and I don't know how to cross it, or if I even want to.

Why does this have to be so complicated? I remember a phrase I heard once – that friends are the family you choose. I think about Seb and Sophie and Holly with a pang. Right now my friends in Verbier feel more like family than my blood relatives, Ben excepted.

Like I said, he always made time for me. Maybe because he's the closest to me in age or maybe just because he has a big heart. When John and Tom went out to work as beaters on the local laird's estate hunt days Ben and I would hide in the barn and read comics. Sometimes we'd take the dogs up on the hills or into the forest for long walks.

Those are the things I miss.

I'm still standing, arms hugging my chest, even though the defensiveness of the posture irritates me.

'You'll help with the funeral tea.' Mum eyes me like I'm a recalcitrant servant who needs putting in her place.

'Of course,' I try hard not to sound snappish. 'I want to help any way I can. . . I'm so sorry to hear the news, Mum. It must've been awful for you.'

She stiffens and glares at me. There's real malice in her eyes that breaches my defences and breaks my heart.

'You'd have known how it was if you'd been here,' she replies tartly.

Aunty Sylvia pats Mum's arm. I'll get no help from her.

I try really hard to put myself in Mum's place. I can imagine the long wait for the air ambulance, how incredibly stressful that must've been. It's one of those things you have to accept if you live somewhere remote – emergency services won't be able to get to you quickly. It's why the fundraisers for the air ambulance get such good support in our area. You never know when it might be your turn to need the service.

'Mum, I. . .' I'm struggling to find the right words to make things better between us when Mum cuts in sharply.

'Maybe you could've saved him if you'd been here. You did that first-aid course, after all.'

She glares at me again with real venom. I feel like I've been punched. Ben shifts awkwardly at my side.

Mum needs to focus her anger at losing Dad somewhere and she's chosen to lay it all on me. Right. I take a deep breath.

'I couldn't have saved him if it was massive stroke. I'm not a doctor.' I force the words out between clenched teeth and turn away from her, blinking hard. 'I'm making tea, would anyone like some?'

As I take the kettle off the ancient stove and put tea bags into the teapot a thought nags at the back of my mind. Aspirin. I read somewhere on the web about how if you put a dispersible aspirin under the tongue of someone having heart attack it might lessen the effects. Is it the same with a stroke? I couldn't have saved him, could I? And if I had lessened the effects of the stroke, Dad would have hated being an invalid. He always said he wanted to die in his fields, on his own land. He loathed hospitals with a vengeance.

Anyway I wasn't here. It's not my fault that Dad died, whatever Mum is choosing to believe. I'm a grown woman, an adult and I can choose my own life. What's so terrible about leaving home? I hate how Mum gets to me so easily. She never fails to make me feel guilty.

As I pass around the cups of tea I realise the next two weeks are going to be very stressful. I wonder how Seb is getting along. I wish I could be with him, I'm missing him already. The thought pops into my mind and I instantly feel guilty for it. What is wrong with me? Dad is dead and Mum needs me. If she wants to take out her anger on me I'm just going to have to suck it up.

When I hand Mum her tea she looks at me as if she can see everything I've been doing with Seb. Do I look different for losing my virginity? I refuse to feel as though I've done something wrong. I don't have to live by her rigid rules any more.

I sigh and sit down on the sofa with my own tea. Ben rests a hand on my shoulder. Normally he'd have stood up for me, but I can sense he's at a loss with how to deal with this fragile yet volatile version of Mum.

The next couple of weeks stretch out in front of me like a prison sentence to be endured. As for my own feelings about Dad, I barely know where to start with processing the grief and the loss of the relationship we could have had in a different dimension maybe.

Perhaps if I'd been a boy . . .

I swallow down that idea along with my scalding tea. I need to do something with my hands too much to wait for it to cool. Briefly I close my eyes and remember Seb holding me, caressing me as though I'm special and I know that thinking about him is the only way I'll survive these weeks at home.

Chapter 17

BETH

'Hi, Dan, I got your voicemail.' My mouth is dry and my pulse racing as I stamp my boots on the camper steps to knock the snow off.

Once in the van, the warmth of the heater hits me and I strip off my jacket and scarf before they turn me into a one-woman sauna.

'Cup of tea?' he asks calmly, as if this is just another one of my visits.

'Maybe later. You, um, said you had some news.' I sit down on Dan's bed, resisting the urge to demand he just get on with it and tell me already.

'I made some enquiries for you. He was convicted.'

I blink hard and suddenly I can't remember how to breathe.

'When?' I whisper, knotting my fingers in the fringed strands of Dan's cotton throw. My fingers are as rigid as claws. My whole body has tensed, though what good fight or flight is going to do me here, hundreds of miles from London, I don't know.

Dan sits next to me, thigh not quite touching mine. The expression on his face is grave and I wonder if he's read the full reports. If it was the same, what happened to those other women? What he did. . .

Without warning my mind flashes back to the park where it happened to me. I can still hear the thunder and loud, angry rain drops pelting the ground around us. Once I'd frozen, realising the impossibility of fighting off a man twice my size I'd switched off from what was happening to my body and just waited for it to be over. I shrank into my mind, focusing on the torrential rain instead of the invasion of my body and in the process it felt like I lost a part of myself.

But it's over now. It's over. I force my mind back to the present. I'm safe here with Dan in this cosy campervan haven.

'A few weeks ago, but the sentencing wasn't reported in the press,' Dan replies and I try to concentrate on what he's saying, on his presence beside me. 'I have a friend who's a law reporter, he found out for me.'

'Thank you.' I unclench my fingers from around the throw and tentatively make myself reach out for Dan's hand, fighting the impulse to withdraw into myself again. 'I really appreciate it.'

I won't ask Dan how long a prison sentence was given. Otherwise I'll be counting down in my head and calculating the possibility of parole and early release. Then even having international borders between us might not be enough to stop me going slowly insane.

'How do you feel?' Dan lightly squeezes my hand.

'Fine. You must be the only boyfriend in the world who

actually wants to talk about feelings.' I roll my eyes and attempt a smile to soften the snarkiness of my words.

'Am I your boyfriend?'

'I don't know. Are you?' I turn and meet his eyes.

'Do you want me to be?' His gaze is on me, intense and penetrating.

'If you promise to keep me in chocolate digestives, you can be anything you want.' I try to smile, to lighten the mood.

'So, Beth, tell me the truth. How are you doing?'

It seems my attempts at deflection have failed to throw Dan off in his quest to assess my emotional wellbeing.

I shrug helplessly. I can't find the right words, or any words at all, in fact.

'On a scale of one to ten, one being totally freaked out and ten being totally cool, what number are you?' Dan asks.

I take a deep breath into my lungs and force myself off pause mode. 'About six, I suppose.' Although in reality the number keeps fluctuating from about three or four to eight. I don't want to go into the conflicting emotions of satisfaction that the man who raped me is now in prison and fury that he will never be punished for what he did to me.

It's so easy to interpret the CPS's cited 'insufficient evidence to proceed with a prosecution' as an excuse, a criticism that I didn't fight back harder, even. If I'd pushed him into injuring me badly then it would've helped my case. Bruised arms from being gripped so tightly I couldn't move and bruising between my legs could be viewed as merely evidence of consensual, rough sex. That was how it was explained to me.

So going through the subsequent medical examination and

detailed statement – both so excruciating I wanted to die – were all for nothing.

I don't know why I froze, but I did. Until it actually happens to you it's impossible to say how you'll react. Am I afraid Dan will judge me? Is that why the words I need won't appear for me?

I swallow down the lump in my throat and tighten my hold of Dan's hand.

'Six is good,' Dan says.

'What were you up to before I came round?' I change the subject.

If he doesn't stop questioning me I'll have to leave. It's my ever-helpful fight-or-flight instinct kicking in again and I don't have the energy for a fight or anything much at all, in fact. Tension has drained and exhausted me.

'I'm reading. I've just started a Scott Mariani, one of the Ben Hope thrillers. I've got it on audio on my phone, so I suppose, technically, I'm listening. Would you like to stay and listen with me?'

'Yes, for a bit, if that's okay. I really, really don't want to talk any more.'

Sitting quietly with Ben and listening to a book that will fill my mind with other words, other images and a different world sounds like just what I need right now.

'Of course it's okay.' Ben gets the book up on his phone. 'I'll start from the beginning again. I was only twenty minutes in.'

He presses the play button on the Bluetooth-linked Bose speaker and as the audiobook plays Dan reaches for me. We lie down on the bed together. I'm on my side with Dan lying behind me, holding me. We fit together perfectly and I rest my head back against his chest. His warm and solid presence comforts me. My muscles slowly unclench and tension seeps out of my body.

I feel. . . safe. Safe enough to lose myself in the story.

Safe with Dan.

Frankly it's exactly the kind of therapy I need right now. I thought I knew what I needed. I had a plan, but the universe sent me Dan. Lying here with my cheek against the soft cotton throw and his arms wrapped protectively around me I feel a profound gratitude.

After an hour Dan gets up and makes a cup of tea.

'Chocolate biscuit?' He offers me the packet as he presses pause on the Bose speaker.

I take two and grin at Dan. 'Thanks.'

'What does two biscuits get me?' He asks, raising an eyebrow.

'A kiss, maybe more. We'll see.'

'You really don't want to talk?' He checks, eyes serious, too serious for my liking. 'You're sure.'

I munch on the biscuits. Once I've finished, I sigh.

'I really, really, really don't want to talk.'

Or think.

'You don't think it would help?'

'I know it definitely wouldn't help.' I squeeze my eyes shut and sigh again, more deeply this time. 'Look, I only want to have to say this once. It's bad enough that I have to try and forget about what happened, but telling you any of the details means if we're having sex I not only have to forget about it myself but I'll also worry you're thinking about it. I don't want you to treat me differently. I don't want to be treated like a rape victim. If he carries on affecting me he's won, whether he's in prison or not. Do you understand?'

'Yes, I think I do,' Dan says slowly. 'I suppose everyone has to deal with trauma in a way that works for them. I know there's not a one-size-fits-all cure. Have you ever talked about it, though?'

'Yes, once.'

And once was enough. Every horrible ugly detail. The terror and the torrential rain and all the ifs. . .

If it hadn't rained. If I'd turned left instead of right on the path. If I'd been more careful. If I'd run when I first noticed him staring at me. If my sundress hadn't been so low-cut. . .

You're not supposed to think like that, I know, but at three a.m. when I'm lying wide awake, those ifs attack me like swarming wasps, stinging me no matter how hard I try to swat them away.

It's best not to think. Not to talk. It's over. He's in prison, not for what he did to me but still. . . It's done. I could go back to England now, if I wanted. I never felt safe knowing he was walking around London, free. It's a big city, granted, but even so. I'm also over the silly crush I had on Mark. I think now that was more about wanting to be a proper part of Eva's family, to feel properly safe, not just an invited hanger-on who might be asked to leave at any time.

Coming to Verbier was the right thing to do. I had to leave the safety of Eva's nest and fly away.

'I want to move on, please.' I meet Dan's eye, try to convey how much I need him to move on too. I'm not Beth the Rape Victim or Beth With the Dead Bipolar Mother, I'm just Beth.

'Okay. Do you want to listen to more of the book or maybe you want to do . . . something else?'

'Something else.' I nod and reach out to stroke Dan's hand. There's been a shift inside me. Sex with Dan took the lid off the pressure cooker last time. Now it's not anger driving me but desire for Dan and a longing to reconnect. Or maybe it's just plain basic desire. I need this.

'You're sure?' Dan hesitates.

'Please don't ask me that again. Don't treat me differently.' My jaw clenches. 'What that man did . . . I won't let it spoil sex for me. I appreciate you being thoughtful, but could you try being less so?'

'Okay. Be more insensitive. Got it.' His lips twitch. 'How about 'get your kit off, woman, I want to fuck you.' Is that better?'

'Much better,' I giggle. 'But not very convincing. You can do better than that. Tell me what you want to do to me.'

Dan leans forward, gaze fixed on me as he runs his hand up and down my thigh.

'I want to strip you naked and kiss every bare inch of you until you're wet and ready for me. Then I plan to make you come, over and over. I want to see that smile you do when you're about to come. To know the privilege of being the one who gets to see you lose control.'

He continues to stroke me rhythmically. The action ignites fiery darts of desire beneath my skin and between my legs. My breasts ache to be touched and my nipples harden.

'That, uh, sounds good. You get an A-plus for effort.'

I swing my legs up beside Dan and lie on the bed again. My breath quickens as Dan pulls my hoodie over my head and undoes my jeans, tugging them down.

Then he runs his hands over my body, over the top of my knickers and bra, eyes darkening. When he lowers his mouth to my neck and kisses his way down my body, my feet begin to tingle. He kisses between my legs, over the damp cotton of my knickers.

I arch up to meet his mouth, wanting more, but he moves away, kissing down my thighs again. The need for him obliterates all other thoughts. I groan and then suck in my breath as he tugs my knickers down.

'Is this what you want?' He lowers his mouth again, this time teasing my clit with his tongue.

'Oh yes,' I gasp. 'And maybe something more.'

I reach out and run my hand over the hard bulge in his jeans, taking delight in the low moan he utters, knowing I'm responsible for it.

Once he's undressed and sheathed with a condom, he presses between my legs – I'm ready for him. Ready to choose sex. Ready to choose living over surviving.

And ready to be fully present when I do.

I stare into Dan's eyes the whole time he thrusts into me. My body welcomes and contracts around him. I don't tune out. I stay with him and it's the best sex I've ever had.

It's moving on. It's winning.

When I come and pull Dan into his own release a millisecond later my obliteration of thought is complete.

I'm not a victim. I'm not even a survivor. I just am.

Dan and I. We are one and the knowledge of it almost fries my brain. I thought choosing to trust a man again would be difficult, maybe impossible, but with Dan it's been easy. It just feels right.

Afterwards we lie in companionable silence.

'I'm so glad last year is over and done with. I wonder what this year is going to bring.' I stare at the campervan's ceiling.

Dan doesn't answer immediately and it occurs to me I'm not the only one trying to cope with life-changing events.

'So, I suppose throwing away a career as a barrister is a pretty big deal.' I roll on my side and look at him.

'Yes, it is.' He turns and meets my gaze. 'It was the right thing to do, though.'

'No regrets?'

'None.'

'Tell me more about you, Dan. That one-to-ten thing, do you know that because of your sister?'

'Yes, we had a few family-therapy sessions and the therapist suggested it. It's meant to be an easier way to express how you're feeling when you're not up to talking.'

'So your sister, she's okay now?'

'She wasn't for a while. She tried to kill herself and was in hospital for a few months. She's much better now, but she's with my parents, because she's not up to being on her own.'

'Oh, I'm really sorry.' I try to imagine my mother attending family-therapy sessions and fail utterly.

Dan squeezes my arm. 'You've done so well, Beth. You don't believe me but you're incredibly brave.'

'I had some help. My friend's mother was a counsellor. She helped me. I even moved in with them for a while. Mum had died and there was a problem with the housing. . .' I sigh. 'I don't know that I'm especially strong. Truth is, if Eva hadn't scooped me up and taken me in I might well have tried to kill myself too. She saved my life.'

That was when the crush on Mark started, a part of a bigger longing to be a proper, permanent part of their family. What I'm experiencing with Dan is completely different. For a start, it's not all in my head. It's like the crush times a thousand. A burst of feeling I never anticipated.

We cuddle and listen to more of the Ben Hope novel and eventually fall asleep together. At six a.m. the next morning I crawl out of bed ready to get back to Chalet Repos to help out.

I can't believe I slept all night through. I crouch down next to the bed and kiss Dan on the cheek.

'Bye, Dan.'

He mumbles incomprehensibly. Not a morning person, then. I smile, almost glad to discover he has a flaw.

'Thanks so much, for finding out the news and for everything,' I whisper. Even though he probably won't remember, I still need to say it.

The freezing air hits me as I slip out of the van. On the walk back I realise that last night was the first night in years I haven't had a nightmare. They're so much a part of my nights I've grown used to them. Yet last night I don't actually remember dreaming at all. Weird.

Good but weird.

I sigh. It could be so easy to get used to this. I mustn't. This is a temporary thing, it has to be. Dan is a traveller, a free spirit on some kind of commitment-free bender. This can't last. If I want to find a man who'll always be there for me I suppose I need to keep looking, stick to my original plan.

Only that plan isn't looking so great right now. The idea of partying and meeting more pricks like Thomas doesn't appeal.

I realise I never got round to making any New Year's resolutions this year. Maybe it's time for a new plan and a new me. Where Dan will fit in that new plan I honestly don't know.

Chapter 18

From: Sebastien@whitelineproductions.fr
To: lucy.ross@hotmail.com
Subject: Sad news

Lucy Lu, I'm so sorry to hear about your father. I'd like to send some flowers to the funeral, if you could let me have your address.

I got the get-well e-card you sent me :-) It has obviously done the trick as I'm out of the hospital now and feel perfectly okay. No worse than the time I got hit by a surf board and got concussion. I have a hard head, used to knocks, don't worry. I've been forced to cancel a day's filming but should be fit for the Xtreme in March, so that's fantastic news.

I can't wait to see you again. I hope things are okay for you at home, I know it can't be easy at the moment given what you told me about your parents.

Thinking of you,

Seb

LUCY

I stare out of the window at the clouds scudding over the hills. I wish I could climb on board one of them and race my way back to Seb in Switzerland.

Instead I'm stuck in purgatory, eternally punished and with no chance of atonement. It feels like I've gone back in time, trapped in this house with the family Bible on prominent display and the ancient rug on the floor with worn patches where we used to be made to kneel to pray as children. I have to keep reminding myself I'm an adult now and will be leaving again soon. I didn't have free choice then but I do now.

At the same time I'm desperately sorry for Mum. I hate to see her tightly controlled grief and it's upsetting that she won't accept comfort from me. It also hurts to be the target of so much anger. Mum even said to me that worrying about me getting up to 'high jinks' probably caused Dad's stroke in the first place.

So I'm a murderer now, too, apparently.

Mum showed Aunt Sylvia the *Daily Mail* article about the supposedly depraved lives lived by chalet girls and they both stared at me, tight-lipped for the rest of the evening. I can't believe she actually cut the article out of the newspaper and has kept it. All the better to taunt me with, I suppose.

As well as the difficult relationship with Mum I'm still trying to process the fact Dad has died. I keep expecting him to come in from the barn and sit by the range in his favourite chair with worn patches on the arms. The chair no one is allowed to sit in now. I try to feel something, anything, but today is a numb, no-feeling day. I've had periods of numbness interspersed with acute sadness for what I've lost and what I never had. Sophie was right about that. I'm grieving for what our relationship could have been.

If it weren't for Ben I'd have gone mad cooped up here with Mum and Aunt Sylvia.

I hear car wheels on the gravel outside and my heart sinks. Surely Mum isn't back from the shops already? A car door slams and I hear Ben's voice from the yard outside.

'There's someone here to see you, Lucy.'

When Ben walks in his eyebrows are raised upwards towards his slightly receding hairline. All the males in our family are cursed with early-onset baldness.

'Who is it?' I get up from the sofa. My old school friends have moved to various cities in search of work as there's very little year-round employment to be found here.

I feel guilty knowing I'm just counting the days until I can go back to Switzerland, but any distraction from the tension between me and Mum is welcome. She won't even let me help her with any of the legal paperwork or admin because 'The boys have it all under control'. Of course my poor little female brain isn't equipped to cope with anything like that. Honestly, Mum left everything legal or financial to Dad to deal with. Now she'll rely on her sons instead.

I can scarcely believe my eyes when Seb walks through the door. It takes a second for my brain to catch up with what I see, so incongruous is his presence here.

'Seb, are you okay? What are you doing here?' I spring up and throw my arms around him. 'You didn't tell me you were coming. I thought you were supposed to be resting at home?'

'I was, and while I was resting I found all these flights going from Geneva to Inverness on the internet. So I thought I'd hop on one.' He shrugs. 'Compared to what I normally do I'd call this resting.'

'Did you hire a car at the airport?'

I'm still trying to adjust to the collision between my two worlds. I can hardly believe Seb's actually here, really here.

'Yes, it's outside. I thought we might have more freedom that way.'

Ben snorts and I realise how rude I'm being.

'Seb this is Ben, the youngest of my brothers. Mum is out at the shops with my aunt at the moment so it's relatively quiet.'

I send out a silent plea that she'll stay away a little longer. My pulse is racing. Seb came all this way for me!

'Ah Ben, so this is your favourite brother then, Lucy?' Seb turns to me, his eyes twinkling, his arm resting possessively around me.

'Yes, I'm the favourite brother.' Ben's eyebrows are still arched. 'And you're Seb. So, are you a friend from Verbier?'

Ben puts special emphasis on the word 'friend'.

'That's right.' I say, trying to will Ben to shut up, that I'll explain more later. No chance.

'Would that be a special friend?' Ben persists.

'Let's just say I'm one of her favourite friends,' Seb replies gravely, but his arm doesn't drop from around me so I've no doubt Ben has the right idea, he's just trying to torment me.

'Why don't we go for a walk, Seb?' I interrupt. 'I'm sure you want to stretch your legs after the journey? Also Ben's got other things he needs to be doing, haven't you?'

I look pointedly at Ben, who snorts.

'Great idea,' Seb agrees. 'You can show me your Loch Ness.'

'It's not exactly mine, but yes, there's a good view across the loch if we walk up the hill.'

'I hope you're fit, Seb? It's a bit of a climb,' Ben adds.

'Oh don't worry, Seb could do it in his sleep. He's very... er... fit.' A flush creeps up my neck and I ignore Ben's smirk. Even post-concussion Seb could manage it in his sleep.

'Don't forget to look out for the haggis, they're vicious wee buggers.' Ben smiles slyly at Seb.

Seb frowns and turns to me, confused, his command of English momentarily failing him.

'Don't worry, I'll explain once we're out.' I glare at Ben in a 'don't wind up the boyfriend' way. Not that I expect it to work. Seb will be subjected to all the usual teasing outsiders to the Highlands get, plus all the potential boyfriend-teasing too. Add onto that Mum's inevitable disapproval and it's going to be one fun evening. And Seb came here willingly?

Even with all the agro I can expect later I'm still thrilled to see him and amazingly touched he came here to support me.

'Thanks for coming.' I link my arm through Seb's as we set off on the stony path up behind the croft. 'I'm so glad to see you, you have no idea how much.'

'I missed you and thought you could do with some moral support.'

'Definitely,' I agree and squeeze his arm. 'I've missed you too.'

'It's very beautiful here, the air is fresh, like in Switzerland. You were lucky to grow up here.'

'Um, it's certainly beautiful and it gave me a love of mountains. I'll always be grateful for that.' I hesitate, if I've learnt anything it's that a beautiful backdrop isn't enough, you need more than that in life to be happy.

'But you're not happy here?' Seb's dark eyes seem to penetrate my mind, diving deep into my emotions.

'No,' I reply shortly. 'It's different here from in Switzerland, Seb, it's not exactly cosmopolitan. Strangers will get smiled at but it's easy to mistake friendliness for genuine openness. Unless you can trace your ancestors back three generations you'll never be truly accepted, not really.'

'It is a little like that in the Pyrenees, in my home village.'

Seb is shortening his strides, but even so I struggle to keep up with him and talk at the same time.

'You'll appreciate the difference, then. A lot of the older generation here don't travel much out of the Highlands. You'll find people here who've never been on a plane, don't have a passport and that's fine. They're good people, but it makes things. . . narrow. If you don't fit in between the lines it's difficult. In Verbier there are people drawn from all over the world, it's a lot more cosmopolitan. Does that make sense?'

'Yes. Like I said. Where I'm from in France it's not that different from this.' Seb says.

'Where is that exactly?'

'A small village in the Hautes Pyrenees. A friend I grew up with who is gay found it hard to find acceptance there. He moved to Paris in the end.'

'So we're both from similar backgrounds. Well, except there are no Winter Games medalists in our family.' I smile. 'How are you feeling anyway, post-avalanche?'

'I'm okay.' He shrugs. 'I'm lucky to be alive. Sorry, that seems an insensitive thing to say given you just lost your dad.'

'It's okay. You know things weren't always great between me and my dad but him being there still gave me stability, a kind of safety net.' I look down at the stony ground. 'Despite our differences I think I always knew deep down he loved me, in his own way.'

Seb puts his arms around me and holds me close. It's a bright blustery day, puffy white clouds racing above us up towards Inverness Airport and the sea. Maybe they did bring Seb to me after all. It's warm and cosy here in Seb's arms. I feel as if they could protect me from anything. But what good is that if he gets taken from me on his next film jump? Or if he takes just one risk too far to retain the Xtreme title this year?

I look up at him. How honest do I dare to be? 'What I'm trying to say is daughters need their dads. I know it's totally your call, but what happened to you . . . the avalanche, it scared me stiff and I know it terrified Gabriella too.'

'Do you think I haven't thought about this?' Seb asks with a frustrated grimace. His face darkens and it feels as if a cloud has obscured the sun.

Have I gone too far?

'Yes, I'm sure you have. It's just, with Dad going so suddenly and on the same day as I got the news about you. . . It was the worst twenty-four hours of my life.' I say quietly.

Seb's expression softens.

'I know, I wish I'd been there for you when you got the news from home instead of being stuck in hospital for observation.'

'I honestly don't know what the answer is, Seb.'

We walk on, further up the path, eventually cresting the hill to the point where Loch Ness is visible.

'I have to teach my daughter how to live a life without fears, without limits, to always push herself to be better, to be the very best she can be.' Seb gesticulates with his hands as we walk. 'Life is about more than being safe.'

'I know that, I admire what you do but what you said about the pressure on you to cut corners in the Xtreme. . . It frightens me.'

'It frightens me too.'

'Really? I thought you didn't feel fear?'

'Of course I do. I've lost friends to the mountains. Every time I do a jump I have that moment before I do it when I wonder if it'll be my last.'

Every time? What sort of man chooses to live like that? Is it bravery or a push for excellence?

'So, why do you do it?' I stare at the glimmer of loch. It's blue today but can so often be dark grey and stormy.

'Because when I push past that fear and I'm in the moment, that jump, taking a line no one else has ever taken, it's the best feeling in the world. I want Estelle to see me push past my fears, to grow up to do the same, to achieve excellence.'

He stares at me, eyes gleaming. 'You get it, Lucy. I saw your face when you watched the film. And you know for me it's about more than getting an adrenalin fix or having fun. I'm trying to show the world the beauty of the mountains. Also, by going to places like the Antarctic I would love to do more to highlight environmental issues.'

'Can't you do more of that side of it, then? Situations where you're in control and not under pressure? I know accidents can happen anytime but. . .' I break off and bite my lip.

I stare down at the view I've known all my life and think about the wider world out there I used to dream of seeing. I didn't let anyone else stamp on my dreams. Is that what I'm trying to do to Seb? It's out of fear, a desire to protect, not wanting to lose him. But I bet Mum would say she tried to stop me for exactly the same reasons.

I think I understand a little more about why Mum's so angry. She's lost control of me, lost the power to manipulate me and my being out of her sphere of influence terrifies her. I might think her fears are misplaced, but maybe Seb feels the same about mine.

I can't put limits on a man who prides himself on breaking them. He wants to live a life without limits, but is that so bad? Maybe. Commitment is limiting, and so is marriage. Do we really have a future together?

As the wind whips my hair around my face it occurs to me that the biggest limit of all is death. No one can escape that.

'You mean I should stop competing?' Seb's face is unreadable for once.

'Maybe, no, I don't know. I don't want to lose you, Seb, I'm sorry.' I squeeze his arm. 'But I don't want to stop you doing the things that make you unique, either. I'm trying hard to be honest here.'

If I push too hard it'll look like I'm forcing him to choose. I'm guessing that's exactly what Gabriella did and look where that got her.

Seb strokes the side of my face.

'I'll think about it. Okay? There's an awful lot to think about.'

'Okay.'

That's enough for now.

We walk back down to the croft house hand in hand.

'I take it your mother wouldn't approve of us having sex under her roof?' Seb asks.

I snort with laughter. 'No, and not anywhere else either. Sorry, it'll have to wait until we can be properly alone. We could take your hire car off to do some sightseeing maybe?'

'I have checked into a hotel,' Seb's eyes gleam. 'I thought it might be a bit crowded here and from what you said I guessed your mother wouldn't approve of us sharing a room.'

'I've been relegated to the sofa anyway.' I kick at a stone on the path. 'Maybe we could fit in a quick visit to your hotel? I can't stay overnight, though. It wouldn't be worth the grief Mum will give me. Well, maybe it would, but I'd rather avoid the extra conflict.'

'That sounds good to me.' Seb pulls me to him again before

we reach the house and runs his hands over my back and down to my bottom, cupping and squeezing. It sends a shiver of desire down my spine.

He kisses me, hard and deep, reawakening my sensual side. If it weren't for fear of one of my brothers finding us I'd pull Seb into the barn and let him have me here and now.

'If you need a cold shower in the meantime just hang around, we get plenty of freezing rain here,' I joke.

Reluctantly I pull back from the embrace, before my body overtakes my brain. I don't know why I'm so bothered about Mum disapproving of Seb. Her opinion of me couldn't matter less at the moment.

I approve of Seb, very much indeed. Right now that's the only approval I need.

Chapter 19

SOPHIE

I'm trying to deal with the wedding situation in my customary way. i.e. ignoring anything to do with weddings and not thinking about how I'm going to send a cease-and-desist order to Mum.

My plan is being foiled by Amelia. It turns out I was underestimating her when I predicted daily emails. I'm getting at least three or four a day, on average. If I don't reply to her she finds an excuse to drop into Bar des Amis to ask me face to face. Sometimes I get a half-smiley, half-snarky enquiry, asking if our wifi is down or I'm having email problems.

'I didn't realise agreeing to let her use Bar des Amis meant I agreed to be her unpaid wedding planner.' I huff to Holly, who's taken to bringing Maddie in each day so they get out of the apartment. 'I tell you, if she thinks I'm staying up all night for a week tying silver ribbons or spray-painting pine cones with fake snow she's got another think coming.'

'Do you remember why I gave up organising ski weddings?'

Holly grins. 'I just don't have the patience to deal with bridezillas and I seemed to be permanently stressed out.'

'Thanks, you're making me feel so much better.' I narrow my eyes. 'Oh crap, that's her now. She's coming in again. Do I have time to hide?'

'Tell you what, why don't I offer to help? I'm bored at the moment. I love Maddie to bits but my brain is suffering atrophy. We could all do it together, it'd be more fun and I'll take some of the heat off you.'

'Really? Would you? You're a total star. Thanks.' I force a polite smile to my face. 'Hi Amelia, it's lovely to see you. . . again.'

Holly turns a laugh into a cough.

'I've found some more winter wedding decorating ideas, Sophie.' Amelia says before she's even made contact with a chair.

I avoid Holly's eye, knowing we'll both get the giggles if we look at each other.

'Uh huh? Can I get you anything, Amelia?' I ask pointedly. If she's going to be here every day I may as well try and turn it into business for the café.

'No, I'll just have a glass of water, thanks. I'm detoxing for the wedding.' She gets out several ring binders and her iPad. 'I've brought you over a spare wedding planner. I couldn't have managed without mine and you really do need to start planning your own wedding, Sophie. I'd be happy to give you some tips, if you like. We could follow the same detox diet.'

'I'm good, thanks,' I mutter and grind my teeth as I fetch her a glass of water.

'I've found some lovely ideas on Pinterest for decorating tables and making wedding favours.' Amelia takes the glass from me and beams.

Has she really used the 'w' word in every sentence she's uttered since she crossed the threshold?

Give me strength.

I look politely at her iPad screen.

'Oh, that one looks beautiful, Amelia,' Holly says, pointing at a reception room that has tall silver trees dotted around the room, lit with tiny white lights.

I'm taken aback by a surge of longing as I look at all the images, at the snowflake wedding-favour bags, tiny skis as name placeholders, white and silver cake pops, ice and snow sculptures and candles in glass holders dotted around in the snow.

'Did I show you a picture of the fur stole I've got to go with my dress?' Amelia opens up a photo on her iPad that shows a white faux-fur stole draped over an elegant dress that shimmers with pearls and white beads.

A sigh escapes my chest before I can stop it. If Amelia and Holly notice I've been consumed by the green-eyed wedding monster they don't say anything.

Before I know it I'm drawn into the discussion, only breaking off when a customer needs serving. I always love decorating the café for Christmas and this is like that, only on a much grander scale. Feeling ashamed of my jealousy makes me agree to do far more than I should to help Amelia. I put the donated wedding planner and detox guide behind the bar instead of tossing it in the bin as I'd planned to.

'So, do you think Luc will do you another treasure hunt for Valentine's Day this year?' Holly asks when Amelia pops to the loo. Maddie is starting to grizzle and Holly rocks the car seat gently with her foot.

'I don't know, he's been really busy. I doubt he's had time.'

I know I'll be disappointed if Luc doesn't do his usual treasure hunt, though, which isn't really fair, given the pressure he's under.

'Two years in a row kind of sets a precedent, I think it's really romantic,' Holly says. 'Although, given he declared himself to be your secret admirer at the end of the first one and asked you to marry him at the end of last year's it'll be hard to top what he's done so far.'

Maddie begins to cry, screwing up her cute little pink face and balling her tiny fists. I have to grip a dishcloth in my own hands to stop myself from picking her up to comfort her. Maddie doesn't want me anyway, she wants her mother. She wants milk I can't produce.

'I need to get her home.' Holly yawns and stands up, too tired to notice my reaction. 'I think our Valentines' night will consist of a takeaway and us both trying to stay awake past nine p.m. Hope you enjoy whatever Luc has planned.'

On Valentine's Day morning I find a clue envelope on my pillow and feel a leap of pure joy. Luc bothered, despite everything. He's also let me sleep in. He must've cancelled the alarm on my iPhone without telling me.

I open up the clue and read:

CLUE 1
Aloha Sophie, Happy Valentines Day,
Use these clues to find your way,
Feeling hungry? You know what to do,
Seek the pink insect for your first clue.

Once I'm dressed and downstairs I bump into Tash, Rebecca and Lucy.

'Hi, Lucy, how are you? How was it back in Scotland?' I give Lucy an extra-long hug. She looks shattered, poor thing.

'Hmm, you know, difficult.' Lucy sighs, her face pale. She's also looking a little thin. I must check she's eating properly.

'But guess who flew into the Highlands to hold her hand?' Tash grins.

'Really? Seb came out to you in Scotland once he was discharged from hospital?' I can't help beaming. Lucy has been single for so long. Not that there's anything wrong with that, but it's lovely she's finally found someone.

'Yes.' Lucy's cheeks flush pink.

Luc comes up behind us and kisses me on the cheek.

'Have you got the clue? Good. Off you go and have fun then Sophie. I'll take care of things here today.' Luc smiles and I know it's no coincidence the girls are here. He's arranged the whole thing.

'Let's see the first clue, then,' Tash says eagerly, holding out her hand for the envelope.

I already know the answer and, from Tash's smile when she reads the clue, I guess she does too. Luc obviously decided to give us an easy first clue, given I've not even had a cup of tea yet.

Rebecca and Lucy look blank.

'It's that surfing-theme place, you know,' Tash says. 'The Offshore Café.'

'A surfing café called Offshore, in a country that doesn't have a coastline?' Rebecca sounds dubious. 'But what about the rest of the clue. . . the insect?'

'You've never been there?' I ask. 'Tash is definitely right. The pink insect is a pink VW Beetle, it's inside the café.'

'They do the best salted-caramel pancakes,' Tash adds. 'I'd love to get the recipe – we could try them out as a breakfast alternative for Chalet Repos.'

'It's not far, shall we get going?' I blow a kiss at Luc and wave as we head out.

Tash and I strike out ahead.

'Are you okay, Soph? You haven't seemed yourself lately?' Tash links arms with me.

'It's been a tough time,' I lower my gaze to the fresh snow beneath our boots, focusing on the satisfying crunch underfoot. 'It looks like we're not going to be allowed to adopt and the whole process has been really stressful. Plus Luc's dad is. . . dying.'

I pause and squeeze my eyes shut for a second, determined not to cry on what should be a nice day. It's the first time I've allowed myself to use the word, to tell the truth out loud.

Tash squeezes my arm. 'That's really tough, Soph, I'm so sorry.'

'It's just weird, having to accept that your parents aren't going to be there forever. It's scary.' I admit. 'Lucy's dad dying of a stroke made me realise how easy it is to take people's presence in your life for granted. Life is so much more fragile than we want to admit.'

I squeeze my eyes tight shut again and manage to keep the tears back.

'And what about your wedding, though?' Tash frowns. 'I mean, I share a chalet with Amelia and I swear if she mentions her wedding one more time I'm going to get creative with the fire tongs.'

I grin. 'What on earth is she going to talk about after the wedding?'

'Oh, I'm sure she'll find something. She'll probably get pregnant and bore us all endlessly about that instead. Can you imagine what a smug mother she'll make?' Tash glowers. 'But I seem to have got distracted with violent fantasies featuring Amelia again, that's happening a lot lately. My point was going to be that in comparison to her you never talk about your wedding plans. Why is that?'

I know I'm not going to be able to deflect Tash, no chance.

'It's so difficult pleasing everyone,' I sigh. 'I don't know how to do it in a way that won't upset the people I love.'

'Can't you elope or something?'

'Not without really pissing off our relatives, no.' I exhale and my breath escapes into the cold air in a puff of white mist.

'What do you want, Sophie? Assuming you could choose your own wedding and we assume for a minute that the people who love you would support your decisions?' Tash turns to me as we reach the café and wait for Rebecca and Lucy to catch up.

'You obviously haven't met my mother,' I reply flatly, shaking my head and then plastering on a smile as the others approach.

The Offshore Café is exactly the opposite of what you'd expect to find in a ski resort of a landlocked country. Surfboards adorn the walls and it has the feel of an old-fashioned American diner. It's a popular spot for breakfast with the ski instructors. Tash is right, the pancakes are to die for and Luc knows they're my favourite.

We find the clue quickly. It's tucked under the windscreen wipers of the pink VW Beetle.

Once we've sat down at a booth and ordered breakfast I open it and read aloud:

'CLUE 2
To find the location of clue number two,
Ask Aladdin or Solomon what to do,
It would probably suit an Arabian Night,
Or if you know the right words it might even take flight!'

'Is there a café that has a genie-type lamp as part of the decor?' Rebecca suggests.

'Not that I know of.' I sip gratefully at the hot chocolate that's appeared in front of me. I love Swiss hot chocolate, the richness of the milk from alpine cows makes it impossible to recreate back in England. I have tried.

'What's the Arabian Night connection? And Solomon?' Lucy frowns.

'Let's ask Mr Google, shall we?' Tash gets out her phone and types.

'Hmm, the top results are mostly about genies or Jin. I think that's another name for the same thing, though.' She scrolls down. 'But there is something about magic carpets and that would fit the flying-away part of the clue.'

'Les Moulins, you know, the children's beginner slope. It has a magic carpet moving walkway to take the kids back up to the top of the slope.' I smile. I love that Luc has gone to the bother of making up clues and arranging today for me despite everything he's dealing with. 'We'll head down there once we've paid.'

But when we go to pay our bill we're told by a smiling waitress that it's already been taken care of.

We head outside again; it's turning into a blue-sky, sunny day. One of those days when the mountain tops look crisp and sharp, a vivid white against azure blue. The reflected sunlight off the snow is almost too much to bear.

I slip my sunglasses on.

'You are so lucky to have someone like Luc.' Rebecca's tone is wistful.

'You'll meet someone, Rebecca,' I reassure her. 'I went for seasons with no one on the horizon. I thought I'd be single forever. You never know what's going to happen, who's waiting for you around the corner.'

'Yes, just look at me and Nate,' Tash beams, a ‚cat got the cream' smile.

'And you know I was single for years before I met Seb,' Lucy says shyly, a rosy-pink blush blossoming on her cheeks.

Aw, young love is so sweet.

I'm not sure pointing out we're all attached except for Rebecca is all that reassuring, especially not on Valentine's

Day. I used to hate being single and hoping for cards and flowers that never arrived. But Rebecca seems more cheerful and I'm glad that Luc included her today. It's another example of his thoughtfulness and kindness.

I really don't deserve him.

I take a deep breath. I don't have the courage to let him go, I couldn't bear it. But I can't let go of the guilt that it's my fault we can't have the family he's always craved. Will it haunt me forever? Will Luc end up resenting me? I wish I could just let it go, but the idea is like a wriggling tapeworm, burying deep inside me and feeding on my fear.

'Are you seeing Nate later?' I ask Tash, keen to stop my train of thought. Its destination isn't anywhere I want to go, I'm sure of that.

'Yes, he's flying into Geneva this afternoon, he's taking me out this evening.' Tash beams again. 'I can't wait to see him. I'm so glad he decided to go into business with Scott.'

'I'm glad it's going well.' I can't help smiling back.

'It is.' Tash's eyes shine, clear of the waves of hostility that used to lurk there. 'I'm hoping to persuade him to move out here or at least buy a chalet in Verbier and spend part of the year here if he doesn't want to leave London.'

When we get to the beginner slope in town a line of pink-faced small children are waiting to get onto the Magic Carpet to take them up the gentle incline.

We get in line.

'You haven't got any skis, silly, and you're too big to use our slope.' An English boy who looks about five years old sticks his tongue out at Tash.

She promptly sticks her own tongue out at him and rolls her eyes. Maybe there's still a touch of the old, not so grown-up, Tash alive and kicking after all. I find that reassuring.

When we get to the head of the queue someone hands me another envelope.

We stand back, out of the way, and this time I open it up myself and read.

'CLUE 3
Time for a hike, off you go,
To the Sanskrit way of saying hello.
For a Kir Royale and a Mont Blanc view,
Then a speedy way down is waiting for you.'

'I'm liking the sound of a Kir Royale.' Tash takes the clue from me. 'Anyone know any Sanskrit?'

'No, they didn't exactly teach it at school.' Rebecca shakes her head.

'Shall we ask Google again?' Lucy suggests.

Tash checks her phone signal and types into her browser.

'Here we go.' She turns her phone screen towards us. 'Useful phrases in Sanskrit. Hello means Namaste.'

'Le Namaste,' I exclaim. 'It's a cosy chalet café, a little way out of town. I think its terrace overlooks Mont Blanc. It's a bit of a walk up, but worth it.'

'Do we need snow shoes?' Lucy eyes our boots doubtfully.

'No, our boots will be fine, the path up there is kept relatively clear for the snowmobiles,' I say. 'I wonder what our speedy way down will be?'

'Maybe a snowmobile,' Lucy suggests. 'That would be fun.'

As we head out of town Rebecca and Lucy fall back, chatting. I love the peace of mountain trails, the fresh air and the heavy silence beneath the towering, snow-laden pines.

'What's it like at Chalet Repos now Amelia's in charge?' I ask.

Tash purses her lips. 'She's a pain in the neck, so full of herself and her sodding wedding. I still don't get why Holly put her in charge.'

'I think she did it so you'd be free to go off and spend a lot of time with Nate whenever he's over from England,' I say gently. 'Would you really want to be in charge? You wouldn't be able to leave the chalet to go off with Nate for a weekend like you do now.'

'I suppose.' Tash scowls. 'If only Amelia were less smug about it, though. She's always asking me pityingly if Nate's popped the question yet.'

I laugh. 'If it makes you feel any better she's always asking me if I'm following my wedding planner or doing my detox diet and making me worry about things I didn't even know I needed to worry about.'

Le Namaste is very different to the Offshore Café. It's a traditional mountain chalet cantine. The only unusual features are sculptures made from agricultural paraphernalia. Apparently the chef makes them in his spare time.

The walk is worth it for the stunning view, but still we all sink gratefully onto brightly coloured deckchairs on the terrace and are just as pleased with the view of the tray of Kir Royales brought out to us. On the tray sits the next clue.

We're facing the distinctive crooked mountain top of Mont Blanc, covered with pristine snow. It literally translates as the 'white mountain'. The air feels even fresher up here, pure and cold. With the extra height the temperature has dropped and now we've stopped moving we really feel the chill. We pull the super-soft blankets laid out on the chairs on top of us.

'To Luc.' Lucy raises her glass and we all toast my fiancé.

'If only all men were as lovely as your Luc,' Rebecca says. 'Poor Beth has been through a horrible time with a nasty piece of work called Thomas. Lucy and I were talking about it on the way up here. He was all charm at the start, but once he got what he wanted he turned abusive and since then he's done his best to humiliate her in front of his friends whenever he sees her out and about.'

'Thomas?' My heart thumps hard, almost painfully so. 'Thomas who? Do we know any more about him?'

Tash catches my eye.

'I'm not sure, he's a semi-pro, I think. Very good looking, apparently.' Rebecca frowns at me. 'Why, do you know him?'

'You think he might be your Thomas, Sophie?' Lucy asks quietly. 'I did wonder.'

Not my Thomas. Not mine. Nothing to do with me.

The words can't stop guilt, never that far away, from rising up inside me.

Should I have warned Beth somehow? But how. . . how could I have known? How could I have stopped him? He didn't break the law, he was just a complete shit.

'It sounds like him.' I stare down at my glass of blackcurrant bubbles. 'I might have a word with Beth.'

A chill trickles down my spine, numbing me like an anaesthetic. Oh God, what if he never got treatment and infected Beth too? What if she can never have children? I could never forgive myself if she's infertile and I could've prevented it.

'How could you have known, Soph?' Tash's voice cuts through the panic, her tone kind, her perception spot on. 'How could you reasonably have stopped this from happening?'

I gulp down the rest of my drink and welcome the warmth spreading through my chest.

'I'm so sorry, Sophie, I didn't mean to ruin your day.' Rebecca looks stricken. 'I didn't know.'

'It's fine, don't worry.' I force a smile to my lips. 'Let's open the next clue.'

Tash opens it for me and reads:

'CLUE 4
It's time to go AWAY, relax and let go,
Get into warm waters and away from the snow.
Rewind and unwind, back to the start,
Enjoy the gifts, they come from my heart.'

'Sounds like a Jacuzzi or thermal springs,' Lucy suggests.

'Can I see it?' I ask and take it from Tash. 'Oh, AWAY is all in capital letters, it's the W's spa, AWAY is its name. Also the 'going back to the start' part makes sense. We had our first ever date at the W hotel. Oh look, there's something else at the bottom. It reminds us to 'ask at the bar for our quick way down.'

'I'll go.' Tash springs up.

When she gets back she's grinning. 'We're tobogganing down, there are two waiting for us. Fancy a race?'

It turns out tobogganing is a great antidote for stress. We're giggling like children as we zip back down to town, rushing past snow-laden fir trees, runners sliding over crisp compacted snow. Tash and Rebecca hit a ridge and come off their sledge into a snow drift, laughing hysterically.

Lucy guides our sledge expertly. She has more of an affinity with the snow, seeming to know exactly how to take the bends and where the deep drifts lie.

Unsurprisingly we beat the other two to the bottom. We prop the sledges up against the log store at the end of the track, where we were instructed to leave them.

'Should we change before we go to the spa?' Rebecca asks, dusting snow from her jeans.

'I think we're okay to turn up in jeans and ski jackets. It's not like we're going for dinner,' I reassure her.

At the spa reception we're handed another envelope. I open it to find a longer poem, in French this time, and some pieces of folded printer paper.

I read the poem to myself, the vocabulary is simple. I can usually translate written French if it's not too complicated, especially with the help of the translator app Luc put on my phone.

> *Sophie. Mon amour,*
> *Mon chouchou et mon cœur.*
> *Mon rayon de soleil,*
> *Et ma moitié.*

Sophie. Ma chérie,
L'amour de ma vie.
Mon destin et mon avenir,
Mon souffle et mon désir.

Sophie. Mon préféré,
Mon ciel étoilé.
Tu as mon cœur,
Je n'aime que toi. Toujours.

I don't need the app for this one. I blink back sudden hot tears, the words swim in front of my eyes.

'What else is in the envelope, Sophie, apart from the poem?' Tash asks.

I look at the other pieces of paper. One is an email booking confirmation for us all to have massages at the spa. The other is a booking confirmation for return flights to Manchester for me and Luc for two days next week.

Wordlessly I hand the paperwork over to Tash. She doesn't seem too surprised.

'You knew?' I raise my eyebrows.

She shrugs. 'When Luc mentioned the surprise to us, Holly and I thought the idea of going home to talk weddings with your mother might leave you in need of a relaxing massage.'

'You're not wrong there.' I laugh, still feeling a little stunned.

'I didn't know he'd booked massages for all of us too, though,' Tash says. 'That's really generous of him.'

'What does the poem mean. Is it another clue?' Rebecca asks, peeking over my shoulder to see the poem.

'Okay if I translate?' Tash asks.

'Sure.' I hand the poem to Tash, reasoning Luc wouldn't have made it part of the treasure hunt if he'd wanted to keep it private.

Tash recites:

'Sophie my love,
My sweetie and my heart.
My ray of sunshine,
And my better half.

Sophie, my darling,
The love of my life.
My destiny and my future,
My breath and my desire.

Sophie. My preferred one,
My starry sky.
You have my heart,
I love no one but you.
Always.'

'Aw, that's so sweet.' Rebecca smiles.

'The only word that's hard to translate is 'chouchou'. Mon chou literally means my cabbage or possibly my sweet pastry. I opted for the second option.' Tash grins. 'You're lucky he didn't call you *ma petite puce*. I looked it up after one guy called me that and it means my little flea. I was ready to clout him one, but apparently it's a term of endearment.'

Rebecca's eyes are starry. 'He really loves you, Sophie. Like really loves you. To go to all this effort. You are so lucky.'

'Yes, I am,' I reply quietly.

'Are you looking forward to going home?' Rebecca asks.

I snort with laughter. 'Let's just say it's going to be interesting.'

Lucy grimaces sympathetically. 'I have a challenging mother too. I sympathise.'

A challenge is one way to describe taking my mother on. If she's in full-on blinkered mode I'll have to stage a protest and lie down in front of the steamroller to bring her wedding plans to a halt.

Chapter 20

SOPHIE

Going home to the Lake District with Luc always feels strange. He belongs to my new life, not the old. The drive from the airport brings back memories. The gently rolling hills gradually turn into craggy mountain tops. Fields are populated with Herdwick sheep and broken up with hand-built stone walls. It's sleeting, but I always think the Cumbrian landscape is still beautiful in rain and mist, just in a different way.

Dad is driving us and he chats to Luc about the bar business and Swiss taxation, his retired accountant genes asserting themselves. I tune out, unable to concentrate, my fingers twisting in my lap as I contemplate trying to talk Mum round.

I hate, hate, hate upsetting people. This time I can't see a way round it. Mum's waiting for us at home because she's got cakes in the oven. I half long to see her, half dread it.

Luc's presence at my side helps keep my jitters in check. I know he'll help me say what's needed.

Mum hugs me tight when she sees me. 'It's so good to see you both. I've really missed you, darling.'

Guilt squirms inside me and my chest is tight. I feel hot as we sit at the kitchen table with Mum.

Dad is out in the garden doing goodness knows what. He's probably hiding in the shed, having sensed impending conflict. The coward. He's happily delegated the referee role to Luc.

Mind you, I'm not much better. We both avoid confrontation wherever possible. I think it's a side effect of living with Mum. I'm sure part of the reason Luc has come to England with me is because he doesn't trust me not to back out. He says he's come along to support me, but whatever his reasons it will help me get the deed done.

Mum has put out enough Victoria sponge and fruit cake to populate a bake sale and has already fetched the wedding binders, magazines and swatches for me to look at. I gaze at the pile and try to control my rising tide of panic. Luc takes my hand and the tide recedes a little.

'I'm so pleased you've come home, darling. We don't have much time, so I thought we could get started right away.' Her eyes are bright with excitement and I feel a fresh wave of guilt.

I'm pre-programmed to please. It's the way I'm wired. The problem is now, with too many to please, I'm frozen, my brain fused.

I open my mouth to say something and then shut it again. I feel the weight of expectation from Luc at my side. This isn't good enough, I have to try harder. I can't disappoint Luc and now I'm getting married keeping him happy should take priority over placating Mum.

'Mum, before we discuss details there's something we need to talk about.' I begin firmly, before I can back out again.

Her gaze drops to my stomach and I flinch, knowing she's thinking I'm pregnant, that the doctors got it wrong after all.

I falter and Luc squeezes my hand under the table.

I clear my throat. 'We need to talk about where we're going to have the wedding.'

'I thought we decided on the hotel with garden frontage onto Ullswater?' Mum frowns. 'I've already spoken to the events planner there.'

'No I. . .' I want to say *we* haven't decided anything and she's been ignoring my emails.

'You really can't keep changing your mind, Sophie, it creates a lot of extra work for me.' Mum huffs and brings the teapot over from the kitchen counter to top our mugs. 'More cake, Luc?'

She smiles tightly at him and fails to offer me any extra cake. I grind my back teeth, rendered temporarily speechless.

'Maybe in a minute, Sandra, the sponge is delicious.' Luc smiles back at her while giving me another hand-squeeze, stronger this time. Mum's frosty demeanour melts. 'The thing is my dad is seriously ill, and he's not been given a great prognosis. He's not allowed to travel and he really wants to see his only son marry. So the wedding is going to have to be in Switzerland.'

Mum's forehead creases and she sits down with a bump, her lips pursed.

'Why didn't you tell me about this, Sophie?'

Aargh. What? Are you kidding me? I resist the urge to smack my head against the table. I'm about to defend myself and produce the emails I sent her as evidence when Luc puts a hand on my knee.

I get the message. He wants to handle this. And I am perfectly happy to let him.

'The thing is, Sandra, Sophie has been terribly upset. She wants nothing more than to make you happy, even if it means going along with a wedding she wouldn't have chosen for us. She also wants to make me happy, and my parents. In fact the only person she doesn't seem bothered about making happy is herself and I don't think that's right, do you?'

My cheeks grow hot and I stare down at my hand linked with Luc's.

'Well of course. . .' Mum nods, but fails to finish her sentence. An unusual state of affairs Luc takes full advantage of.

'I know you and Derek would hate your daughter to be getting so stressed and unhappy about planning what is meant to be a happy day for her. We can't have her getting so unhappy that she feels the need to postpone getting married indefinitely.' His tone implies that Mum must surely agree with him. It's a clever move to mention putting the wedding on hold. Somehow I think that might be a more persuasive argument than my stress levels. 'I'm confident we can work out a compromise that will enable both you and Derek and my parents to be present.

Amazingly Mum is nodding. I almost fall off my chair in shock.

'Well, of course, all we want is for Sophie to be happy. She only had to say if she didn't want what I've been planning for her.' She smiles guilelessly, looking utterly innocent.

I almost implode with the effort to keep my mouth shut.

Excuse me? I've been trying to do exactly that for weeks! Clearly I should have deployed my secret weapon, namely Luc, much earlier. My secret weapon tightens his hold on my hand, but his warning for me to stay quiet isn't needed. I have no intention of interrupting a master at work. If the bar ever fails perhaps I should suggest a job in Geneva at the United Nations for him. Anyone capable of managing Mum could easily sort out warring countries.

'What we'd like is to marry in Switzerland,' Luc continues. 'It seems to be the only viable solution. We can help you apply for a pet passport for Toby and make the arrangements for the pre-return vet appointment at our end. For other relatives there are plenty of cheap flights from the UK to Geneva and we're perfectly happy to forgo wedding presents to help with travel costs. Simply having the presence of those who care about Sophie at the wedding will be gift enough.'

'If you could help with the pet passport arrangements that would really ease my mind.' Mum smiles tentatively at Luc.

I grind my teeth in earnest now. How many times have I offered to do exactly that? But I hold my tongue. I don't want to spoil the good job Luc is doing. I push my annoyance aside. The important thing is that Mum listens – it doesn't matter who she listens to.

'I was thinking you could help me pick my dress, Mum, while I'm here. I also still need shoes and to decide what to put in my hair. Maybe we would go shopping tomorrow?'

I hand over my peace offering, mentally crossing everything that it'll be accepted.

Her face brightens. 'Yes of course, love. I've got a list in one of my binders of the best places to go. Some of them are appointment-only so I'd better get on the phone.'

'And maybe I could give you my mother's email address?' Luc suggests. 'We can think about how to plan this in a way that will suit everyone. We just need to come up with the right compromise.'

As Mum bustles off to make some calls I exhale loudly.

'My hero. I think you missed your calling, you should be negotiating peace treaties for the UN.' I lean my head against Luc's shoulder. 'I've been trying to make all the points you made for the past few months and she ignored me. You say the same thing *once* and she gives in immediately! It's really not fair.'

I can only think she must be susceptible to Luc's charms. That and she knows she can't manipulate him like she can me so she doesn't dare try. The threat of wedding postponement was a good incentive too, I'm sure.

'What sort of wedding would you choose if you didn't have to think about pleasing anyone else?' Luc asks, putting his arm around me. I lean my head against his shoulder.

'I like what Amelia has planned – a chapel surrounded by the snow and mountains we love so much. A winter wonderland reception with our friends and the relatives who care enough about me to travel out to Switzerland. Max running around trying to con guests into feeding him the contents of the buffet and the wedding cake. Problem is, how exactly are we going to arrange a wedding to take place in the next few months?' I sigh into his chest. 'According to Amelia's wedding-planner checklist I should've started six months, if not a year ago.'

'Actually, I think I have an idea about that,' Luc replies. 'Leave it to me.'

Chapter 21

From: benross21@yahoo.com
To: lucy.ross@hotmail.com
Subject: Famous Boyfriend

You didn't tell me Seb was famous, Lucy! Have you seen the news? There's an article I found here on the BBC news website: 'Snowboard Addict Cheats Death'

Be careful, okay? I'd hate to see you get hurt. Although I have to say, apart from the high-risk lifestyle I thoroughly approve of your choice. Anyone who can charm Mum has to be a sound bloke.

Ben

LUCY

'I've decided, Lucy, that this year's Xtreme will be my last.' Seb exhales loudly. 'It's the right time to withdraw, while I'm on top of the game. The film side of *White Lines* is taking off in such a huge way it makes more sense to focus on that.'

I feel something unclench inside me, a releasing of tension, of a fear so powerful it was twisting me up inside. We're lying in bed in Seb's flat, our limbs entwined, resting after another of his highly enjoyable sex education lessons. When he said he intended to teach me everything he knew he hadn't been joking.

We've been back in Switzerland for over a week now and every time I think about the Verbier Xtreme coming up I feel sick. Knowing it will be his last competition helps a little.

'I can't say I'm not glad that you won't be in as much danger,' I reply, choosing my words carefully.

'You know I'll never do a safe job, don't you? Can you imagine me chained to a desk job? And it was while we were filming that the avalanche happened.' He fixes his intense gaze on me, questioning me and searching for an answer. We are lying so close that when our gaze locks it feels as if he can see into my soul.

I do realise his work will always include an element of danger. The filming is dangerous, but at least he can stay in control of his decisions. He won't be constantly pushed to take a risk too far to stay ahead. It was his admission that the younger guys coming up against him in competitions were willing to be increasingly reckless to win that gave me nightmares, more than anything else.

'I know and I can't ever see myself doing a desk job either. I understand what drives you, that your work will always have some element of danger and I promise I'll do my best to support you,' I reply carefully, meaning it.

'Thank you.' He pulls me to him and plants a kiss on my lips.

It's the least I can do after all the support he gave me in Scotland. I'm still amazed that he managed to win Mum round. But then Seb is very charismatic – he can't help charming people, even when he's not trying, and he did make an effort with Mum. He expressed deepest sympathy for her loss, complimented her cooking, asked lots of questions about Highland culture and wowed her with tales of travel to the Arctic and Greenland. He even talked about my growing skill on the slopes. Gradually she thawed a little and I think she even smiled a few times.

It definitely helped having him there. He filled awkward silences and took me out for drives when I needed to escape. Mum was nicer to me in front of him. I suppose she had no choice, really. Bitchiness is reserved as an 'only in front of the family' speciality. In front of strangers and guests a polite front must be maintained at all times.

When it was eventually time for me to leave I felt things had shifted between us. She saw me more as an adult following a serious career choice, rather than a girl who ran away to drink cocktails and frolic in the snow.

Personally I don't think the two options are incompatible. Not since I met Seb, anyway.

I think Mum has reluctantly accepted I've escaped her sphere of influence and she can't control me with her usual passive-aggressive emotional blackmail. It was great being able to compare notes with Sophie about difficult mother-daughter relationships on the Valentine's Day treasure hunt. It's reassuring to realise I'm not the only one who struggles to get on with her mum.

'I bet Gabriella is happy about your decision to stop competing,' I say, watching Seb's face for a reaction.

'She doesn't know yet – you're the first to know.'

'Oh.' I smile, more pleased about that than I probably should be. 'It'll make her happy, though.'

'I gave up working out how to keep Gabriella happy a long time ago. It was an impossibility.' Seb pulls a face. 'It's much better now we're just friends. I know she wants me to stop altogether. She never got why I needed to do it. It was one of the main things we argued about.'

'Well, I do understand giving up isn't an option for you. It's not going to happen. I get it. The mountains are like eating or breathing to you. They're in your blood.' I rest my cheek on his bare chest. I can feel his heart pulsing. I don't get why you'd want someone to change who they are if you claim to love them. Seb wouldn't be Seb if you took the mountains out of his life.

'I know you get it. Gabriella always said I loved them so much I had no room to love anyone else, but she was wrong. I love Estelle and now I think I'm definitely falling in love with you, Lucy Lu.' His dark eyes are fixed on mine and my pulse quickens.

'I think I'm falling in love too.' I admit, but as he pulls me closer I can't help wondering if I'm being naïve to believe him. Maybe this is how he talks to all the women he dates. I don't know enough about dating, I'm not worldly wise enough. How am I meant to tell?

I lied to him, though. I've already fallen in love with him. It happened a long time ago. I'm invested in Seb, body and soul, and if he doesn't feel the same about me I'm in for a big fall.

Chapter 22

SOPHIE

'Are you sure you don't mind, Amelia?' I ask cautiously, eyeing her over the café table. We've been back in Verbier for a while now and Luc has refused to talk about his plan until today, just insisting I trust him. He obviously took that time to approach Amelia and Matt.

'Of course not, we've been friends for years. How could I refuse to help you out, especially given you came to our rescue with a reception venue? It'll be fun.' Amelia's smile appears genuine.

'But agreeing to share your wedding, well, it's incredibly generous of you.'

Luc's idea, to make it a double wedding, is genius – after all we'll both be inviting lots of the same guests. Also it's probably the only way we can marry this season, while Luc's dad is well enough to attend.

Plus Amelia's wedding is exactly what I'd choose if given the choice.

'Well, you've already done lots to help plan the reception

and, as I said, we wouldn't have a venue if it wasn't for you and Luc.' Amelia smiles again.

I feel guilty of misjudging her. It looks as if there are depths to her shallows after all. I get on with her but never considered her a friend in the same league as Tash and Sophie. I didn't know she had it in her to be unselfish.

'It makes sense, given we've got the same friends coming. Also this way we can share the cost.' Amelia's smile now has a hint of smugness about it.

Ah, there's the Amelia I know and love.

Holly enters the café, Maddie's car seat in one hand.

'Does Sophie know yet?' she asks excitedly.

I nod, smiling. I can still hardly believe it's happening and without Mum going into meltdown. There's still time for that, I suppose, but the early signs remain good.

'I've had an idea.' Holly sinks onto a chair and puts Maddie's car seat down gently beside her.

I peer in and see Maddie is fast asleep.

'Hot chocolate on the house?' I offer. 'Amelia?'

They both accept the offer and as I'm stirring rich chocolate powder into frothy milk Amelia joins Holly at her table.

'Sophie, can you sit down for ten minutes?' Holly asks.

I glance around the bar, we're still quiet.

'Okay.' I slip in next to Amelia. 'What's your idea then, Holly?'

'Well, we've not got any guests booked in next week so I thought we could use the other girls, draft them in as assistant wedding coordinators and pine-cone painters. Also, given you're getting married at the end of the season we could block out Chalets Amélie and Repos for accommodation for your families. Amelia, your family may as well join you at Repos and Sophie, your family could use Amélie. You should stay overnight with them so you're not with Luc the night before the wedding. We can send Matt to stay with Luc or Scott the night before maybe?'

'Are you sure? But you might get a booking in.' I don't want to protest too much. I feel a thrill at the idea of staying in Chalet Amélie. It would be nice to use the spa. Mum would love it.

'I doubt it, it's not school holidays anywhere.' Holly says. 'Anyway, it's only for a couple of days and it can be our wedding present to you, if that makes you feel better.'

'It'll be fun to all work together again.' I smile. 'We might have to do most of the planning here at Bar des Amis, though, especially with Luc going up to Vex most days.'

'Don't forget we also have something else to plan.' Holly's eyes glint.

'Oh?' I glance warily at her.

'Hen night.' Holly grins.

'Hmm. I remember yours, Holly.' I raise my eyebrows. 'And a game of truth or dare that lead to a certain chalet girl called Flora doing very naughty things.'

Amelia cackles. 'That was hilarious. I still can't believe she accepted the dare to kiss the sexiest man in the bar. Holly, you must get Tash involved in planning our hen night.'

I really should have kept my stupid mouth shut. Although it turned out okay for Flora, dares aren't my idea of fun.

'So, we've got the chalet-girl workforce at your disposal. Let's work out what needs *doing*.'

* * *

The following week I'm sitting at the large dining table in Chalet Repos with piles of pine cones in front of me. Beth and I have the job of painting them white, blue and silver. Lucy and Rebecca are making snowflake-themed wedding-favour bags and Tash and Holly are working on the tiny ski placeholders, having sourced what they need on the Internet. Emily is spraying tree branches white, to be used to construct table centrepieces and Amelia. . . Well Amelia is sipping a cappuccino and 'Supervising', checking one of her innumerable lists.

I take a deep breath and steel myself to bring up a difficult subject. It's been bothering me since Valentine's Day.

'Beth, there's something I want to talk to you about.' I put another duck-egg-blue pine cone onto old newspaper to dry and don't meet her eye.

'What's that?' She adds another pine cone to the pile.

'I understand you ran into someone called Thomas this season.' I try to keep my tone as gentle as possible. I don't want to scare her off.

'Yes, you could say that,' Beth replies cautiously.

'I wanted to say I'm sorry.' I stare down at my hands, they're speckled with duck-egg-blue paint. Then I force myself to face her.

'I don't understand.' Her forehead creases. 'Why are you sorry? How on earth can Thomas being a prick be your fault?'

'Um, well. . . I had my own run in with him a few years back,' I mumble.

'So?' She chews her lip.

'I feel like I should have warned you,' I admit. 'I've been feeling really bad about it.'

'But how could you have known?' Beth asks.

'I don't know. I just feel like I ought to stop him. I. . .' I take another deep breath. 'He, er, gave me an STD. It led to an infection that scarred my ovaries and left me infertile.'

The words come out in a rush and my cheeks burn. I hate talking about this, but maybe I should've talked more openly about it in order to warn other girls like Beth.

'Oh God, I'm sorry, Sophie.' Beth looks appalled. 'I had no idea.'

'He refused to use protection and I've been. . . afraid he might've done the same with you.' My cheeks burn even hotter, turning me into a human furnace.

'Oh, no.' She shakes her head. 'I mean he tried to but I was really bolshy about it and stormed out of the flat. He tried to force me to go through with it, but I threatened to call the police and he backed off.'

If only I'd had Beth's confidence back then, but I'd been so insecure and too flattered by the attention. Besides I'd been on the pill, so pregnancy wasn't an issue. That's the thought I'd comforted myself with as I'd tried to push worries about STDs to the back of my mind.

Oh the irony.

'I wish I had been. More bolshy, I mean.' My words are barely audible, but at this exact moment there's a break in the conversation and everyone is listening.

'Are you talking about that slimy bastard Thomas?' Tash asks, eyes hardening.

'Yes,' I say flatly. I've kept quiet for far too long. It's best to bring it out in the open if I can help someone else not to make the same stupid mistake.

'We should do something about him.' Tash's mouth compresses into a hard line.

'Like what?' Holly stops what she's doing and picks a grumbling Maddie up out of her car seat.

'Lynch mob?' Tash suggests. 'Or waterboarding?'

'Please don't tell Luc his name.' I bite my lip and look around the table. I don't think I'll be able to keep it from him now. Too many people know. 'Luc is gutted about not being able to have a family and with his father ill and dying I wouldn't put it past Luc to track Thomas down.' I glance anxiously around. 'He's not a violent man normally but I have a feeling he might try to defend my honour.'

'He adores you, that treasure hunt and the love poem show it.' Rebecca says. 'Don't worry, we'll keep Luc out of it if it's going to stress you too much.'

'So what can we do, if physical violence is definitely off the table?' Tash has a gleam in her eye I don't like the look of.

I can just imagine her accidentally letting a ski pole whack Thomas between the legs. The thought is surprisingly cheering.

'It's off the table.' Holly says firmly, unbuttoning her top to feed Maddie. 'Let's think about this. What do we want to achieve?'

'To stop him treating other girls like crap.' Beth says. 'And stop him infecting them if he's still a carrier of whatever he gave to Sophie.'

'Yes.' A firm resolve rises up in me. Even if this leads to Luc finding out it's too important to keep quiet about. Women should know. What if Beth had gone through with it and been left infertile too? 'How though?'

'We'd have to be careful, legally speaking, not to commit slander or defamation,' Rebecca adds. Given her dad's a High Court judge I suppose she knows what she's talking about.

'Maybe a YouTube video? Women talking about their experiences. Or Facebook. We could get enough shares going around the Verbier crowd to get it widely spread,' Beth suggests.

'Or we get someone like Matt or Jake to talk to him and record it. Thomas is always bragging about girls. He could probably give us enough to hang him with, metaphorically speaking, of course.' Tash grins at Holly. 'That way we wouldn't have to say a thing, Thomas could do all the talking.'

'I know Dan would be up for helping with that,' Beth says quietly. 'He used to be a barrister back in England, so he'd be a good choice to make sure we don't cross any legal lines.'

'Okay, let's do that, then. Okay with you, Sophie?' Holly says, still cradling a feeding Maddie.

'Yes, I think it's better Thomas gives us the material to damn himself with. I don't fancy spilling my guts on Facebook if I don't have to.' I take a deep breath in.

'Okay, then, leave it to us.' Holly smiles. 'Think of it as another wedding present, Sophie.'

'A toaster would've done,' I say. 'Only joking. Thanks, this really means a lot.'

Chapter 23

SOPHIE

Not long after our pine-cone painting session Luc suggests getting out of Verbier for a drive one afternoon.

'So, where are you taking me?' I turn to glance at Luc in the driver's seat. Max is in the back of the car on his blanket, one ear quirked forwards, as though he's waiting for Luc's answer too.

'I thought it was time to get a friend for Max. You've always said you'd like another dog and I think Max would enjoy the canine company.' He turns to look at me. When our eyes meet I get the feeling he sees everything, that there's nothing I can hide from him. I need someone or something else to nurture.

'Are we going to the same rescue place you got Max from?'

'Yes, they've got quite a few dogs I think could be a suitable match for us, but the choice is up to you. And Max, of course. We need to introduce him to the dogs on neutral ground to make sure they'll get on.'

I look back at Max again, both his ears are pricked forward now. I swear he understands far more of our vocabulary than dogs are supposed to, according to scientists, that is. He's certainly picked up that where we are going will involve him.

I stare out at the view as we're nearing the valley floor, the snow is patchy down here. It's only down in the valley I get a sense of just how breathtakingly huge the mountains are.

It's on the tip of my tongue to ask why we're doing this now, but I hesitate. Never ask a question you don't want the answer to. Some things are better left unsaid. Like pulling at a loose thread I can't help it, though, even if it risks unravelling too much.

'Won't people think we're getting another dog because we can't have children?' I stare down at my hands and pick at a loose bit of nail.

'Do you really care what people think?'

'Um, a little,' I admit. 'But not that much, I suppose. So, what made you think about doing it now?'

'You've got a lot of love to give,' he says quietly. 'And I'm sure there's a dog waiting you could make the world of difference to. You do that all the time, by the way – make a difference in people's lives. It's just so natural for you, you barely realise you're doing it.'

We pull up at the rescue charity carpark. Luc smiles, a smile that tugs at my heart and soothes away my stress. I'm not alone. I'll never be alone while I'm married to Luc. He sees a better me than I recognise. I want to be that best version of me.

I'm not sure if I actually believed things might really be okay with Luc until now. I've been waiting for the rug to be yanked out from beneath me, expecting that one day Luc would wake up and realise he'd made a huge mistake the day he chose to send me that very first Valentine's clue at the start of our relationship. Once out of the car Luc links hands with me, threading his fingers through mine.

'I think I might have mentioned that I love you.' He squeezes my hand.

'You have, the poem was lovely. The others were really impressed. If you ever change your mind you won't be short of offers.' I grin up at him.

'I'm happy with the choice I've made.' Luc leads me towards the office. 'Now we've got another one to make. We'll look at a few of the dogs and then try a meet with Max.'

Because of our tiny flat, we decide to look only at the smaller dogs. We then narrow it down further to dogs who are good with other dogs.

Luc eyes up a larger terrier mix, a scruffy doormat of a dog a little bigger than Max, but I can't help being drawn to a little Yorkshire terrier who walks with a strange, shuffling limp. When he runs it looks like he's skipping.

Luc talks to the member of staff on reception duty. Her speech is so rapid I struggle to pick up what she's saying.

Luc turns back to me and translates. 'He was found tied to a lamp post with really bad injuries to his front leg. The vet has put a metal plate in it and it's healed nicely now, so he's ready to be rehomed.'

'Did someone injure him on purpose and then abandon him?'

The idea is overwhelming. I don't understand the mentality of anyone who deliberately hurts animals. It's inconceivable.

I crouch down and extend my hand for the Yorkshire terrier to sniff. He backs away at first, so I stay still and wait for him to come forward.

'What's wrong with people, Luc? I don't understand how they can be so cruel.' I frown.

He rests a hand on my shoulder. 'I know you don't, it's just one of the reasons I love you. You want him, don't you?'

I nod my head and produce one of Max's liver treats for the Yorkshire terrier, who tentatively takes it and then licks my finger with a tiny, darting tongue.

'*Et i'll est bien avec les autres chiens?*' Luc asks, while I tentatively stroke the sandy fur of the little dog.

'*Oui*.' The lady nods.

Luc goes to fetch Max and the Yorkshire terrier has a lead put on him.

On a nearby patch of land they meet and after a brief mutual sniffing session they walk alongside each other quite happily.

'She says we can take him home today if we want.' Luc crouches down to let the terrier sniff him. 'I was home-checked when I adopted Max, so they don't need to do it again.'

'Can we?'

'Of course. Maybe you should take him on your lap for the journey home, though. He seems fine with Max but I don't want to shut them in the back of the car together until they know each other better.

I settle in the seat with the terrier on my lap, knotting his lead to my seatbelt. It'll have to do until I can get him a car harness.

'What shall we call him?' Luc asks.

I think for a minute, staring down at the tiny dog nestled in my lap, taking it all in his stride. He is at least half the size of Max.

'Pipsqueak.' I smile down at the terrier and stroke his back. 'He's such a cute, funny little thing.'

'Pipsqueak?' Luc raises his eyebrows, his accent makes the word sound odd. 'I don't think I know the word. What does it mean?'

'It's hard to explain. It means small, but in a nice way. We can call him Pip for short.'

'Pip.' Luc nods. 'Yes, I like it. I think he's taken to you already. Look how he's cuddling into you.'

'And I like him already.' I stare into the little dog's soulful brown eyes. 'In fact, I think I'm falling in love. How is it possible to love so quickly?'

'I don't know, I think it's very possible,' Luc replies slowly. 'I fell in love with you the first time I saw you reading a book on your Kindle in the bar. You had such a sweet smile on your face and this amazing light in your eyes. I thought I'd give anything to be the one making you smile like that.'

'Really? You never told me that.' I continue to stroke Pipsqueak, my fingers tracing lightly over the ridge of the metal plate beneath the skin on his right leg. I still can't conceive how anyone could break a little dog's leg on purpose and then leave him in pain.

'You're okay now, sweetheart.' I murmur. 'I've got you. You're safe and you're going to be so loved.'

'You've got a lot of love to give, Sophie.' Luc turns briefly to look at me. 'Just because we might not have children doesn't mean that the love we would've given them has nowhere to go. You give love wherever it's needed. To your friends, to animals in need. . . You've helped so many people. You love Holly and Tash and you'll be a great godmother to Maddie.'

'I know, but I still feel this big hole inside me.'

'A hole?'

'An emptiness,' I struggle to put it into words. 'A loss, a sadness that I don't think will ever go away, not completely.'

'Maybe not, and I'm not trying to say it's okay, just that the love you wanted to give, that nurturing instinct. . . Well, you can still give it. You do still give it.'

'I suppose.' I look down at Pipsqueak. I've been so afraid to love Maddie, would it be safe to try or will it hurt too much?

'We'll be okay, Sophie, it'll be okay. My mother says life takes unexpected turns, like a mountain stream twisting and turning its way down to the river. We plan out what we want, what we think is best and then get pulled in quite another direction. Fighting the current doesn't change our direction, it just makes us exhausted.'

'We have a lot, don't we, Luc?' I look up. 'We live in an amazing part of the world. We have great friends, a business, a home, two dogs and we're healthy. Maybe we should focus on what we have rather than what we don't have.'

Luc briefly takes one hand off the wheel and reaches for my hand. He intertwines my fingers on top of Pipsqueak's fur. 'We do have a lot and we have our own little family. Fifty per cent of it happens to be canine, that's all.'

'I am so glad we persuaded Holly to organise the hen night.' Amelia steps forward to press the buzzer on the intercom at the Appartements Belle Neige.

'Me too.' I pull off my gloves and brush the snow from them before putting them in my pockets. Holly knows public humiliation isn't my idea of a good time. 'Do you really think Tash didn't manage to worm her way into the planning, though?'

'I hope not. I told Holly I'm doing a serious detox before the wedding.' Amelia's mouth compresses into a hard line. She looks immaculate, as always, her highlighted blonde hair tied back in a high, swishy ponytail.

'Really, you think Tash will let you get away with not drinking on your hen night?' I laugh.

'Do you think I'd let Tash intimidate me?' Amelia's tone is frosty.

'Hmm, no comment.' I raise my eyebrows and my mouth twitches, but I manage to suppress my smile. I'm pretty impressed they've managed this long without either of them murdering the other.

The door buzzes open and we traipse inside. Amelia and I were told we had to be the last to arrive so the others could set everything up.

A home spa and cocktail party is my ideal hen night. The last place I want to go on my night off is another bar.

The door to Holly's apartment is ajar and we let ourselves in.

There are candles and tea lights everywhere and an aroma steamer is piping the scent of orange blossom throughout the chalet apartment. Calm lounge music is playing via the iPod dock.

'The place looks amazing. Thanks so much for doing this.' I hug Holly tight. 'Is Maddie asleep?'

'Yes, she's sleeping much better now. Thank God. I was beginning to understand why they use sleep deprivation for torture.' Holly laughs.

'There are going to be healthy snacks and drinks, right?' Amelia glances suspiciously at the bottles of alcohol. 'Remember, I'm doing a detox.'

'Of course. All the cocktail recipes we picked have fruit in them, and there are always the fruit liqueurs.' Tash tries to look innocent and fails.

'We have lots of healthy face masks ready, they should help with the detox.' Holly steps in. 'You can have a virgin cocktail if you want, Amelia.'

'And I have some games planned for later including a Mr and Mrs quiz we got Matt and Luc to fill out beforehand.' Tash has a glint in her eye that tells me participation won't be optional.

Oh joy.

'I think we might want to be drunk for Tash's games,' I say to Amelia and then settle down on the sofa next to Lucy. 'Oatmeal and honey? Are we eating porridge?'

'It's for a face mask,' Tash replies.

'We have an oatmeal, honey and yoghurt mask and a scrub made from sea salt, almond oil and lavender oil.' Holly perches on the arm of the sofa. 'We have ingredients for strawberry daiquiris, sex on the beach, raspberry mojitos, appletinis and woowoos.'

'What on earth is a woowoo?' Lucy puts a finger into the honey and licks. 'Are you sure we can't eat this?'

'A woowoo is peach schnapps, vodka and cranberry juice and, no, you can't eat the face-mask ingredients.' Tash slaps Lucy's hand away. 'To eat we have salted caramel ice cream, toffee pop corn and a fruit salad for Amelia.'

'I love salted caramel. I am so glad my wedding dress isn't a tight fit so I'm free to indulge,' I say.

'Sensible woman. I can't understand those brides who buy a dress two sizes down from their normal size and then diet to fit into it,' Emily says. 'They must get so miserable.'

From the pinched look on Amelia's face I'm guessing she's one of those. When her back is turned and she's in deep conversation I catch Tash tipping a good helping of vodka into Amelia's virgin cocktail.

She puts a finger to her lips.

'Tash, are you sure?' I hiss in her ear. Amelia and I are never going to be BFFs but she's come up trumps for me with the wedding so I feel a little sympathy for her. On the other hand, this evening will go a lot more smoothly if Amelia's able to loosen up a little.

'I'm sure. I owe her a little revenge for all the unsubtle reminders that she's in charge at Chalet Repos, not me. Not to mention all the digs about how you only really know a man loves you when he proposes and, by the way, has Nate popped the question yet?' Tash's whisper is practically a growl in my ear. 'Relax, I'm not going to do anything terrible, just get her sloshed enough to be honest for the Mr and Mrs quiz.'

'Hmm, okay then. I saw nothing.' I back off, feeling small

pricklings of misgiving about this quiz Tash has prepared. What exactly did she ask Luc?

When the quiz starts I find out. I'm up to be tortured first. Mixed in with innocuous questions like 'what would your bride rescue first in a fire?', to which Luc correctly guessed Max and Pipsqueak, Tash has added plenty of 'favourite sexual position' and 'sexual fantasy' questions. It appears Luc knows if I got him to dress up as anyone it'd be a 'cowboy from one of those romances she reads' and now everyone else knows it too.

It's pretty tame compared to the confessions the cocktails are inducing. Tash reveals far more than I ever wanted to know about what Nate can do with an ice cube.

When it's Amelia's turn to be humiliated I decide to make my escape to find Holly, pretending I need the loo.

I find her in the nursery feeding Maddie.

'You don't want to feed Maddie in the living room?' I ask, closing the door softly behind me.

'It's a bit too raucous out there. I'd never get my little night owl back to sleep again. She hates missing a party.' Holly rolls her eyes. 'Plus Maddie's a little young to be corrupted just yet. I hear the confessions are getting a bit racy.'

'Tash has mixed the drinks with a heavy hand on the vodka bottle,' I admit.

'I thought she might. Why do you think I've kept my drink with me?'

'Me too.' I lean back against the chest of drawers and sip my appletini. 'Holly, I just want to say I'm sorry.'

'What on earth for?' Holly frowns.

'I feel like I haven't been here for you much,' I admit.

'You've had a lot going on. I've worried I haven't done enough to support you.'

'What are we like?' My lips quirk. 'I'd like to be there for you more, once the wedding is over. Luc and I would love to babysit sometime, if that's okay.'

I'm trying hard to send out 'I'm not going to steal your baby but I think I'm ready to love her now' vibes. No amount of appletinis could ever give me the courage to actually say that, though.

'That would be great.' Holly beams, relief suffusing her features, and I think she knows how I feel without me saying it.

'Just promise me one thing, Holly.'

'What?' She gently places Maddie back down into her cot.

'Don't ever use the phrase 'you're not a mother so you couldn't possibly understand' or I may have to kill you.'

She laughs. 'Okay, I promise. Now let's go and see if there's any toffee popcorn left.'

Chapter 24

BETH

While I'm painting yet another sodding pine cone Holly comes to sit next to me. Sophie and Amelia have left, but we're trying to get a bit more prep done while all the materials are out.

'Thanks for offering to help.' Holly scrubs absently at a blob of dried paint with a fingernail.

'I don't mind, it makes a nice change.'

I'm not exactly lying. It's not that I object to helping out with Sophie and Amelia's wedding, just that Amelia seems to need so many duck-egg-blue pine cones that I've got pine-cone blindness.

'I meant with the other business, you know, Thomas.' Holly looks directly at me then, frank eyes appraising me kindly.

'Oh, yes.' I look back down at my pine cone. 'I'm sure Dan will help us.'

'I'm glad you've found someone you can talk to, Beth,' Holly says softly. 'I know I'm not around a lot, but if you ever need another pair of ears you're always welcome to come round to the flat.'

'Thanks.'

'I know how much Thomas hurt Sophie.' Holly has lowered her voice so the others can't hear her. 'He's a nasty bastard and, whatever happened, I just want you to know you're not alone.'

I raise my eyebrows and quirk my lips. 'No chance of that.'

The only time I'm ever on my own is when I go to the loo. Getting used to sleeping in a dorm room after living a fairly independent life has been interesting.

Holly smiles. 'You know what I mean, there are different kinds of being alone.'

Don't I know it. I hadn't realised that Holly knew it too. A flash of understanding passes between us. I wish I knew how to talk about the encounter with Thomas and the humiliation in front of his friends, but I still can't. In order to explain why it affected me so much I'd have to talk about what happened at home and I don't want to do that. Here I'm just Beth. I don't have the labels I acquired at home: 'rape victim' or 'daughter of a bipolar mother'. People are so much more complicated than that. My life is about much more than that. I am more than the sum of how other people have treated me.

'I'm okay,' I start to say automatically, then decide Holly deserves more than that from me. She seems to really want to check I'm alright. 'Well maybe I'm not totally okay but most days I am. I'm definitely getting there and. . . Dan is helping.'

As I say it I realise it's true. Six months ago I might not have been strong enough to tell Thomas to piss off and walk away. I'm stronger than I was, and happier. Thinking about it, most of that happiness is down to meeting Dan and learning to let go a little. The strength must be purely my own, given the Thomas thing happened before I really knew Dan. Tapping into my anger helped. Eva says depression is anger turned inwards. Well, I think I've now discovered how to direct that anger outwards, to the deserving recipients.

'Good, I'm glad.' Holly nods and gets up from the table, seemingly having seen what she wanted in me. 'Don't forget, my offer is there if you ever want to take it up. You'll be doing me a favour, Maddie and I love company.'

'I will, thanks.' I smile and store the seed of friendship carefully away, treasuring it. Sympathetic friends are always appreciated, but empathetic friends are scarce and should be treasured.

When I've finished the specified number of pine cones I scrub the paint from my hands and head over to see Dan. I need to broach the Thomas issue with him and while I'm sure he'll agree, I can't help feeling anxious as I knock on the door of his campervan.

Dan grins when he sees me. 'I was hoping you'd come early. Fancy helping me cook dinner?'

'Okay.' I nod and then gasp when he pulls me into a sudden embrace. This kind of action would normally trigger a panic attack in me. I wait for the symptoms, but they fail to appear. I relax gratefully into the kiss.

'Now, I've got a present for you.' Dan says when he releases me. 'Close your eyes.'

I obey, another sign of how much I've come to trust Dan,

and hear him opening a drawer. Then I feel his hands brushing the back of my neck and a cold, thin chain settles against my neck.

'Can I see?'

'Go on.'

I open my eyes and turn to the mirror fixed to the front of one of the cupboards. There's a pretty silver pendant around my neck with an engraving of a picture of Pooh and Piglet and the quote ,it's so much friendlier with two' on it.

'I love it, thank you.' I throw my hands around his neck and hug him.

We kiss again, a slow and lingering kiss that almost distracts me from what I need to ask him to do. It nags at the back of my mind, though, stopping me from letting go.

He seems to sense it, pulling back and regarding me quizzically.

'Everything okay?' He goes to the campervan's fridge and gets out tomatoes, minced beef and Gruyère cheese. He's still watching me from the corner of his eye.

'Yes, I'm okay, but I've got something to ask you.' I get a chopping board out and begin to chop the tomatoes.

We're standing close. In a camper van there's very little option. Funny how I hate the close quarters of the dorm room but am happy to be cramped and intimate here with Dan.

'Actually, I've got something I wanted to ask you too.' He tips oil into a pan and turns up the heat.

'You go first.' I take the coward's way out.

'Okay. When the season's over I want you to think about

coming travelling with me. We can see a bit of Europe, pick up some yacht work. You can do the kind of job you're doing now, it'll just be on a yacht instead of in a chalet.' He pauses. 'And we'll be together. If we sign up as a couple we'll get a cabin to share.'

'Oh, I wasn't expecting. . .' I will myself to shut up. Just because I wasn't expecting commitment from Dan doesn't mean I don't want it. But joining him in this kind of lifestyle, it's tempting, but so far from what I planned.

Am I doing the right thing? It would be fun, I've no doubt about that, but life is serious. Being safe is what matters.

Having security.

Somehow that old argument isn't as convincing as usual. Isn't loving and being loved more important? Would I rather be with my lovely, sexy Dan or a guy with a steady nine-to-five job who bores me rigid but promises to stick to my side forever?

I run my eyes over Dan's athletic body and then meet his smiling eyes.

Daft question. That whole sticking-to-my-side-forever thing sounds a lot like stalking, now I think of it.

'Take some time to think about it. You don't need to give me an answer now.'

'Okay, I'll think about it.' I bite my lip. 'Dan, the thing I need to talk about – I've got a favour to ask you.'

'Ask away.'

I take a deep breath. Not because I think he'll say no but because it'll be difficult to talk about.

'Would you be willing to help expose someone who's hurt

a lot of people,' I say, eyes down and words coming out in a breathy rush.

'What sort of someone?' I hear from the change of pitch of Dan's tone that he's noticed. It's the way he is when he's trying to sound relaxed but there's an underlying alertness. I think it's the latent barrister in him. When something piques his interest it flicks a switch inside him, sharpening his mind.

'The worst sort. A complete bastard.' My mouth compresses into a thin line. I swallow hard.

'Okay, tell me more.' Dan's tone is light but the alertness is still there, waiting to hone in.

I realise I don't mind him knowing. It wouldn't be too awful to tell him. He's given me so much, I can offer him up this layer of me. It touches on the deep vein, leading to the worst things, the terrible memories. . . but I trust him now.

'Do you remember that day you found me at the cantine, when I was upset. . .?' I meet his eye. 'Well there was someone called Thomas there who. . . upset me and has treated Sophie dreadfully. It's really terribly sad.'

By the time I've finished telling Dan about Sophie the meal is ready.

'I'll help. Of course I'll help, it'll be my pleasure.' Dan hands me a bowl of pasta bolognese. 'But I would like you to tell me why this is personal for you. You've said he upset you, but not what he did to get you into that kind of state.'

'What?' I suppress a dart of panic and take the bowl.

'I can read people, Beth, it's what I used to do.' He sits down beside me. 'I can read you.'

'Hmm.'

'Don't pull that face, I think you like that I can read you, that I can see the things other people miss. It must get lonely hiding all the time.'

I turn sideways, pulling my legs up underneath me so I'm facing Dan. I won't be a coward. I do like that he found me, that he reads me and sees me. Keeping my real self hidden from the world became second nature with Mum being, well, Mum. I've been pretending everything is okay for so long it's ingrained in me. The truth can be dangerous and shameful. But Dan's right, I'm tired of being lonely, of being trapped behind so many layers. Stripping them away is exhausting.

'Okay, maybe you're right. I do like it, but it's still . . . scary,' I admit, and exhale loudly. I take a spoonful of pasta. 'This is nice, do you cook a lot of Italian food?'

'No deflection. Tell me why this is personal to you, Beth.' He leans towards me. 'I need to know if he, if he hurt you.'

A muscle twitches in his neck and I know he must be thinking about his sister. I've triggered his primeval response to protect and defend. He couldn't protect her, but maybe now there's a physical enemy to grapple with, a tangible outlet for his rage.

I tense and am engulfed by a flood of mixed emotions. I like that Dan wants to defend me, but it's not necessary. Thankfully on this occasion I was able to defend myself. It occurs to me I've been looking at the Thomas incident as a failure, but really it was a triumph.

'Let's just say he doesn't like hearing the word 'no'?' I say cautiously.

'Did he... force you?' There's a dangerous glint in Dan's eye.

'No,' I say hastily. 'Well, he tried to, but I dealt with it. I don't need you to defend my honour. I'm not asking you to help with this for me but because of what he did to Sophie. She's lovely and she really doesn't deserve to pay for the rest of her life because of his actions. Plus, we want to warn other women about him. We'd do it ourselves, but really we need a guy to get him to talk and I thought, with your knowledge of the law...'

I break off and take a breath.

'You're lovely too, Beth,' he replies softly, a tiny frown line appearing on his forehead. 'If he was a bastard to you I'll happily crush him into the dust for you. You matter, you realise that, don't you? You matter to me.'

I don't reply, but stir the pasta in my bowl, staring down at it, my appetite gone.

I'm too choked with emotion to swallow. His words have touched that deep vein, that terrible fear that I don't matter to anyone, not really.

'And I'm bloody sure you didn't deserve however he treated you either,' he adds forcefully, reaching over to hold my hand still and stop it stirring.

He takes the bowl off me and puts both our dishes up on the tiny counter.

'Come here for a cuddle.'

Obediently I climb onto his lap and put my arms around his neck.

'It doesn't matter,' I mutter and wonder how many times

I've said that about myself. The old belief that I don't matter took root when I was a child and it swiftly shot up to become a towering weed, tangled around my sense of self and strangling the hope out of me.

I don't feel so tangled up any more, though. I can finally breathe again.

'It does matter.' Dan nuzzles my neck, his lips lightly grazing my skin with the gentlest of kisses. The tendrils of the evil weed inside me curl, withering and dying. 'I meant it. You matter to me very much indeed.'

I exhale and relax into his embrace. The weed carries on shrivelling inside me, weakening by the second.

'Do you want to tell me more about it?' Dan asks quietly.

I'm surprised to find I do.

'I went home with him after that party. You know, the night when we met,' I say, trying to keep my tone matter of fact. 'Thomas was . . . a bit rough with me and he said some really horrible stuff that upset me. But I got angry with him and said I'd call the police if he didn't let me go.'

My voice is very quiet. I find I can talk about it a little if I'm not looking at Dan and my face is half buried in his hoodie. I inhale the clean scent of fabric conditioner and catch the edge of Dan's own masculine scent, mixed in with shower gel and deodorant.

Dan doesn't reply, he just squeezes me tightly as though I might float away from him. Eventually I relax enough to squeeze back.

'I wish I'd stopped you going home with him,' Dan replies quietly. 'I almost came back to find you that night, but I met a friend, a girl I work with who'd just broken up with her boyfriend and wanted to talk. And I was so sure you were giving me the brush-off when you wouldn't accept a drink and virtually accused me of being a potential rapist.'

'Oh God, I'm so sorry.' I press my face hard into his hoodie.

'Don't be, I understand now why you're so cautious. I just wish I'd looked deeper.' Dan sighs. 'If only I'd come back to find you.'

'It's not your fault. I can see why you thought I was giving you the brush-off, but I've learnt it's not a good idea to tread the 'what if' path. I find it doesn't go anywhere,' I say carefully.

Dan pauses, holding me closely to him. 'So, what happened the day I met you at the cantine?'

'He was there. I saw him with his friends. He talked about me and said some things that triggered memories, you know.'

I don't want to say it, to have to spell it out. I'm not going there, not today.

Dan holds me tight until the discordant cries of the memories recede and I'm fully present again.

Dissociative disorder. That's the neat scientific term for the survival strategy I adopted to cope. I can't help wondering if I never had anything worth staying present for.

Until now.

'Of course I'll help, Beth. I'll do anything you want.' Dan's breath is warm on my neck, on the chain of the pendant he placed there. 'Don't you know by now that I'd do anything for you?'

Chapter 25

From: sophietrent@hotmail.com
To: sandratrent@gmail.com
Cc: derektrent@gmail.com
Re: Vets

Yes, Mum, we've booked you an appointment with our vet here in Switzerland and, yes, I'm positive the appointment is more than 24 hours and less than five days before your Eurotunnel crossing. Toby won't be put into quarantine. I did send Dad all the details. Then all you need to do at Calais is just report to the pet control booth before you board the train at the Eurotunnel terminal, hand over Toby's passport and get him scanned. It's really easy, I promise.

Luc and I both look forward to seeing you. I'm so glad you're finally getting to see Switzerland and my home.

Lots of love,
Sophie
xx

SOPHIE

'Look, it's had a thousand Facebook shares already and almost as many YouTube views.' Tash holds up her phone, a triumphant catlike smile on her lips.

'Dan won't get into trouble, will he?' I try to ignore the knots in my stomach. I'd rather not be worrying about this on my wedding day, but we need to talk now before Mum and the others are finished in the steam room and join us. Chalet Amélie's treatment room, where Tash and I are now, has been transformed into a temporary wedding make-up and hair station. Our outfits are hanging in the bar area, where champagne is cooling and flutes are waiting to be filled.

Emily and Jake have been fantastic getting everything ready for us. Dad is upstairs with Jake; both are staying well out of the way. Both Dad and Mum raved about the chalet when they got here and Toby has been running around outside woofing excitedly and eating snow with Pipsqueak and Max, so it seems, miraculously, that everyone is happy. Mum's friend, Rita, came with them and the fourth seat was taken by Gran, who miraculously got better when she realised a free holiday was up for grabs. She's resting in her room until the reception, convinced she'd catch pneumonia in the mountain chapel, in spite of the space heaters we've hired.

Tash is delighted she got to spend the night here with a room to herself while Amelia is at Chalet Repos with her family. Beth, Lucy and Rebecca came over this morning to get ready with us, but Tash is my only bridesmaid. I would've asked Holly, but she wants to be free to take Maddie out if she cries.

A few months ago her decision might've upset me, but I'm in a better place now. Nothing stays the same forever. Life changes and good friendships change with it.

Amelia hasn't asked any of the Chalet Repos girls to be her bridesmaids, but instead has chosen Matt's sister.

'Beth says Dan doesn't care if he does get into trouble. It's unlikely, though. I expect Thomas might be able to persuade Facebook and YouTube to take it down eventually, but as there's no swearing, nudity or defamation in it, it's unlikely he'd be successful,' Tash grins maliciously. 'He gave enough material without us having to say a word. Dan did a good job getting him to talk. He's a sound guy.'

I connect the dots.

'Are Dan and Beth a proper item, then?'

'I think so,' she nods. 'And if not they should be.'

'Talking about people who should be together, things seem to be going well with you and Nate,' I smile. 'I heard he was over here looking for a chalet for himself this time, not just for investment.'

'Did you now? He was looking. I went with him for the viewings, but I don't think he's made an offer yet.' Tash beams, her whole face lights up, making her look much younger. 'I think I'll pop off for my shower now, if you'll be okay on your own, Soph?'

'Sure,' I nod and close my eyes to enjoy a few minutes peace and quiet before everything gets hectic.

With no distractions it's hard not to think about the video

doing the social media rounds. I didn't watch it and I've no desire to. I know Dan got Thomas talking about Minger Wednesday – competing to take home the ugliest girl in the bar. He also expanded on his theory about fat girls trying harder in bed and boasted about never sleeping with the same girl twice.

Dan also told Thomas he'd heard some girl claim he'd given her an STD and left her unable to have children after complications.

That's the reason I can't watch it. Thomas's response was to shrug. What did he care, he'd said, he didn't want to have children after all. Just hearing that made me so livid I had to spend a whole evening reassuring Max he wasn't in trouble. I channeled the anger into furious housework, taking out my feelings on the dust and grease smudges. I even cleaned the oven and attacked the growing block of ice in the freezer, hacking away at it with a satisfying ferociousness.

I must've cleaned for hours – bleaching, scrubbing and scouring Thomas out of my life. Housework is a great way to deal with anger. You get to work it out of your system and have the satisfaction of ending up with a clean flat.

I stare around at all the lotions and make-up primers, it's so weird to think it's actually happening – I'm getting married. It feels like I'm skipping inside, in spite of the odd flutter of nerves in my stomach. I'm in a much better place than I was at the beginning of the season. I have to work with what is, rather than stay hung up on what I wish could be. I have plenty to be grateful for. Luc especially.

Thankfully Luc is one of the few people I know who isn't

on Facebook. He always says he's too busy talking to people face to face, and at the end of the day the only person he wants to connect with is me. I'm finally going to tell him, but not until we're on honeymoon in Geneva. I'm hoping the physical distance from Verbier will give him time to calm down.

Today is our wedding day and Thomas isn't invited in any shape or form, especially digital.

I am glad the truth is out there now.

Mum bustles into the room with the girls, her face very pink in contrast with her white towelling robe. I think she overdid the steam room.

'Are we on schedule?' She picks up the clipboard containing her master lists, having refused the offer of an iPad, and surveys its contents.

She and Amelia have a lot in common. For the first time in ages I'm actually glad of Mum's bossiness. She and Rita took over the last-minute decorations and organised everyone else, which meant I could have a luxurious soak in the bath last night. Amelia also now directs any questions at my mother instead of me. So it seems there are some advantages to having a steamroller mother.

'I think you've got it all under control, Mum. You don't need to worry about anything.'

She frowns, clearly not believing me. I suppose Mum wouldn't be Mum if she didn't have something to worry about.

'We should be drinking champagne now, before we get our make-up done.' She peers closely at the schedule. 'Let's go. You're not using the steam room, Sophie?'

'No, sometimes it gives me a heat rash and I don't want

to look like a beetroot for the wedding photos.' I ease out of my chair and follow Mum. While we drink Kir Royales I take a minute to stop and admire my dress. Its magical tiny pearl beads and silver embroidery on the bodice glimmer in the light. It seems like a blink of an eye before it's time to get ready. Once the dress is on, the silk skirt skims my hips and the shape flatters my curves. Especially with the horrendously expensive but highly effective shapewear underwear I bought to wear underneath. There's a white fur- trimmed cape too. Amelia's style of dress is simpler and more modern, but this more traditional style suits me much better. Mum and Dad brought it out with them in the car so we wouldn't have to worry about transporting it on the plane back to Geneva. Rita and Gran had to travel with it laid out carefully on their laps for the entirety of the journey out here.

'You look lovely, Soph. I'd marry you.' Tash beams at me.

The make-up artist has finished working on us, although Tash insisted on her own distinctive style of eye make-up.

'You look lovely too.' I reach out and gently stroke the shimmering, silver silk of Tash's elegant bridesmaid's dress.

Both our dresses are long enough to hide the fact we're wearing ski boots underneath, but not so long we're going to trip over our hems. I have some comfy cream ballet flats to change into for the reception. They're waiting for me at Bar des Amis, which I haven't been allowed to see since the preparations started in earnest.

'So, are you ready to go and get married?' Tash asks.

'Yes, absolutely.'

'Come on, Sophie.' Mum appears, to chivvy us along. 'We should have left the chalet two minutes ago.'

I meet Tash's gaze and her lips quirk, suppressing a giggle. The urge to giggle rises up in me too, the earlier skipping feeling bursting through like a ray of sunshine through cloud.

I give in to the emotion; it's such a welcome change from being ambushed by fear. Soon Tash is giggling too.

'Girls, what's so funny?' Mum's forehead creases in confusion.

There's something about being treated like a child that makes you want to act like one. I manage to get myself under control but can only stop laughing if I avoid looking at Tash.

Which could be a problem, given she's my bridesmaid and it's my wedding day. What if I get the giggles at the chapel? Luc would just think it was funny but Amelia would never forgive me.

'Never mind, let's just go.' Mum smiles indulgently. 'Come on, quick quick.'

I feel a rush of affection for her. I hate to admit it, but Mum's bossiness has actually turned out to be pretty useful. It's been much less stressful being able to take a step back from the details.

We file out of the room like naughty schoolgirls. I catch up with Mum and squeeze her arm.

'Thanks, Mum.'

'What for, darling?'

'Everything you've done to help.' I bite my lip. 'I want you to know I appreciate it.'

Mum blinks hard. 'Don't make me cry, Sophie, there's no

time for re-doing my make-up in the schedule. Anyway, you don't need to thank me. You're my daughter, I'd do anything to help you.'

She says it as though it's obvious. That it's an immutable law that parents will always love and support their children unconditionally.

'You say that like it's a given Mum, but I've got friends who don't have mothers who are always there for them,' I say quietly, not wanting Tash to overhear. 'I'm sorry if I've taken it for granted in the past.'

Mum squeezes my arm back. 'That's nice of you to say, Sophie. I'd hug you but we can't risk crushing your dress. Come on, let's get you married.'

The ceremony flies by in the blink of an eye. I try to fix the memories in my mind, taking mental photographs of Luc's serious eyes as he says his vows, the smiling faces of the guests and the bright-blue sky.

I'm overwhelmed by an intense relief. No more soul-searching. I'm married; it's done. I'm now a Mrs, not a Miss. A Madame, no longer a Mademoiselle.

'I can't believe we're married,' I say to Luc as we enter the marquee back at Bar des Amis.

'*Ma femme*,' he squeezes my hand.

'My woman'. I like that. The French word for wife is primal and possessive, but I like it. I'm happy to be Luc's woman.

I gasp when I get to see the Winter Wonderland that Mum and her press-ganged team have created in the marquee. Silver and white branches and pale-blue pine cones are artfully arranged around glowing lanterns. The larger branches are fixed to table centrepieces so it looks as if there are trees growing up through each table. There are white twinkling lights everywhere and with tall church candles flickering in brass lanterns the whole room shimmers in a magical silvery light.

The buffet looks incredible. The white chocolate cake pops and snowball cocktails look particularly tempting. Amelia has pulled off her helter-skelter, ski-slope cake complete with tiny fir trees and a snowboarding bride and groom.

Pipsqueak, Max and Toby are all lingering close to the buffet tables, tails wagging and eyes huge in typical doggy begging style. Pipsqueak trails behind the other two dogs, canine company helping him to grow in confidence.

I smile when I see him. Someone has tied black bow ties to each of the dogs' collars, Tash probably. I feel a rush of love for Pipsqueak. He's so willing to start again, to try to trust me and so heartbreakingly grateful for every treat and cuddle. It's awe-inspiring that I can make such a difference to another creature.

Luc and I have also talked about fostering. Apparently the authorities are so desperate for foster carers they apply 'lower standards' when it comes to selection. That's kind of shocking and insulting all in one. Although it does open up new possibilities. When I think about a young Tash or a young Holly needing help and not getting it I think maybe it might be something I could do. Maybe it's even what we're meant to be doing. Luc would make a good foster father.

I don't know, I'm not usually hung up on fate or ,meant to be's'. I think you make your own destiny, but I've got a feeling about this, that we've been pushed in this direction for a reason.

I don't recognise the music playing. It's slow-tempo chill-out music, the kind they play at the W cocktail bar. It's only meant to be background music; we're supposed to eat first and then dance, but I don't object when Luc pulls me into a slow dance.

I get it, he wants a quiet moment of it being just the two of us, to feel it's our wedding, not just a big orchestrated party we've been invited to participate in.

'We're not supposed to have our first dance yet, it's not in the schedule.' I whisper.

'I'm happy to risk your mother's wrath to dance with my wife.'

'My hero.' My lips twitch.

My wife. I really do like the sound of that.

'Luc, you know that Mr and Mrs quiz Tash made you do. . .' I hesitate. 'You know I'd choose you over a brooding cowboy any day, right?'

'Are you sure?' Luc asks. 'How about a Regency duke?'

'Definitely.' I rest my head against his chest.

'Or a billionaire boss?' Luc's lips curve in a smile.

'Uh huh.'

'More than a playboy prince with his own tropical island?'

'Tropical islands are so overrated.' I grin.

'True. I hear the best romances end with a girl and a bar owner. And a couple of rescue mutts.'

'The very best,' I reply, letting happiness wash over me.

It makes such a nice change from niggling anxiety. Maybe I've been more like my Mum than I realised – always looking for something to worry about. That way of living is pretty exhausting. I'm doing things differently from now on. Being honest with Luc, even if I think it might hurt him, will be a good place to start. Even when it's done for the best reasons selective disclosure creates barriers.

It's as though the wall I used to feel trapped behind has been gradually dismantled, brick by glass brick, each time I've opened up to someone. I was the one who walled myself in. The bricks were all the things I didn't say, the weight of them pressing in on me until I couldn't breathe.

Now the wall has gone I can breathe again.

Luc's lips brush the top of my head. He holds me tight and we sway to the music bathed in silvery light. We're the only ones dancing, but I couldn't care less about looking silly.

It's my wedding and I'll dance if I want to.

Luc recites his poem, his lips close to my skin.

'Sophie. Mon amour,
Mon chouchou et mon cœur.
Mon rayon de soleil,
Et ma moitié.

Sophie. Ma chérie,
L'amour de ma vie.
Mon destin et mon avenir,
Mon souffle et mon désir.

Sophie. Mon préféré,
Mon ciel étoilé.
Tu as mon cœur,
Je n'aime que toi. Toujours.'

The whispered words of Luc's love poem wash over me and a warm peace seeps into every corner of my soul. All the stress of the wedding preparations and handling Mum floats away, as insignificant as a wisp of smoke. It's done. We managed it.

We're married.

I'm Luc's *ciel étoilé* – his starry sky. We're going to be okay. Life won't be perfect or trouble-free but next time we hit a bumpy patch I'm not going to ride it alone. I'll reach out to Luc and hold onto him tight, so at least if we're thrown off course we will still have each other. Without stars our night skies would be very dark indeed.

'*Je n'aime que toi. Toujours*,' I repeat, looking up to meet his eyes. 'Only you Luc. Always.'

Chapter 26

LUCY

I think Estelle's wide eyes are as big as the dogs' eyes when she sees all the white and silver cake pops on the wedding buffet table. It's the first time the three of us have gone out together. It was Seb's weekend to have Estelle and Sophie said it was no problem to bring her along with us to the wedding.

Amelia is busy showing off her ski-slope wedding cake to anyone who indicates a glimmer of polite interest. To be fair, it does look amazing, but I can't help thinking it's a shame Matt is off drinking with his best man while she is, well, I can't think of a nicer word for it, showing off. But if showing off makes her happy, who am I to interfere?

Once we've got drinks and found seats Seb puts an arm around Estelle. 'What shall we do tomorrow, Estelle?' He asks. 'We could go to the snow park?'

Estelle rolls her eyes. 'You know Mum doesn't let you take me to the snow park unless she's there too. Not since I broke my wrist.'

Seb's eyes darken. 'I thought you explained what happened?'

'I've told her like a million times, Dad,' Estelle replies indignantly. 'She just keeps on saying you're, what was the word? Reckless, that was it, or was it feckless?'

She attacks her cake pop with relish, apparently unaware of the pain her words are causing Seb.

'Surely she knows I would never, ever endanger. . .' Seb stares into the middle distance and mutters, his hands clenching into fists.

I rest a hand on his forearm, feeling the tension in his muscles. I move my hand down to cover his and tease his fingers out of their hard knot to interlink with mine. I'm coming to realise Seb's moods are as transient as mountain weather – dark clouds one minute and glorious sunshine the next.

I feel a momentary flash of annoyance on Seb's behalf. I'm completely positive Seb would never take a risk with his daughter's safety.

'What did happen?' I ask.

'Another child lost control of his snowboard and crashed into her. Estelle was standing nearby, she wasn't even moving at the time.'

'Oh.' I bite my lip. I really shouldn't get involved. But maybe Gabriella would be happier if I promised to go to the snow park with Estelle and Seb. I could always ask. It would be a fun thing to do together.

I glance over at Sophie and Luc. They're slow-dancing and seem totally oblivious to everyone else. A smile spreads across my face. They are so sweet together. Luc utterly adores Sophie. Just look at the trouble he goes to, setting treasure hunts for her. From the besotted expression on her face, I think she might finally believe he loves her.

'They look so happy,' I murmur to Seb.

'Can we dance, Daddy?' Estelle asks, wiping her mouth with a napkin, cake pop finished.

'It wouldn't be polite to leave Lucy sitting on her own, sweetheart,' Seb replies.

'Oh I don't mind. . .'

Estelle interrupts me. 'Why can't Lucy dance with us?'

'Why not?' Seb raises an eyebrow.

'Okay.' I stand up and Seb and I form a protective circle around Estelle.

When it comes to dancing, let's just say Estelle's enthusiasm outstrips her abilities. Soon we are all giggling and after many missteps on our toes it's decided we'll do much better if she rests her feet on top of Seb's.

I can't remember laughing so much. When we sit back down, Seb is dispatched to fetch us drinks. He hobbles away, pretending that Estelle has crippled him.

'You have to marry my Daddy, Lucy. I've decided,' Estelle proclaims, fixing me with a determined stare. 'You will, won't you?'

'Um, well he hasn't actually asked me to marry him, you know. It's quite a serious decision and we haven't been together for very long.' I feel hopelessly out of my depth. Am I supposed to be honest? What's the proper grown-up answer? I have no idea, so it's going to have to be the truth.

'Oh he'll ask you, Lucy. I've already told him he has to.' Estelle fixes me with a gimlet glare. It's so like Seb's expression when he's determined that I have to keep myself from laughing.

Okay, then.

'I love your daddy very much, Estelle,' I say the only true thing I'm sure of.

'So do I.' Estelle slips her hand into mine, so trusting.

I decide I'll do my best to encourage and support her. I'm determined whatever happens, I'm not going to repeat my mother's behaviour patterns.

Seb looks over at us from where he's trying to balance two cocktails and a fruit juice. He smiles, his craggy face splitting wide with a grin. I'm reminded, as always, of sunshine breaking through the clouds.

'Okay?' He mouths.

I nod. I most certainly, definitely am.

From: lucy.ross@hotmail.com
To: benross21@yahoo.com
Subject: Good News

Hi Ben,

Seb has asked me to move in with him and I've said yes :-)

Do you fancy breaking the news to Mum for me?

Lucy

xx

From: benross21@yahoo.com
To: lucy.ross@hotmail.com
Subject: Seriously?

No no no no no no no!

I'm very pleased for you, little sis, I think you're great together, but you want me to break the news to Mum you're going to be living in sin? I'd rather poke my eyes out with a pitchfork. Does she know he has a child from another relationship yet?

Mum is always going to be Mum, I'm afraid. She won't take it well.

Just a thought, but do we really have to tell her? Maybe you could come back in the summer with Seb and break it to her then. Or, better still, wait until you're engaged, that would probably pacify her. I hope!

Seriously, though, congratulations. I am happy for you :-)

Ben

From: gabriella@gmail.ch
To: Sebastien@whitelineproductions.fr
Subject: New Girlfriend

Hi Seb,

I like Lucy a lot. I think she's good for you, she seems pretty grounded. I know Estelle adores her. After a visit to you I hear nothing but 'Lucy this' and 'Lucy that'! It's very sweet.

Anyway, I'm emailing because I've had a chat with Lucy about snow-park visits and I've changed my mind. I'd be happy for you all to go to the snow park together this weekend.

It's not that I doubt your love for Estelle for a second. It's always been about my fear that she'll learn to be a risk-taker from you. We're always going to have to agree to disagree on that subject. I do think Lucy's calm, practical nature will help to balance things out. At least then Estelle will have two different approaches to observe and learn from.

Have fun at the snow park and I hope you nail it in the Verbier Xtreme. You know I won't come to watch and won't be bringing Estelle and why. Sorry. Just promise me you'll stay safe. Okay?

Take care,

Gabriella

Chapter 27

BETH

'So Beth, are you coming with me for the summer?'

Dan pulls me closer and I rest the side of my head against his chest.

It feels bizarre to be slow-dancing in the middle of a shimmering, silver forest. That's what the marquee feels like, anyway. I get a burst of pride whenever I see my pine cones. Amelia might be a task-master, but she definitely has an eye for design. It's satisfying that I helped create something so beautiful. It was fun too. It made a change from cooking and cleaning.

Somehow my plan to come to Verbier to find security has gone by the wayside, but I really don't think I care. The lure of fun, of life being about more than surviving or staying safe is intoxicating. It fizzes with possibilities, like champagne bubbles on my tongue.

'To be a yacht girl? Would we really be able to get work together?' The Kir Royales must've gone to my head because I feel a little giddy. I sway with Dan to the music, trusting him to guide me and hold me upright.

'Sure, my mate Hal is the captain of one of those mega-yachts. They need a staff of thirty and if I ask him you can get taken on as a stew.'

'A stew? Like braised beef and onions?' I laugh.

'Stew is short for stewardess.' Dan kisses the top of my head. 'I'd love to have you with me. You know my favourite Winnie the Pooh quote – 'It's so much friendlier with two.' What do you think?'

'I think it could be fun.' I gaze up at him.

'Fun? You're choosing to do something because it could be fun? That is definitely progress, Beth.' He lowers his voice. 'So . . . there's no other reason?'

'Maybe.' I smile into his chest.

'There's another quote I love.' Dan holds me close. 'One word frees us of all the weight and pain of life: that word is love.'

'Another *Winnie the Pooh* quote?' I ask.

'No, Sophocles.' Dan laughs.

'Dan . . .' I bite my lip.

'Beth?' He quirks an eyebrow.

'Why me?' I swallow hard, trying to put the brakes on, to hide my feelings of insecurity. I feel like damaged goods. I know I'm not, but knowing and feeling are sometimes worlds apart. I look up at him. We've stopped dancing. We're surrounded by glittering silver and people wearing their fanciest clothes and best smiles.

'Are you fishing for a compliment, Beth?'

'Absolutely.' My pulse quickens and my insecurities jump up and down, hollering like naughty children. I ignore them, focusing only on Dan's smiley eyes and kind face and how it feels to have his arms around me.

'I love you. Every little bit of you. You know you said you liked Piglet best because he was brave despite his fears?'

I nod.

'Well, that's you, you're brave and strong and smart. Also I can be myself with you. Do you know how rare that is?'

'Yes, I do,' I whisper. 'I feel the same. I love you too.'

'So, come away with me, Beth. We can travel and see the world. There's more than one way to live.'

The pull of a potential adventure hand in hand with Dan is irresistible. It occurs to me that while he might believe in living in the moment, in the 'now', as he calls it, he's never given me any cause to believe he's a 'just for now' boyfriend. Quite the opposite, in fact.

'Okay, let's do it,' I grin. 'There's got to be more to life than settling down and financial security. It's not like I've got a mortgage to pay.'

'Actually, I've got one of those. I kept my London flat and I'm renting it out, so it's paying for itself. I said I was adventurous, I never said I was foolish. Anyway, you'll earn a lot on the yacht. It's hard work, but the tips alone will be more than you've made all season here.'

'I knew there was a sensible lawyer hiding in there somewhere,' I grin.

'Just do me a favour and don't tell anyone,' he mock-whispers into my ear and whisks me further into the shimmering forest to dance.

* * *

The season is officially over and I'm stowing my bags in lockers and climbing into the passenger seat of Dan's campervan.

'Ready to go?' He puts the key in the ignition.

I nod. Holly said I could stay on if I wanted, as they've got lots of summer bookings for mountain-biking and hiking groups, but I said thanks but no thanks, with absolutely no doubt in my mind that my future lies with Dan.

'You're sure about this?' Dan reaches over and lightly rests his hand in mine.

'Yes, I'm sure,' I smile.

'You're sure you're sure?'

'Yes. I'm absolutely positive I'm sure I'm sure.'

Dan fixes his penetrating gaze on me. 'Why?'

'Are you fishing for a compliment?' I ask, wondering if he remembers our conversation the night of the wedding.

'Absolutely.' Dan grins as he repeats the answer I gave him back then.

'Because in the words of a certain bear 'any day spent with you is my favourite day' and 'As soon as I saw you I knew an adventure was going to happen'.' My lips twitch.

'You listened to the *Winnie the Pooh* audiobook I bought you?' Dan grins, delighted I've not only listened to it but taken the time to memorise some quotes.

'Uh huh.' I click my seat belt on and settle back into the seat. 'And you're right, it's just as much fun listening to it as an adult. But I still think you're a big kid. It's just as well I'm coming along to keep an eye on you.'

'How about we agree to look out for each other?' Dan backs the camper van out of its space.

'You're a bit close to that concrete post.'

'Hmm. That wasn't quite what I meant.' He rolls his eyes. 'And if we're going to talk about spatial awareness, how about we discuss the time you took out a whole queue of skiers on the button lift?'

'How about we don't.' I say, but can't help muttering. 'I had to jump sidewise to avoid that little girl, what happened next wasn't really my fault.'

'If you say so. Just don't knock anyone overboard when we're on the yacht, okay? They tend to frown on that, especially if it's a guest you give an unexpected swim.' Dan smirks and if he wasn't driving I'd probably clout him one. In love, obviously.

As we pull onto the road out of Verbier, the sun is setting, turning the mountaintops gold and streaking the sky with hues of rose and amber.

I'm done just surviving. Dan is right. And so is Winnie the Pooh! Life shouldn't be just a problem to be solved, but an adventure to be lived. Otherwise what's the point?

I turn to look at Dan. He catches me looking and grins, that sunny, easy smile that always makes me beam back and never fails to make me feel floaty and light. If life is an adventure then love is one of Dan's smiles.

I've got it bad.

We reach a fork in the road – left for Italy via the St Bernard tunnel or right for France.

'Left or right? You choose.'

'Seriously?' I ask.

'Yes, we can go both ways, there's no great hurry to get

down to the Riviera. We can take our time getting to the yacht.'

'Left, then. I've never been to Italy.' I bring up the map on my phone so I can see our route.

Dan takes the left-hand lane and a sign with a St Bernard dog, complete with barrel around its neck, informs us we've entered the St Bernard Valley.

'You know I did have another favourite children's book series growing up. *Dr Dolittle*.' I smile. 'The bits of the stories I loved weren't the talking-to-animals parts, but when they opened up a map and randomly planted a pin into it. Then they had to go wherever the pin landed on the map.'

'I remember that. And they always had these amazing adventures. Why don't we do it? You could open up the Italy map so it fills your phone screen and drop a pin with your fingertip. The modern way.'

'You promise we'll go there?'

'I promise.'

I do as he says and then close my eyes and put my fingertip on the map. 'Okay then, let's go.'

As I spell out the Italian town name for Dan to put into his satnav I finger the Winnie the Pooh pendant at my neck and know Dan is right. Whatever happens next it will definitely be much friendlier with two. He has opened my eyes to see the world differently and, somehow, with stealth and snowballs he has opened up my heart too, allowing me to feel, to trust and to love. With each day that passes I have a feeling Dan might turn out to be an adventure that lasts a lifetime.

From: lucy.ross@hotmail.com
To: beth.chapman@yahoo.com
Subject: News!

Hi Beth,

I have news!!! Seb won the Verbier Xtreme for the third year running :-)

I'm so relieved he's retiring from competitions on a high. He'll be spending more time film-skiing now. *White Lines* is going really well.

The other bit of news I've got is that Seb asked me to move in with him and I said yes! I've told Holly I'm still happy to work for her this summer, I just won't be living in. I know we've only known each other for a few months, but it feels right. I still can't believe I'm using words like 'feels right', but I guess you know what I mean, given you're off travelling with Dan the van ;-)

I can't believe you're off to the French Riviera to join a super-yacht! I know you'll be working, but it still sounds super-glam. Hope it all goes well for you and Dan.

Stay in touch.

Love,

Lucy xx

From: tash.cat@hotmail.com
To: holly@theluxurychaletcompany.ch
Subject: Amelia

Hi Holly,

Could you have a word with Amelia please? She's being a right royal pain in the arse and has got super-bossy. You know I can do my job, right? I've been doing it for years.

Please tell her to scrap the performance charts before I do something she'll regret. I don't think I'd regret it one bit ;-)

Ta,

Kisses to Maddie,

Tash x

From: amelia@theluxurychaletcompany.ch
To: holly@theluxurychaletcompany.ch
Subject: Employee Appraisals

Holly,

I'm trying to implement employee appraisals in accordance with HR best practice but I'm encountering some resistance. If you could send a group email backing me up that might help.

Thanks,

Amelia

From tash.cat@hotmail.com
To holly@theluxurychaletcompany.ch
Subject: Moving Out

Hi Holly,

Thanks for being so understanding about my decision to move out. I can't wait to move into the chalet Nate's buying. It's that ultra-modern one I was pointing out to you the other day. I think it'll be fun to split my time between Verbier and London.

Nate thinks I'd be really great at helping with his mentoring charity. Can you imagine? Me giving advice to someone! He seems convinced, though, and if I can help, I think I'd like to.

I'd never leave you in the lurch, though, you know that. If you and Scott are ever short-staffed and need a hand, just give me a shout.

I think we both know if I spend another season under the same roof as Amelia I'd end up sticking her ski pole where the sun doesn't shine.

Love Tash x

From Danthevan@hotmail.com
To hal@thejunocaelestis.com
Subject: This Summer/The Juno Caelestis

Thanks, Hal. It'll be great to be back on the Juno and working together again. It's really good of you to give Beth one of the stew positions. You'll like her. I do, a lot :-) I can't wait for you to meet her.

Here's to having a blast on the Juno this summer.

See you in Monte Carlo.

Cheers,

Dan

From: sophietrent@hotmail.com
To: holly@theluxurychaletcompany.ch
Subject: Fantastic News!

Hi Holly,

I know I'm seeing you soon, but I can't wait to share the news. You won't believe it but Luc and I have been approved as foster parents!!! I cried when I read the letter. Luc did too, but don't tell him I told you that ;-)

We've got an appointment to meet a two-year-old girl called Ana they think would be a good match. I know it's going to be challenging and probably really tough when we're given children for temporary placements and have to say goodbye. But who knows, maybe if we do a good job fostering we can re-apply to adopt. We could be recommended internally, the foster-placement social worker said it was a possibility, so we'll see.

For now cross your fingers and maybe soon I'll have a new friend to introduce to Maddie. Give my lovely goddaughter a kiss from me. See you both tomorrow for coffee.

Love,

Sophie

xx

Printed by RR Donnelley at Glasgow, UK